With the first
GOODBYE

a novel

With the first GOODBYE

a novel

LEN WEBSTER

emtippettsbookdesigns.com

Books By
LEN WEBSTER

The First Touch of Sunlight

The Sometimes Moments Collection
Sometimes Moments (Sometimes Moments #1)
Sometimes, Forever (Sometimes Moments #2)
Sometimes. Honestly? Always. (Sometimes Moments #3)
Coming Soon

Thirty-Eight Series
Thirty-Eight Days (Thirty-Eight #1)
Thirty-Eight Reasons (Thirty-Eight #2)
What We'll Leave Behind (Thirty-Eight #2.5)
What You Left Behind (Thirty-Eight #3)
All We Have (Thirty-Eight #4)
With The First Goodbye (Thirty-Eight #5)
With The Last Goodbye (Thirty-Eight #6) Coming Soon

The Science of Unrequited: The Story of AJ & Evan
The Theory of Unrequited (The Science of Unrequited #1)
Coming Soon

She was there all along but he didn't recognize her because the time wasn't right. He needed to wait.

-Carter Hall, *Smallville*

For all the Maxes of this world.
You're the hero in your story.
Your story just takes time.
And every story has a lot of bends in the road you take.

For all the Josies of this world.
Don't ever let disappointment lead you.
You deserve a lot more love in your life.
It will find you.

Chapter ONE

Max

Eight months ago

"You should probably tell him," said Robert Moors, one of Maxwell Sheridan's best friends.

Max let out a lengthy sigh as he tore his gaze away from Nolan Parker dancing for the first time with his new wife.

His best friend was right.

Max should tell Noel about what happened in New York almost six months ago, but Noel was now married. And from the smile on his face, Max knew he was *happily* married. Noel had the dream. He had what Max had always wanted.

True love.

Someone to love him.

He'd never known that kind of love. When he was seventeen, he thought he had true love when he had betrayed one of his best friends and slept with Alex Lawrence's girlfriend. Max had been infatuated with Sarah Collins since he was eight. He had seen a side of her that she had never let anyone else see. On that step outside her front door, she had opened up to him.

But she had dated Alex, and she was hands off.

Until one drunken night when Sarah had told him that she

1

and Alex were over. It had been a lie. And for almost seven years, he had kept his deep, dark secret from seeing the light. Alex still didn't know. Max had sworn he'd never betray another one of his best friends again.

Until I met Andrea.

The thought had Max wincing. Andrea Wallace had been the woman Noel had dated to try to get over Clara. It had been a stupid bet. Who could win at golf. An innocent kiss that turned into so much more for him. An attraction they shared but couldn't act on. She was Noel's, and Max could only stand by and watch. Andrea had no idea how in love her boyfriend was with someone else.

"I'm sure he won't care," Rob added.

Max shifted so he could see the concerned frown on Rob's face. Growing up, Rob was the focused one. He was going to be an Olympian and win gold. He was the one who always had their backs.

"He loved her, Rob. I can't do that to him. He's happy, and it's his wedding. I can't do that. Not to him. And not to her. Noel deserves this; we both know that."

Rob's brows furrowed, and then he shook his head. "You realise he's just married Clara, right? He married the love of his life. I'm pretty sure Andrea is the least of his concern."

The guilt doubled in his chest. The pain had him searching the room for a waiter, for anyone to save him from his traitorous memories and actions. Having kept Sarah a secret all these years hurt, but keeping what he had with Andrea a secret was killing him alive. So much so that he had gone back to Sarah and wanted her to take it all away. To make his infidelities seem non-existent. But no amount of sex with her could make him forget.

He had betrayed Alex when he slept with his girlfriend, Sarah.

And he had betrayed Noel when he had kissed Andrea.

Sloppy seconds was what they called it. And he had indulged in the concept more than once. But Andrea … he couldn't forget her. Couldn't wash her off his skin nor scrub her from his thoughts. He wanted her. He wanted to speak to her and see her.

But she lived in Boston, and he lived in Melbourne.

It was never going to work.

"Doesn't matter," he mumbled. "She'd never want to see me again anyway."

"You don't know that," Rob countered.

I do.

She's said it so many times.

Instead of saying that, Max opted to divert the conversation. "Has Julian's flight landed yet?"

Rob shook his head. "Nah. Not yet. He said he'd call once he left the airport." He paused and then scratched the back of his neck. "Max, I really think you need to tell Noel. And I really think it's time you told Alex about Sarah."

Max's eyelids fell closed. After he had taken a deep breath, he glanced over to see Alex dancing with his fiancée. He had a right to know just whom his girlfriend had cheated on him with. Even if it was with his best friend. Max had done a lot of bad things in his life, but sleeping with Sarah had been the worst. Trying to hook up with Andrea came close.

"Yeah," he finally agreed. "I've gotta tell him. I'm just not ready to lose him or Noel just yet."

"Excuse me, Rob," a soft-spoken woman said, interrupting them.

Both Max and Rob spun around to find Ally O'Connor standing before them with a hesitant gleam in her hazel eyes. Ally was stunning—sexy when she needed to be, but all around the girl-next-door that no one in society saw. She was Sydney's it girl. An heiress with more money in her pockets than everyone at the wedding combined.

Out of the corner of Max's eye, he noticed Rob's posture stiffen.

"Yes," Rob said, almost sounding as if he were dismissing her.

Max had known Rob had been interested in the nineteen-year-old since he had first laid eyes on her at Clara and Liam's rehearsal dinner. Luckily for everyone, Clara had backed out, opting to spend the rest of her life with Nolan Parker rather than Liam O'Connor.

Ally flinched at his abrupt reply. She had dug her teeth into her bottom lip before she released it. "Could we talk for a moment?"

3

Rob sighed. "Allison, I'm with Max—"

"No, no," Max said, shaking his hands. "I'm going to step outside for some fresh air. I'll let you two have a moment. We'll talk more about that thing we were discussing later. You look beautiful as always, Ally."

The blush that took over her cheeks was so innocently cute that he was jealous of Rob. Max knew deep down that their feelings were mutual. However, Ally's public image wasn't really one to be linked to an Olympic hopeful. But Max had every faith in the world that they'd figure it out. If anyone deserved love, it was Rob. The guy had run away from it for so long that it was only about time it cornered him. And a woman like Ally was perfect for him.

Max sent a wink Ally's way and then slowly backed away. The two stood there staring at each other until Max spun around and made his way towards the ballroom doors. Once he'd reached them, he slipped out of the wedding reception and stepped into the hallway with a heavy exhale. Digging a hand into the pocket of his black dress pants, Max made his way towards the glass doors. Wrapping his fingers around the steel handle, he pulled the door open and went outside. He took in the vast hills and golf holes of the Eagleridge golf course. Then he distanced himself from the wedding reception and headed towards the bridge connecting the gazebo Noel and Clara had said 'I do' under to the main course.

When he noticed a woman in a purple dress standing on the bridge, he paused and smiled at the way her brown curls fluttered in the wind. She'd had black hair the last time he'd seen her before the wedding, but the light shades of brown suited her, giving her a softer appearance. Though her black locks brightened the colour of her blue eyes, when he had stood in line to walk her down the aisle, they appeared gentler. Even sweeter.

Josephine Faulkner.

Max watched the way she gazed at the water ripples after she dropped a small rock into the lake. Unlike Clara's other friends, Max barely knew Josie. He'd said hi, and when they'd been paired together for the wedding, he hadn't minded. All he knew was she was a law student with black hair dating a DJ. Next thing he knew, she was this beautiful brunette looping her arm through his.

He took her in. Max had never seen someone so lost in thought or so graceful as she stared at the lake. Josie was beautiful. He'd known that the moment he'd laid eyes on her. But he knew nothing about her. And maybe that was what he liked about her. She never asked for anything from him. Josie Faulkner was a mystery he wanted to solve. It was a strange thought to have. There was no explanation as to why he began to walk across the bridge towards her. For once, he wanted to speak to someone not linked to his past. Max wanted to speak to a woman who he had no interest in anything other than finding out about her day.

"What are you doing out here, Jos?" Max had asked once he stood next to her and rested his arms on the wooden railing of the bridge.

Josie moved her hand closer to his, presenting a handful of small rocks. "Thinking. Throwing rocks into this lake. What about you?" she asked as she lifted her palm higher to offer him a rock.

When her eyes met his, a smile graced her lips in a slow and perfect motion. For a second, the way her eyes glimmered caused his beating heart to spike. It was an odd phenomenon and something he had never experienced before. He swallowed hard, hoping to dislodge that lump in his throat. "Thinking. Just about to throw rocks into the lake with you."

Josie's perfectly pink-lacquered lips deepened as her smile grew wider. "Well, go for it," she urged.

He nodded and took a small charcoal-coloured rock between his fingers. Then he turned and peered over the railing. Breathing out, he let the rock fall away from his touch and watched as gravity pulled it into the lake. The rippling water fascinated him. Ripples were just like life. One action affected the other. The ripple effect. Life's cruel tricks. One mistake led to another and then another. Just like his involvement with Sarah Collins. She was the mistake that just kept coming. Literally and figuratively. He hated that he couldn't forget what it felt like to just be with her. It had him returning to her no matter how poisonous she was.

"So our best friends are married," Josie said, interrupting his thoughts.

5

Max peeked over to find her lining the rocks on the wood in the space between them. "Yep," he agreed.

She nodded. "I feel compelled to ask you this, but are you okay?"

His brows met, and he turned his body to face her. "What makes you think I'm not okay?"

Josie sighed while she set the last rock down then mirrored the way he had turned his body to hers. "Max, I may not know you well, but I can see the trouble in your eyes. That guilt in your eyes. I know it all too well. I saw it every time I saw my dad return from Germany after spending all his time there with his daughters."

Doesn't she mean her sisters?

"What?" he asked, confused.

She pressed her lips together. "My dad left my mum when he became the Australian Ambassador to Germany. Met this German woman and had kids with her. Watched them grow up and not me. Missed all my dance recitals. I needed him, and he had a new family that he never invited me to join. He comes back each year, and I get to spend two weeks with him and his guilty eyes and conscience. So, yeah, I know what guilt looks like, Max. So I have to ask again. Are you okay?"

Am I okay?

No one had asked him that. No one had cared enough to warrant concern towards him. Not Sarah. And not Andrea. Only Josie. The realisation warmed his chest. She cared enough and that caused him to smile at her.

"I'm okay, Jos," he said.

She took a deep breath and surprised him by taking his hand. The jolt in his chest startled him at the connection of their hands. His lips slowly parted as he found it difficult to breathe. Found it difficult to comprehend such intense feelings. Max watched as she gazed down at their hands and then returned those beautiful blue eyes to him.

"If you ever need someone to talk to, I'm here for you. You seem like you need a friend. And honestly, I could use one, too," she admitted.

He squeezed her hand, feeling content with such an innocent act. In fact, he enjoyed her touch. "Consider us friends."

Her small laugh had him grinning at her. "Well, Max,

now that we're friends, you wanna go abuse Noel and Clara's generosity at that free bar?"

"I love the way you think, Josie," he said, afraid to lose her touch.

Something about Josie and just the touch of her skin alone was different. And she wanted to be friends.

This.

This was something Max wanted.

Josephine Faulkner, in all her mystery, was a friend he needed.

Just as he was about to lead the way, his phone rang. Sighing and believing it was the current client he was dealing with, Max gave her an apologetic smile. Josie nodded for him to take the call, and Max dug his phone out of his jacket pocket. He glanced down to see Sarah's name flashing and dread instantly filled his body. Out of all the days for her to call, today was most definitely not a good day. Noel and Clara did not need to see that woman—the one who had caused their separation—on their wedding day.

Max lifted his chin and had clenched his jaw before he said, "I'm sorry, Jos, I've gotta take this. I'll meet you inside?"

"Is everything okay?" she asked. The worry in her voice was something new. No one had ever directed such concern towards him.

Warmth spread through his chest, and he nodded. "Yeah, nothing to worry about. Save me a dance, okay?"

She let out a sweet laugh. "Sure. I'll see you in there, Max."

Then she walked past him, off the bridge, and made her way back to the wedding reception. Quickly spinning around, he watched her take step after step away from him, loving the way her skin glowed from the bright sun and how her hair blew because of the warm wind.

The phone vibrating in his hand caused him to shake his head. What he felt around Josie was different, new, and he wasn't sure if warranted. She seemed nice and sweet. But he wanted them to be friends. Something about her and the idea of a friendship between them had changed something within him. Whether his outlook on life or his approach, he would be the better man he knew was somewhere deep inside him.

With a confident and reassuring nod to himself, Max let out

a sigh and answered the call.

"Sarah?"

Josie

Present day

*T*ightening her hold on the bouquet of peonies she had picked up from the florist at the gift shop, Josephine Faulkner took a deep breath as the doctor exited the hospital room. He had brushed his grey hair out of his face and behind his ear before he turned and faced her.

"Good morning, Josie," Dr Frederickson said with a smile. Not too large or small. It was perfectly mastered not to show off too much or too little. She was sure it was the same kind of smile that had broken news to families for years.

The thought had Josie's heartbeats accelerating. They were already living through more bad news, and she wasn't sure how she would cope with any more. Right now, she wasn't. On the exterior, she seemed fine, but the reality of the situation was that she was only just passing law school, and she was sure she was on the brink of failing one of her units. More bad news and she could kiss her law career goodbye.

"Good morning, Doc," she said as kindly as she could.

The elderly doctor sniffed and shoved his hands into the pockets of his white coat. "We'll have to wait until your mother recovers from the neutropenia fever caused by the first round of chemotherapy. She'll have to stay in the hospital for at least a couple of days, and we'll keep her on antibiotics. This isn't rare, Josie. It happens. You were right to have her admitted."

Okay.

At least, we haven't hit worse.

But the thought continued to linger. There was no way Josie could continue with her day and not know. After a deep breath and squaring her shoulders, she decided to ask. Not asking meant she'd end up knowing far too late to be able to prepare herself.

"Doc, is there any chance this could …" She trailed off, hating the fear that laced her voice. She had once been confident and so sure of herself, but since her mother's diagnosis of breast cancer ten months ago, Josie's life had spiralled into uncertainty. It meant changes for not only her but also for her mother. It also meant re-evaluating her life.

Her rebellious days were over. Days spent dating lowlife DJs were behind her. It was time to stop punishing her father by getting lost in men who would never treat her the way her mother would have liked. They had never done anything for her. The sex had been mediocre. It lacked at best. Her last boyfriend had been less than a lover. But her father, when he cared, hadn't approved, and it had been just what she was looking for.

But when her mother had told Josie of her cancer, life was no longer about her. Her mother needed her attention and time. That was when law school took a tumble. Though her tutors were disappointed, she hadn't confided in the details of her life. Not yet. Not until it was necessary. Not until she was on the brink of being kicked out of Deakin University.

"Josie," the doctor breathed out. "The cancer coming back isn't uncommon. But we need to run more tests. Yes, it could be aggressive, but we'll have to see how your mother reacts to the chemo. We'll know more soon. It's best if she stays in the hospital. We can't risk her going home, especially since she doesn't have anyone to look after her."

"I could —"

"I know you could," he said, interrupting her. "Looking after your mother won't be as easy as you think it would be. It's a lot of pressure. You do have Power of Attorney, so if you wish to, you can. But I highly recommend you continue life as you have been. It will calm your mother."

He's right.

Continuing life will make her happier.

I can't give up on law school.

I can't let her see how this affects me.

Josie bit the inside of her cheek to stop herself from crying. She was hardly the crier. Now, her tears snuck up on her, and she had no idea how to handle them besides accepting they were forming and then falling.

"You're right. Thanks, Doc. Is she all right to see visitors?"

The doctor removed a hand from his coat pocket and settled it on her shoulder. Then he made a slow nod. "She is. But keep the conversation light. She needs plenty of rest."

She gave him a tight smile, making no promises as she stepped around him and entered her mother's hospital room. The first thing Josie noticed was the paleness of her mother's face and her hollow cheeks. The vision before her was not the warm and bright mother who had raised her. The smiles were no longer the same. Instead, they were broken and never complete. Her mother had tried, but the cancer showed when she attempted to smile. There lay a woman who had already fought one cancer battle and was now enduring battle number two. But this time, Josie wasn't sure how much fight her mother had left. Though she was determined and mentally willing, her body told another story.

"Mornin', Mamma," Josie said sweetly as she made her way to the side of the hospital bed.

"My sweet Josephine, good morning," she said softly and reached for her hand.

Josie tried to hide her flinch at the contact of her mother's cold touch. Emily Faulkner gently squeezed her daughter's hand and attempted one of those tired smiles. Josie placed the bouquet on the side table and pulled her hand from her mother's just long enough to pull the visitor's chair closer to the bed and sit on it. Then she reached for her mother's hand and rubbed her thumbs across her bony knuckles.

"How are you feeling?" Josie asked, unable to remove the concern that seemed to echo loudly in her voice.

Her mother's other hand covered Josie's. "Haven't felt this good in years."

The teasing tone in her voice had Josie chuckling. "You're such a bullshitter."

"Language, Josephine!" her mother scolded.

Rolling her eyes, she let out a groan. "Mamma, I'm twenty-two years old."

"I don't care. You're still my little girl. Use language like that again and watch out—" Emily's wince had Josie getting out of her chair, running her eyes over her mother's frail body to find the source of her pain.

"Do you want me to get the doctor?"

Her mother shook her head. "Don't be silly. I told you; I'm the best I've been in a long time. Now, are you ready to see your father tonight?"

Josie sank back down on the chair and let out a heavy sigh. It was her mother's idea to see him. He would only be in the country for a few days with the German Chancellor. The only reason Josie hadn't refused was because her mother's eyes twinkled when she had suggested she see her father. But her interactions with him were anything but warm and loving. In fact, it felt like an inconvenience for both her and Ambassador Jeff Faulkner.

"Mamma, I don't think seeing him is a good idea. Especially with you being in the hospital."

"Josephine, your father is hardly in the country. It will be good for both of you. You need a nice dinner to unwind. Working at the bakery and uni is a lot to handle." Her mother gave her that 'I am your mother and I am right!' expression, pursing lips and all.

Josie let out a lengthy exhale and conceded defeat. If it made her mother happy, she would do it.

"But no mention of my health," she reminded.

"Stupid instruction, but all right."

Her mother lifted their clutched hands and brought Josie's knuckles to her lips, pressing dry kisses on her skin. Then she said, "I love you, Josephine. You know I will always love you." Emily's voice had softened in that tone that worried Josie. It was delivered in that 'I'd better say I love you in case it's the last time' way, and it caused a crack in her heart.

The tears flowed.

Fucking tears!

She knew it was okay to cry. Josie was sure her mother would appreciate her tears, but Josie needed to show her mother that if she was strong, then she could be, too. That she could beat cancer for the second time in less than a year. But Josie knew the reality of the situation, and that was that the second time could be the last time.

"I love you, too, Mamma," she said as she stood, leant over, and kissed her mother's head. "I love you so much."

Chapter TWO

Max

Julian: Max, do you read me? Over.

Max: I read you. Over.

Julian: Have you checked the results? Over.

Max: No. Been at work and about to go have drinks with some of the lawyers from the office. Over.

Julian: Want to know? Over.

Max: You'll tell me regardless. Over.

Julian: Very true. Over.

Max: This is the part where you tell me if my best friend is the world champion. Over.

Julian: Oh, yeah! Over.

Max: Julian, seriously. You seem not to know the concept of telling people information. Over.

Julian: Settle petal. Rob's the WORLD CHAMPION! Over.

Max: FUCKING KNEW HE WOULD BE!

Julian: You forgot to say over. Over.

Max: Shit. Sorry. Over.

Julian: And get this, HE'S MARRIED! He and Ally eloped last week while they were in New York seeing her specialist. Over.

*M*ax felt his jaw drop. His best friend, the recluse in the group, was not only the Men's Single Scull World Champion but was now a husband. Max had been so busy with clients that the only time he'd seen them was when Ally had moved to Melbourne after being admitted to the hospital for kidney failure. Because of his heavy workload, he wasn't able to travel to France to see Rob's race. But his best friend had done it. Robert Moors was now the world champion and husband to a beautiful and sweet wife. The same wife Max had flirted with many times before. The jealousy he felt engulfed him. Sure, he was happy Rob married the love of his life, but for Max, he wanted that. Rob had always shied away.

For Max, that was all he wanted.

Real, honest, truthful love.

No manipulations like with Sarah.

And no bullshit games like with Andrea.

Unfortunately for Max, neither of the two warranted his interest right now. Work was overwhelming, and Andrea had made it easy by never returning any of his calls or emails. Some days, he hated her. Hated that she didn't act on her attraction the moment she had broken up with Noel. All Max had gotten was a message from her that read: *I broke up with him.* And that was that. He'd messaged her that he'd take the next flight out to her, but she had said no, that she needed to be alone. She was confused and wasn't even sure she had any feelings towards him. After several attempts to contact her, Max had given up. He had thought he'd go running back to Sarah, but he hadn't. And for that, he was proud of himself. Instead, he had submerged himself in work rather than sex.

He had a habit and was working his way to correcting it.

Sarah had left his system months ago.

Eight, if he were honest with himself.

He'd forgotten all about her the moment he'd stood on that bridge with Josephine Faulkner. She'd been hard to forget. He'd promised to dance with her at Noel and Clara's wedding, but a call from Sarah had interrupted them. Then Julian had arrived, and suddenly, she was gone. When he had asked Clara where she had gone to, all Noel's wife had said was that she had to go back to the city. He hadn't pressed for more, refusing to show his concern and his interest in Josie. But he was curious. He hadn't seen her since the wedding. Not even at Noel and Clara's goodbye dinner several months back. It seemed she had vanished. With his growing list of clients and pressure from his father, he had no time to learn more about her.

Work consumed him.

Work set him on the straight and narrow.

Shaking his head, Max pulled the key out of his Porsche's ignition and got out of his luxury car. It had been an unnecessary purchase, but with money sitting in his account, he splurged. He represented men, women, and companies he despised. Truth be told, if it hadn't been for his father, Maxwell Sheridan would have never become a lawyer. When he locked his car, he noticed several of the senior lawyers already gathered in front of Pa La Blue on Lygon Street. The Michelin star French restaurant was one of Melbourne's finest—add in the bar, and it was Gordon Sheridan Lawyers' favourite after-work places to go.

Upon reaching the group of men in expensive tailored suits, Max felt his phone vibrate once more. He glanced down to see that Julian had messaged him again.

Julian: Are you okay? Upset that Ally's off the market or something? Over.

14

Max's brows furrowed. Sure, he had flirted with Ally and thought she was beautiful, but he was in no way interested in being with her. He had sworn that Andrea would be his last. That he'd never be with any of his best friends' girlfriends or exes. Andrea had left him scorned when she wanted to brush that kiss under the rug. Gripping his phone tight, he began to reply.

> **Max:** I'm happy for them. Seeing Rob after she was admitted, I can't doubt how in love he is with her. If giving a kidney isn't love, then I don't know what is. Hey, I'd better go. I'm having after-work drinks with some of the guys. Tell Rob and Ally congratulations for me and that I'm happy for them. I'll call him later tonight. Over.

> **Julian:** I'll let them know. You should have seen her father when he found out they eloped. Best thing I've ever seen. Oh! Blondie says hi! We'll see you next week. Over.

> **Max:** Tell Stevie I said hi, too. See you all when you get back. Over.

Satisfied with his response, Max shoved his phone into his jacket pocket and nodded at Greg, Harry, and Sully. They were all older than Max was, but they were the more welcoming of the lawyers at his father's firm. Most hadn't liked the fact that he was the boss' son. Max didn't care. He'd shown he was more than a competent lawyer with his work. He didn't go around seeking their approval.

"Ready to go inside?" Sully asked, loosening his grey tie as excitement twinkled in his brown eyes. Since his wife had left and then served him divorce papers, Sully had wanted to go out for drinks more often to celebrate his newfound freedom.

Max nodded. "Definitely. Let's get inside."

Harry, in his early forties with his auburn hair and green eyes, held open the door, and the men went inside the restaurant. Max couldn't wait to unwind, have a drink, and forget about his women problems as he cut into a tender steak. He'd charge it to the firm as he always did.

As he passed tables on his way to the bar, he heard a waitress say, "I'm sorry to disturb you, Miss Faulkner, but it's been twenty minutes. Would you like to dine alone, or I could get whatever you'd like wrapped up to go?"

Miss Faulkner.

Max halted.

His heart sped up its beats as he repeated that name in his head.

It couldn't possibly be Josie ...

Spinning around, he noticed Josie sitting alone at a table to his left. She glanced down at her phone and sighed. Her brown hair was curled, and from what he could see, she wore a dark red dress.

"I'll just go, thank you," Josie said and began to stand.

His next actions appeared desperate, but she had glammed herself up, and he wasn't going to let her night go to waste.

"Josie," Max said as he took a step towards her.

Her vibrant blue eyes flashed in surprise, and his heart filled with that familiar warmth he'd felt on the bridge with her.

"Max," she breathed, sounding almost relieved. The thought she was happy to see him caused butterflies to fill his stomach. He hadn't felt that sensation since he was a teenager and had kissed Sarah Collins for the very first time.

"How are you?" he asked as she tilted her chin up at him.

The smile she made was sweet, far sweeter than any other smile ever directed at him. "I'm good," she said. "But I'm just about to leave."

"Stay—"

"Max, you coming?" Sully asked, irritated, behind him.

Max had clenched his eyes shut, breathed out, and said, "Sorry, Jos, give me a second." He then spun around to see the pissed-off expression and stance from Sully. Max ignored it. If Sully wanted to go drink his marital problems away, Max would let him. He hadn't seen Josie in eight months and wanted to catch up with her. He also wanted to know why she was alone in an expensive restaurant. "You guys go ahead. I'll see you all on Monday."

The men from the firm all shook their heads at him and then retreated to the bar. Max turned back to find Josie's brows

16

scrunched together.

"Can I join you?" Max asked as sweetly as he could. It had been easy. It came naturally to him around her.

She peered past him and eyed his co-workers. "You have plans," she stated.

"You're more important." Three words that freely slipped past his lips. He was just as surprised by his comment as she was.

What the fuck, Max?

Seriously, control what comes out of your mouth.

Josie is your friend.

Josie blinked at him and then sat properly in her chair as she gestured for him to take the seat in front of her. He acted quickly and sat facing her. Her smile was breathtaking and filled with relief and joy. He wasn't sure if it was his presence that did that, but he hoped so. It was insane how much he wanted to be the reason for that smile.

"That was nice of you to say," she said, sounding almost unsure of herself. Her gaze fell to the table as she played with the cloth napkin. "I must look pretty pathetic right now, huh?"

His fists became tight balls. It surprised him how enraged he was at her belittling herself. Reactions he had never had before. "Did some guy not show up?"

She let out a small laugh, and her eyes met him. "Yes and no."

"What?"

Josie took a deep breath and shrugged. "My dad didn't show. You're sitting where he should be. I've been waiting almost thirty minutes. I just messaged his assistant and ..." She paused as her phone beeped. She glanced down at it, and her lips had pressed into a tight line before she glanced up at Max. "He never left Canberra."

"What an asshole," Max growled.

"Yeah, well, I'm not very high on his priority list. Guess he did me a favour. I didn't even want to be here," she confessed.

Though she attempted to give him a reassuring smile, Max saw right through it. He took in the pain that flashed in her vibrant blue eyes. A glimmer of longing, as if she wanted her father's attention, existed, but he knew she'd never voice that out loud. From what little he knew of her, she appeared to have

17

a lot of pride when it came to her father.

"Well, he did me a favour. I get to see you and not have to hear about my co-worker's divorce. Can you believe the guy is a lawyer and about to lose everything to his cheating wife?"

Josie brushed her brown curls back and laughed. "You're better off hiring me than that guy, then."

"How is uni going?"

She shrugged. "It's going. Everyone in my units has their placements for next year, and here I am, not even able to convince my father to dinner. Not gonna make a very great lawyer, am I?"

Max ignored the teasing in her voice. Reaching for her hand, he took it firmly. He felt her wince beneath his palm as his thumb gently brushed along the knuckle of her index finger.

That surge of electricity, similar to what he felt on the bridge, had him glancing down at their connection. The smoothness of her skin differed from other women. He loved that. Then Josie's thumb caressed his.

If she can convince me this is something different with just her touch alone, she's gonna make one hell of a lawyer.

"Your father's an idiot," Max pointed out.

No teasing.

It was the truth.

Her thumb strokes stopped. "You just won yourself a free meal compliments of the Australian Ambassador to Germany. Order whatever you want. The more expensive, the better."

"Seriously love the way you think, Josie," Max said. Then she smiled at him, and he swore his stomach did a flip. It was unusual. He had never reacted this way to a woman before.

"Thank you—" The ringing of her phone interrupted her. Josie pulled away from his hand and then glanced down. Seconds later, her paleness had him standing. She clutched her phone and her handbag as if they were her lifeline, and she bolted out of her chair. Her fast breathing caused her chest to rise and fall, and she looked up at him with a pained expression he'd never seen before. "I'm sorry. I have to go."

She hadn't given him any chance to say more as she pushed past him. Max quickly grasped her wrist to stop her. "Hey, are you okay?"

Tears filled Josie's eyes as she nodded and then yanked her

arm free. "I'm fine. I'll see you later, okay? I really have to go."

"Okay," he said, not really wanting to let her go, but she seemed desperate, and Max wouldn't stop her. "I'll see you later, Jos."

She gave him a small smile and then turned toward the exit. Max watched as she rushed towards the doors and then stopped. She stood still for a long moment and then spun back around and returned to him. Josie took a deep breath as she reached up and cupped Max's left cheek. Then she got on her tippy toes and kissed his right cheek.

His heart swelled.

It became too big and consumed the small space in his chest.

The feel of her lips on his skin almost had that beating organ explode within him. The warmth he felt was almost too much.

She was too much.

As quickly as she kissed him, her lips left him. Then she whispered, "Thank you, Max. Rain check on dinner, okay?"

"Okay," he murmured as his fingers wrapped around her right wrist and then slowly pulled her palm from his face. "Good night, Josephine."

Her smile deepened. "Good night, Max," she said in a soft voice then left Pa La Blue, taking a piece of him. One he had no idea if he wanted back.

Josephine Falkner was a complete mystery.

One that Max had every intention of being lost in.

And that in and of itself was something else.

Josie

"There's a chance the cancer has spread to her lungs. However, until we know the results, we'll assume the worst-case scenario, so you need to prepare yourself. Unlike last time, Josie, it might be a lot tougher on your mother," Dr Frederickson said.

Josie peered into the hospital room and pressed her lips together. Once she saw her mother was still asleep, she swung her attention back on the doctor and nodded. "I understand. Thank you for having them call me last night."

Dr Frederickson gave her a tight smile. "Of course. It was

touch and go, but she's stable. We won't be able to run the tests until later this afternoon, so it's best if you go home and get some rest. If anything happens, we will call you. I promise."

"Thank you. I'll just tell her goodbye, and I'll be back." Josie nodded at the doctor and then entered the intensive care room.

Her steps were soft and precise to ensure her mother remained undisturbed as she made her way across the room. Upon reaching the bed, Josie gently set her hand on her mother's shoulder and kissed the top of her head. When she stepped back, she took in her mother's short brown hair and frowned. The cancer had returned before her mother's hair could even grow out properly. She glanced over at the peonies she'd brought with her yesterday and made a mental note to bring fresh flowers later this afternoon.

With an exhale, Josie held her handbag closer to her body and said, "I'll see you soon, Mamma."

Unlocking her apartment door, Josie entered and dropped her bag onto the floor. As she passed the hallway table, she dropped her keys and kicked off her shoes. She had spent the night at her mother's bedside. The nurses and doctors at the Royal Melbourne Hospital had been kind enough to let her stay past visiting hours. Many of them knew her from her waitressing job at Melbourne's most beloved bakery. The Little Bakery on Little Collins Street had been made famous by her former boss, Danny Fletcher, and former baker, Clara Parker. They had both left Melbourne for the States to pursue their futures. Danny had become a head chef at a reputable restaurant in San Francisco, and Clara had married and moved to Boston to be with her husband.

The new head chef, Nadia, was just as kind as Clara was, but she was more demanding when it came to service. The plan to turn the bakery into a dessert restaurant had stalled when the owner, Liam O'Connor, had left for Europe. But that hadn't deterred Nadia; she had adapted, creating her own line of cupcakes. Though they were a hit, they hadn't come close to Clara's recipes—those still sold out in the first few hours of opening. Though Josie loved working at the bakery, it wasn't the same since Clara left. Her presence and the way she baked was missing from the workplace.

Rubbing the kink in her shoulder, Josie headed towards her bedroom of the two-bedroom apartment she shared with Stella Weller, who Josie had met during O-week at Deakin University. They had sparked a friendship immediately, and when second year came around, they had decided to move in together. When she made it to her bedroom door, she gazed at a yellow sticky note with Stella's scribble on it.

Left my phone at West's Missed you last
night. Talk all about your dinner when I come
                                home
                              Love,
                              Stella

With a small smile, Josie peeled the sticky note off the door. It was a system they had. Sure, texting and calling were easier, but it was sentimental and something they'd shared since the very first day they moved in together. Unlike Josie's four-year degree, Stella had graduated the year before and was currently a casual relief teacher. Being on-call for when schools needed a substitute teacher meant their schedules rarely coincided.

Josie entered her bedroom, stuck the sticky note by the light switch, and began to unzip the red dress she had chosen for her dinner with her father. The same dinner he hadn't shown up for. The same dinner where she saw Maxwell Sheridan again. It was strange how connected she felt to him. They had agreed they would be friends, but the hand-holding on the bridge eight months ago and the kiss on his cheek last night pushed the boundaries of friendship.

She had tried not to dwell on it too much, but just the feeling of Max's hand on hers was enough to render her breathless. And her heart had tightened to the point where it was almost uncomfortable. If circumstances were different, if it hadn't been the hospital calling, she'd have stayed and had dinner with him. Max was different from most guys she knew. The guilt she'd seen in his eyes was one she knew, and for Josie, she wanted to free him from it. Those brown eyes were beautiful. And that soft smile of his was incredible and completely unforgettable.

He's your friend, Josie.

She was so lost in thought over him that she had even stopped unzipping her dress as she stood in the middle of her bedroom. Blinking rapidly, she shook her head.

"What are you doing?" she asked herself as she pushed the straps off her shoulders, deciding that her connection with Max was only due to her loneliness.

Her need for companionship on a platonic level.

That was what she needed, and she was sure he did, too.

Nodding to herself, Josie continued to undress and decided that right now, being by her mother's side was more important.

After a shower and dressing in a pair of dark blue skinny jeans and a white T-shirt, Josie closed her door and headed towards Stella's room. When she reached it, she clicked the pen and held up the sticky note pad in her hand to write her roommate a reply.

> *He never showed up. Hospital called, and I had to leave. Mum's okay. Will talk to you later.*
>
> *Love you, too.*
>
> *Josie.*
>
> *P.S. West still owes me $20 on that bet we made. Remind him that I'll be collecting VERY soon. Or we could double or nothing next time?*

Happy that her note had the right level of teasing and reassurance, Josie stuck it on Stella's door and began to make her way to the front door. On her way out, she left the pad and pen on the hallway table and picked up her bag. Once she closed the front door behind her, Josie headed towards to the elevator, ready to see her mother.

It had taken almost ten minutes to turn onto Lonsdale Street on her way to the Royal Melbourne Hospital. Josie would soon have to take another turn onto Elizabeth Street, and she'd arrive at the hospital. Travelling through the busy afternoon traffic, a tall building caught her eye. Slowing down to avoid hitting pedestrians, she smiled at the large golden letters that spelt "Gordon Sheridan" above the glass revolving door.

For a moment, her heart had skipped a beat as she realised Max worked here. She had left him when she had gotten the call from the hospital. She felt guilty, but he appeared to understand, and that made her heart go wild. It felt as if her body had acted before her brain had processed what was going on as Josie indicated left and parked just outside Gordon Sheridan Lawyers. When she pulled the key out of the ignition, she decided she would go inside and thank him for being nice to her last night.

She hadn't realised how much she had needed a friend until he offered. Sure, she had many girlfriends, but Josie needed someone new and unattached. Stella had always pried, and Clara was too busy with her married life in Boston. Although she loved Stevie, she was not only consumed with university, but was also with her fiancé in France for the Rowing World Championship. It had been months since she last saw them. When they returned, she promised herself she'd see them more.

Stepping out of her Mini Countryman—a guilty purchase from her absent father—Josie locked it and approached the parking metre. Digging into her front jeans pocket, Josie took out what she could find and inserted the few gold coins into the machine. She wouldn't be long and didn't need to stay longer than the hour the ticket had given her. Once she had returned to her car, Josie unlocked it and displayed the ticket on the dash before she closed the door and approached the entrance. Josie passed through the revolving doors, entering in the impressive lobby of Gordon Sheridan Lawyers.

If she were ever lucky to work for such a prestigious law

firm, she knew her life would be set. But Josie would be lucky to find a single law firm willing to take her on as a trainee lawyer. If she didn't, she'd never complete her compulsory year of traineeship. By the time she graduated, she'd have a HECS debt of over $120,000. Thankfully, she wouldn't find a job anytime soon that would get her over the threshold to start paying it back. Working for Gordon Sheridan Lawyers would make her debt troubles fade away. It was *the* dream job for any lawyer and law student.

She envied Max. He had a father who helped him achieve his dream career. For Josie, her father hadn't so much as wished her the best for university. Pushing thoughts of him away, Josie made her way to the reception desk. The woman behind it lifted her chin and graced Josie with the fakest smile she had ever seen. Bright white teeth and deep red lacquered lips. Blonde hair and blue eyes. The woman was attractive and scary all at the same time.

"Good afternoon. Welcome to Gordon Sheridan. How may I assist you today?"

Josie glanced down to find the receptionist tapping her finger on the desk as if Josie were forcing the life out of her. The moment to be nice was lost. Josie would be blunt and to the point.

"I'm here to see Max Sheridan."

"Do you have an appointment?" the receptionist countered, going for the direct approach.

"No," Josie answered.

Should have known that I'd need an appointment to see him.

The woman behind the desk did not attempt to hide her eye roll, and that annoyed Josie more than anything. But it was obvious this woman had dealt with no-appointmenters on multiple occasions. Josie was not the first, and she sure as hell would not be the last.

"I'm sorry, but I can't let you see Mr Sheridan without an appointment."

"I'm a friend of his," Josie informed.

The woman's brow raised and then her eyes fluttered down to Josie's casual attire. "A friend … of Mr Sheridan's?"

Josie's nostrils flared in annoyance. "Yes," she bit out. "Could you just call him? He'll tell you that I don't need one."

Not true, but she was bullshitting. In fact, she wasn't sure if Max would be pleased with her spontaneous visit. But she needed to see him and thank him.

"Fine." The woman sighed and picked up her phone. She then pushed a button and glared at Josie. After a few 'Uh-huhs' and 'Okays', the receptionist set the phone back on its hook. "Sorry, you just missed him. Mr Sheridan had an emergency he had to attend to. I can take a message."

Her heart sank.

She had just missed him.

With an exhausted exhale, Josie nodded. "That would be great. Thank you." Leaving him a message was all she could do because she had no other means of contacting him.

"What would you like me to say?"

Josie reached into her back pocket and retrieved one of the bakery business cards she carried around. It had her name and the store number on it. When Danny had been the owner of the bakery, they used to do private orders, and each order went through Josie. Flipping the card over to the blank side, she grabbed the pen next to the blonde receptionist, scrawled her message, and handed it to the less than impressed woman.

"Thanks," Josie said with a little appreciation and then spun around, ready to head to the hospital.

Chapter THREE

Max

The woman who sat in front of him had been everything at one time. Until the real Sarah Collins unveiled herself. A manipulative bitch. A woman willing to take a secret to her grave. A person who would go to extreme lengths to ruin lives. She had been the woman Max had loved.

All the things he had been oblivious to since he had met her were now clear. She wasn't the kind-hearted girl he had helped when he was eight. The one who sat on her doorstep crying as her parents fought. He saw the sad girl. He knew how nice she was underneath it all, but everyone else hadn't. Everyone saw the true Sarah while Max had been in denial.

For as long as Max had known Sarah, she had never been much of a crier. The first time had been when they were eight. But then he saw her shed tears when the truth of her ways came to light. She had told Clara a lie that broke her and Noel apart. Max had ended it with her when he discovered what a blackened heart she had. That was when she had cried. It took seventeen years until he saw those tears of hers again. She had never shown an inch of emotion and never given much in the companionship department. Max had never been an option for her. Instead, his best friend, Alex Lawrence, had. She had chosen the star footballer and the brains. The same man who went to Stanford while Max stayed in Melbourne.

"I wish I had never done it, Max. I can't do this anymore. I can't keep feeling this pain. I don't want to be without you," she sobbed.

He knew she meant it. Sarah had never shown more than her bitchy side. Max had thought it was a portrayal — something to hide behind. A defence mechanism. But he had learnt the hard way that it wasn't a façade. It was real. It was her. All of her.

A heartless bitch.

Max stood from the dining chair where he sat. She had called him in the middle of a client meeting mumbling and threatening self-harm if he did not see her immediately. The love he thought he felt had him excusing himself and driving across the city to her Docklands apartment. The love he thought she felt for him had him at her door. What he had expected was a remorseful woman, not a soulless and sinister woman in lingerie.

It was an act.

One he fell for.

She was quite the actress.

That and his love for her had made him a blind man.

Love made him a terrible person.

And love made him betray his best friends.

"I'm tired of this. Don't call me ever again, Sarah. I told you; we're through. Never again," he instructed firmly, trying to ignore the way his heart shrivelled up inside. He'd loved her since he was eight. At least, he thought he loved her. But after seeing all his best friends in love, he knew his love for her was not the right love. It wasn't how love was supposed to be.

She shot up from her chair. "No!" she begged desperately.

He took two steps away from the table and headed towards the front door, ready to leave her behind and go back to work. His father would not be impressed that he had run out on a client for her.

"Max, don't! I love you, for fuck's sake. I've never loved anyone. No one. None of them. Not Alex. *You*. Just you! I should have been with you. Not him."

Her words had him stop. He was metres from the door and metres from saving his soul. Metres away from starting his recovery to becoming a good man—an honest man worthy of love and worthy of a future.

"Turn around," she breathed. "Tell me you believe me when I say I was meant to be with you and not Alex. Turn around, Max."

Max clenched his eyes shut. Eight months. He had gone eight months without the feel of her. Eight months sober was about to go to waste as he turned around. Max watched her reach behind and unclasp her bra. Then she pulled it off and held it between her fingers. It was slow—painfully slow—in order to hurt him. He would never win in control or teasing. That was all her.

Eight months.

Days before his best friend's wedding was the last time he had slept with her. Moments of weakness and loneliness had won, but he was close to sobriety from her.

Until today.

Until he answered her call. Her damn cheekbones and her long black hair. She was a devil with a body that controlled him. What was even more fucked up was that he loved her. All of her. Loved her tarnished and putrid heart. Hated her blue eyes and the way she'd moaned his name because they'd made him love her all the same. Again and again. It never ceased, and he hated her more for it.

"Sarah," he warned. Max took a step back because he knew how close he was to breaking and how close he was to making the worst mistake of his life.

Then she dropped her red lace bra and shoved her thumbs into the elastic of her skimpy and no doubt expensive panties. Max held his breath, starving his lungs of oxygen. It didn't help that all blood went south. He needed pain. He needed to remember what she did. How she tortured him with her lies and deceit. He wanted light and not the darkness. Max thought he deserved that. He wanted real love. Not this. Not with her. No matter how much his past him wanted this. And no matter how much the eight-year-old he had once been told him that the good was still inside her.

Eight-year-old Max had been a child.

He knew nothing of the nearly naked woman standing before him.

"Say it, Max," she whispered.

His nostrils flared. Attraction and his hard-on were ruining sobriety. He hated her for doing this to him. For ruining him. For making him think he deserved this. That he was never meant for something good or wholesome. Never meant for mutual respect and want. Never meant for anyone but Sarah. She took a deep breath; her chest rose, and it made him ache all over for her.

And then she did it.

Tore his heart out the moment she pulled down her red lace underwear and stepped out of them. She sashayed towards him as if she were a venomous snake and he was the small mouse.

He was completely helpless and completely and utterly fucked.

"Don't do this to us, Max," she cooed in his ear once she had closed the distance and had cupped him where every man wanted to be touched. His erection throbbed with her touch.

No.

She squeezed him gently. The right kind of pressure.

God, yes.

Then her touch disappeared, and for a moment, he thought he was safe. But then her hands were undoing his belt. Yes and no were at war in his thoughts as her mouth began to blaze a trail along his neck. She was trying to make him submit to her. Like he always did. But he didn't want to. Not this time. This was about keeping his integrity. He needed to leave. To be the better man he knew he could be. Max balled his fists, trying to find a way to separate them.

To finally end them.

"Say it. Say you want me. Like you've always wanted me."

His heart thudded violently. Inside him, all his resolve broke into sharp fragments that embedded within him.

"Fuck you, Sarah," he growled. Then he grabbed her hips and slammed her back into the wall behind her.

Sarah let out a moan at his forcefulness. "There you are," she breathed and unzipped his pants.

Wild, animalistic pressure burst as he pushed her legs apart. Max pulled her hands from his pants and forced his pants down to his ankles.

"I hate you so fucking much it hurts!" he hissed the moment her blue eyes met his. Crashing and burning, just like they were about.

"Then show me," she challenged. Her voice filled with desire and need.

Max wrapped his hands around her thighs and helped her up off the ground. Then she wrapped her slender legs around his waist. Sarah's hands were on the back of his neck, pulling him closer to her. She felt unnaturally cold under his touch.

He hated it.

He wanted warmth.

The same warmth he'd felt with Josie's touch.

Josie.

No, no, no.

She was the last person Max should be thinking of. Not sweet Josephine. Her name should not be thought of in all this. He shook his head, hoping to rid her of him as he concentrated on the harsh blues that stared at him. The same pair of hooded eyes that ripped out his soul the moment he had kissed her as a teenager.

This had to be raw.

This had to have no emotions.

"Fucked anyone else since me?"

"No," she said breathlessly. "Just you."

For a second, his traitorous heart skipped a beat. Had this come a year earlier, he would have been thrilled. Make love to her. Show her she should love him. But he was now a different man.

"You saying that to get me back?" he grunted.

"No." Her eyes, for the first time since they were children, had softened. She wasn't lying. Max had been the last man she had slept with.

He decided this would be the last time.

This had to end.

For good.

There would be no foreplay or slow.

No romantic gestures or gentle touches.

This was about destroying her.

Satisfaction swept through him. She might control his heart, but he controlled her pleasure. He remembered every aspect of her face. The way she only showed vulnerability when she was lost in her own selfishness. The way her cheeks flushed, no doubt in anticipation of him entering her. He remembered it all one last time.

"You're going to miss me," he said confidently.

Sarah's eyes widened. "What?"

"I hate you, Sarah Collins. You are the worst thing that has ever happened to me. You denied me real love. So I'm going to not only deny you an orgasm, but also something real and good."

Max set her roughly on the ground. He said no more as he pulled his pants up and fastened his belt, enjoying the shocked expression on her face and the quiver of her lip.

I get this.

I get to break Sarah Collins' heart … if it's possible.

He ran his fingers through his hair, combing his brown locks back. He didn't storm out like he would have liked. Instead, he took short and slow strides. Once he reached her apartment door, he paused, staring at the black paint.

"Have a great life, Sarah. You will never find someone who loves you as I did," Max revealed and grasped the door handle. With a twist, he pulled it open and walked out of her apartment.

Once he closed the door behind him, he leant against it and sighed.

Almost-sex.

Add that to my never want to experience again list.

Max pressed his lips together in a victorious smile, satisfied with his goodbye.

After the short drive back to his apartment, Max had taken a long and scorching hot shower before he returned to work. He needed her touch off his skin. Seeing Sarah enforced his need to live a life without her. And that was what he had done. He said goodbye the only way he knew how and the only way she would listen. She wasn't a woman who sat and had a conversation.

He'd made it raw.

Denied her sex.

She had used sex against him for so many years. But this time, Max didn't give her pleasure. He'd denied her like she had denied him love. Instead, he'd told her goodbye.

Sarah Collins would no longer be a parasite in his life.

She'd be a notch.

Just like he had been one for her.

As Max entered the lobby of Gordon Sheridan Lawyers, the law firm founded by his father, he tightened his tie. He smiled politely at several of the employees from different departments that he remembered and made his way towards the elevator.

"Mr Sheridan!" Ruby, the receptionist hired by HR last month, called out.

He stopped just short of the elevator and spun around. She had already left her desk and met him halfway with her flirty smile. Not the practiced one she normally wore for clients and the other lawyers.

"Hey, Ruby," he said with minimal energy in his voice. He wasn't up for small talk with her. There was no way he was ever going to give her any extra attention. She was an employee. He wasn't going down that road.

"You had a visitor while you were out," she said, brushing her blonde hair over her shoulder. Then her smile faded. "It was a woman."

A woman?

Only one woman would come to his workplace. "My mother?"

Ruby shook her head. "I know what your mother looks like, Mr Sheridan. She was younger. Here, she left this for you. She wrote something on the back." She presented him a small rectangular card.

Max hadn't missed the hint of jealousy in the receptionist's sharp tone. He took the business card from Ruby and smiled. "Thanks."

"No problem. If you need anything, let me know." Her flirty voice and smile had returned.

"Will do," Max said.

The receptionist stood there, staring at him as if she were waiting for him. She glanced down at the card and then back at Max. When he didn't say anything else, she let out a sigh, spun around, and stalked away. He couldn't help but chuckle at her change in attitude. His focus fell to the business card as he held it properly to see that it was from the Little Bakery on Little Collins Street. His chest tightened as he took in the name on the card.

Josie Faulkner.
Baker and cupcake taste tester.
Orders can be placed in store or over the phone.

Josie had come to Gordon Sheridan to see him, and he wasn't there. Instead, he was busy dealing with his ex-whatever-Sarah-was. They were never girlfriend and boyfriend; she had never let them reach that level in their 'relationship.' The honest truth was that they were fuck buddies. If he had just stayed, he'd have gotten the call to go downstairs to find Josie waiting for him. Max flipped the card over to find that she had written, in cursive, a message for him.

I'm sorry about last night.
- Josie.

Stunned, Max had no idea what to think. She had come all the way to apologise for leaving him last night. They hadn't had plans. He had hijacked her night by sitting in front of her so she wouldn't leave. If anyone should apologise, it was Max. Taking in her neat and beautiful writing one more time, Max slipped the business card into his pocket and headed for the revolving door entrance of the law firm.

"Mr Sheridan?" Ruby called out.

Over his shoulder, he yelled, "Something important has come up. See you Monday!"

Josie

Danny: How is my former employee going?

osie squinted at the text from her old boss. There was no denying how insanely hot Danny Fletcher was. She had always harboured a crush, not caring that he was almost ten years older than she was. An attractive man who could cook was a serious turn-on. But he was her boss, and she would never jeopardise her employment or his bakery. Danny had never been a fan of any of her boyfriends. According to him, none of them had ever been worthy of her. Her favourite view of his was always, 'when are you going to take out the rubbish, Josie? You're wasting your time with that dickhead.'

Yeah, she missed him.

Since he'd taken over at the Leopold in San Francisco, their chats were text messages every now and then. Today was one of those days. After she had gone to the hospital, she was told the CT scanners were booked out, and her mother's tests were delayed until tomorrow morning. Josie's mother had kicked a fuss and made her leave after lunch, instructing her to go home and concentrate on her upcoming torts assignment.

However, the moment she left the Royal Melbourne, Nadia had texted her asking if she would fill in for Denise who had called in sick. Josie accepted the shift because baking took her mind off all the stress and pressure around her. Though she was no natural at concocting new cupcakes, she did know how to bake them right. She was no Clara Parker, cupcake genius, but Josie managed just fine. Her regular customers had noticed immediately the change in taste when Clara had left the Little Bakery but commented that Josie had done a fine job replicating Clara's recipes as best as she could.

Josie leant on the stainless-steel prep counter and sighed. As cute as Danny was, and as much as she loved him as her boss, she couldn't tell him how she really felt. Emotionally, she was exhausted. And mentally, she wondered where her thoughts went to most of the time. One thing she didn't have to worry about was her mother's medical bills. Emily Faulkner had money saved away plus private health insurance. Though they weren't rich, they had enough money to pay the bills. And if it got so bad, Josie knew where to go. Her father owed her almost three years' worth of child support. She wouldn't tell him exactly why she needed the money, but she'd find an excuse.

Josie: Oh, you know, the usual. Nadia's working on recipes while I'm here on my phone. Nothing has changed since you left, Danny.

Danny: Thought as much. You heard from Clara lately?

Josie: She's busy with classes since she left that job you set up for her. Seriously, Danny? How could you let her go work for such an asshole?

Danny: I didn't know Mac was taking over. He had a job lined up in New York. Thought she was in safe hands with Antonio. How was I supposed to know he'd leave? It's been three months, Josie. Stop blaming me. I wasn't the one who threatened her marriage.

Josie: You're right. Sorry. With everything that's going on, I haven't had a chance to blame someone. Anyways, how are you?

Danny: Good. I'm thinking about coming home in a few months. Catch up?

Josie: As long as I don't have exams, sure. Let me know when and where.

"Josie!" Nadia called from the shop floor.

Setting her phone down, she pushed off the steel bench and made her way out of the kitchen where she found Nadia holding a serving apron in her direction.

"Do you mind serving for a bit? I have Liam's lawyer on the phone," Nadia said. Concern was evident in her frown and creased forehead, and fear mixed in Josie's Italian boss' dark brown eyes as she brushed her tight brunette curls behind her ear.

"Everything okay?" Josie asked as she took the apron and began to tie it around her.

Her boss nodded. "Looks like Liam's transferring the

With the first GOODBYE

bakery's ownership over."

"To who?" Josie knotted the ties and tilted her head. "To you?"

Nadia let out a dry laugh. "You kidding? There is no way I could afford this place. Ally's taking over."

"Ally?"

"Yep. When she comes back from France with her husband, she'll be over with a new contract and details on what's happening. Liam's lawyer just wants me to be ready. Ally could want a new head baker. It could mean I'd potentially be out of a job."

Josie stepped forward and set a hand on Nadia's shoulder. "Ally's not who you think she is. She's one of the nicest people I know. You'll see — Did you say *husband*?" She hadn't heard from Ally since she left for New York with Rob. Nothing on Facebook had indicated that she and Rob had gotten married recently. All the news and social media told her were that Robert Moors was now the Men's Single Scull World Champion. When Josie found out, she had squealed, happy for Rob. But also because she knew someone famous.

"Yeah. Didn't you know?"

She shook her head. "No, I didn't."

"They are definitely married. Also, Taylor will help serve with you."

Josie nodded. Taylor was the new waitress the bakery had hired a few months ago. Although a little ditsy, Taylor was a good waitress. She was no Clara, but Josie appreciated her enthusiasm at work.

Nadia turned her head slightly and smiled. "You have a customer, Josie."

Smile, Josie.

Your customers make the time fly by.

Three hours and forty-five minutes until you get to go home.

Josie readied her smile and then spun to find a customer she was not expecting. Light brown eyes that reminded her of caramel and dark brown locks. He wore his suit perfectly. Tailored to him, no doubt. How she ever dated sweaty DJs she'd never know. Men in suits were where it was at. However, no man wore a suit quite like Maxwell Sheridan.

"Max," she breathed, mentally kicking herself for sounding

36

so out of breath at his presence.

Seriously?

"You've got this?" Nadia asked, hint of humour in her voice. Josie swung her gaze to her smirking boss and glared at her. "Yes," she said through clenched teeth. "I do. Thank you, Nadia."

Nadia chuckled and retreated to the small office. Josie took a deep breath then faced Max's very cute confused expression.

"Hi," she finally said.

The confusion left his face and joy replaced it. "Hi," he said in a soft voice. Then he dug a hand into his jacket pocket and produced something rectangular.

Josie raised a brow at him.

Max held it up, and she recognised it as her business card she had left with his law firm's receptionist. He had gotten it. She couldn't help but hope he'd come straight to the bakery to show her. Stupid thought, but she seemed to have them around him.

"*You're* sorry, Josie? Really?"

The humour in his voice had her folding her arms over her chest. "Well, I am. I'm sorry for last night."

He laughed. It was light and sweet sounding. "That's exactly what you wrote," he pointed out. "Why would *you* be sorry? I hijacked your night."

It was her turn to laugh. "I guess you did. I just ran off and left you there after you cancelled your plans with your friends."

"Josephine, first, let's get some things straight. Okay?" He leant on the counter and moved closer to her. She was thankful his surprising visit was during the quieter moments of the store's trading hours.

She tilted her chin a little higher. "Okay."

"One, you're more important than they are. Understood?" His brown eyes darkened.

"I guess ..." she said, unsure.

He rolled his eyes at her. "No guessing. You are important to *me*. Two, they are not my friends. You are my friend. Three ..." He paused, reached up, and pulled on her left arm to untangle it from its fold and grasp her hand. "You don't have to be sorry if you need to be somewhere important. Okay?"

Oh, dear heart.

That beating organ of hers tightened at his words.

Goddammit, Maxwell Sheridan, you asshole!

When she first met Max, she had no idea how sweet he could be. She knew bits of his life from Clara and Stevie — how he had slept with the woman who had torn apart Noel and Clara — but Josie knew deep down he was keeping other secrets. Darker ones that hadn't met the light. Ones he was ashamed of. Maybe that was what she felt connected to. His desire to keep his secrets. Just like her desire to keep hers at bay. She was sure his fears were the truth. Her fears were that the reality of her mother's health would be known. That Josie would lose her sooner rather than later.

That this time, her mother wouldn't be able to fight.

She didn't want to accept the fact that the only person who loved her unconditionally was dying.

"Okay," she finally said in a small voice and attempted a smile.

He appeared satisfied with her response as his eyes softened. "Do you have another business card?" he asked, his hand leaving hers.

She felt the emptiness his touch had created with its departure.

Josie's brows furrowed. "Ah, sure." She ducked down and opened the cupboard underneath the register and opened a small box of her business cards sitting next to a few of Clara's that remained. Josie removed one of hers and then stood, handing Max the card.

He took it from her and reached into his jacket pocket to produce a pen. Max set the card on the counter and began to write on it. When he finished, his hand went into his inside jacket pocket and took out his wallet. Josie watched as he flipped it open, pulled out a card, turned it over, and scribbled something on it.

Once he appeared happy with what he wrote, he returned the pen and wallet to his pocket. Max picked up the cards and held them out to her. "I've gotta run. I'm sorry I wasn't at the office when you stopped by. It was good to see you last night and today. I hope everything is okay. If you want to talk, I'm here."

Josie took the cards from him, her eyes never leaving his.

The air around her seemed thick and unbreathable. It was a struggle she didn't want him to see.

"Thanks."

"I'll see you around, Josephine."

She nodded at the large, almost hopeful smile he directed her way. "Thank you for stopping by, Max. You didn't have to."

He leant closer to her and whispered, "I had to," before he left her staring after him as he exited the bakery.

When he had vanished from her line of sight, Josie glanced down at the two cards in her hands. She flipped over her business card and read what he wrote.

> I'm sorry about today.
> Didn't mean to miss you.
> - Max.

She smiled at the sweetness of his note. It caused her heart to flutter in a way it hadn't before. The flutters were heavy and warm as if so much pressure weighed it down, but her heart was fighting against it to break free.

Didn't mean to miss you.

Josie knew he meant that he had just left when she had arrived at the firm. But she couldn't help but love the thought that maybe he couldn't help but miss her. She shook her head at the ridiculous thought.

Max miss me?

Completely stupid.

We're friends.

She set down her business card and took in the other one, realising it was his. Effortlessly embossed underneath the Gordon Sheridan logo were his name and details.

Maxwell Sheridan
Corporate lawyer.
03 9605 2800
MaxwellSheridan@GordonSheridan.com.au

Flipping the card over, she felt her heart swell at what he had written. And at that moment, Josie knew he had ruined the concept of friendship for her.

I feel compelled to ask you, but are you okay?
 Call me: 0428 673 388
 - Max.

Chapter FOUR

Max

He received Josie's text message on Tuesday. Max was at Stevie and Julian's apartment on his lunch break to water Julian's orchid plant. Max had been given specific instructions to keep the pink flower alive. It was an exercise Stevie had given her fiancé. If he could keep the plant alive, then she'd consider a dog. Julian Moors was all kinds of whipped, and Max had been stupid enough to let Julian coerce him into making sure his best friend achieved his dream of a pet.

Max set the small watering can on the glass table and unlocked his phone.

> **Unknown:** You felt compelled? Stop stealing my lines. I'm fine, Max. -Josie.

His chest warmed at the sight of her damn name. He had no idea why or how he had such strange feelings for someone he considered his friend. That was what they were. Josie was far too sweet and smart to want anything other than friendship with him. Max's thumb pressed on her number to save it under her name.

> **Max:** It's quite the line, Josie. Hard not to use.

> **Josie:** I guess I have a way with words.

> **Max:** You do. Don't you have class or something?

> **Josie:** Yeah. Sitting in my contracts lecture. It's hell. And it is very confusing.

> **Max:** You do know I'm a corporate lawyer, right? I deal with contracts every day. I can help you.

She hadn't replied straight away, and that had worried him. Maybe he had overstepped, but he was sure offering his help was a friendly thing to do. He had limited friendships with the opposite sex. Most times, he either slept with them, or they were married or engaged to one of his best friends.

Josie was neither.

As Max checked on Julian's orchid one last time, he quickly took a picture to send later and then left the apartment. By the time Max had driven back to the firm, rode the elevator to the fifteenth floor, and sat at his desk, his phone beeped in his jacket pocket. When he pulled out his phone, Josie's message flashed on his screen. It had been over twenty minutes since he'd last texted her.

> **Josie:** Sorry for the late reply. Lecture ended, and I had to run to my next tutorial. You really want to help me? You'll need a lot of patience. Family law, I know. Contracts and torts? That's another story. You'll see just what a terrible lawyer I'll be.

Max chuckled. He knew she was teasing and had every confidence she would make a terrific lawyer. One that had every right to work for a firm like his father's. She had mentioned she had no placement for next year. Max would look into finding her a traineeship at Gordon Sheridan. His father's law firm was one of the best in the state, so it would be an amazing addition to her resume.

Max: Josie, I wouldn't be offering if I didn't want to help. Is that what's been troubling you? Law school and placement?

His heart thumped as his palms sweat. Soon he would know the extent of their friendship. If it were one where they shared their fears and troubles. Or if it were one where they would eventually tell each other their sins and guilty secrets.

Josie: No.

Josie: I mean, yes.

Josie: Honestly, Max, I don't know. My life is a little full on at the moment.

Just as Max was about to reply, Julian messaged him. He opened it to find a picture of a pear.

Julian: I was always afraid of gardening. Then I decided to grow a PEAR!

"What an idiot," Max muttered as he shook his head. His phone beeped once again.

Julian: Puns aside, how's my orchid? Better not have killed it. I will hurt you when I come home if anything happened.

Max: Relax. Your damn orchid is fine. I'll send you a picture later. I'm just at work.

Julian: Fine. I'll be home in a couple of days. Don't forget that picture of Orchid.

Max: I won't forget that picture of Orchid the orchid.

He then exited his text message conversation with Julian and returned to Josie's.

Max: Just for you, I'll waive my service fee.

Josie: You really are a pal, aren't you? Talk more later?

Max: So that's a yes to tutoring you?

Josie: You're going to regret it, but sure. I'll message you after this class. My tutor's talking about my upcoming assignment for taxation.

Max: Taxation is the worst. Enjoy class.

Enjoy class.
"Out of all the things you could possibly say to her," he mumbled as he set his phone on his desk.

Max shook his head and picked up the contract he had been drafting for his client, Bill, a country dairy farmer. It wasn't the most exciting job on the planet, but someone had to create the contracts businesses signed. But knowing the distributor, Bill and Max had a long negotiation battle ahead of them. To prevent this, and to minimise the cost of what Bill would have to pay for his services, Max had to make sure this contract suited not only the distributor but also helped the dairy business.

The chime from his phone had stopped Max from typing the clauses section of the draft contract. He peeked down to see Josie's name on the screen. It had been almost two hours since he'd last spoken to her. Unable to help the smile on his face, Max reached over and picked up his iPhone. He unlocked it and read the message she had sent him.

Josie: Are you okay for me to stop by your office?

Max: Why wouldn't I be okay with that?

Josie: The receptionist seems to have forgotten me since the last time I was here. Claims you don't know who I am.

Max: What? I'm coming downstairs.

Josie: You don't have to. You're probably busy. I was on my way home from uni and thought I'd drop by. I can go.

Max: Seriously, Josie. Stay there. Give me a couple of minutes.

He didn't wait for her to reply. Instead, Max pressed save on the Bill Erickson contract and stood from his leather chair. He shoved his phone into his pants pocket and then left his office for the elevator. As he waited for it to reach his floor, Sully called out Max's name and made his way towards him.

"Max, we're going out for drinks tonight. Earl from recruitment, it's his birthday. You in?" Sully asked as the elevator doors opened.

Max stepped inside, spun around, and pressed the lobby button. Just before the doors shut, he replied, "Can't. Got plans."

"Since when do you have plans? You're always the last to leave this place." The elevator doors began to close on Sully.

"Since your wife left you," Max teased with a smirk.

"Fuckin' bastard!"

Max chuckled as the elevator descended, bopping his head along with the typical jazz that played. It took several minutes to make it to the ground floor. The elevator had opened and closed on several different floors as employees hopped on and off. Finally, he breathed out when the doors opened, and he entered the lobby.

It hadn't taken him long to find Josie staring up at the large chandelier on the ceiling. Max noticed she was wearing a blue Deakin University hoodie, black skinny jeans, and a messenger bag. She had her long brown hair pulled into a high ponytail with some shorter straight strands loose by the side of her face. He watched as she lowered her chin and those bright blue eyes found him. Her smile developed instantly, and Max's chest tightened. She was beautiful in all her naturalness and comfort.

Damn.

He should not be thinking his friend was beautiful.

Hell, he had thought she was the moment he met her and then at the wedding.

He was too far gone.

Max closed the distance and smiled at her. She was shorter than Sarah and Andrea were, but it was adorable. Not even thinking it through, Max wrapped his arms around her and pulled her into a tight hug. Josie tensed in his hold, but after several seconds, she relaxed and hugged him back.

"Sorry. Was that ... umm ... over the line?" he asked after he broke their embrace and nervously rubbed the back of his neck.

She laughed. "No. Has anyone ever told you that you're actually a good hugger?" Josie stepped forward and squinted at him. "Are you ...?"

His brows met. "Am I what?"

This time, she let out a sweet giggle. "Are you blushing?"

Max groaned at her. "Jos—"

"Maxwell," he heard his father, Gordon, say.

His father had impeccable timing, and Max groaned as he noticed the hesitation on Josie's face. Gordon Sheridan was a feared man in Melbourne. Undeniably the best defence lawyer money could buy with the best win ratio. He had not lost a case yet. Max had never wanted to eclipse that legacy, so instead, he became a corporate lawyer and specialised in contracts.

He gave Josie a reassuring smile as his father made his way to them. Gordon nodded at Ruby and then stood next to Josie.

"And who is this?" His father's eyes roamed Josie—from her beautiful, slender face to her body—and a smile hinted on his lips. His father was one who hardly smiled. Last year, working for him had caused Max to go back to Sarah. Client after client was at Max's door. His father cited it as a growing exercise. To see if he could someday run the firm or become a partner.

46

"Dad, this is Josie, a friend of mine. Josie, this is my father, Gordon Sheridan," Max introduced.

Josie shifted and held her hand out towards his father. "It is a pleasure to meet you, Mr Sheridan."

She sounded sweet and kind as if it really was a pleasure to meet him. If only she knew how forceful and brutal he really was. His father glanced over at Max and eyed him. It was that 'How did this happen?' look he gave when he was building a defence for his clients.

"It's lovely to meet you, Josie." His eyes darted to her hoodie. "Deakin, huh? Good law department. What are you studying?"

It surprised Max how nice and tame his father was being. Though, he was sure his father was wondering how Max even knew someone like Josie. His father had only ever seen him with women like Sarah. In fact, for a long time, Gordon Sheridan had only ever seen him with Sarah Collins.

"Law, sir," Josie said. She sounded shy as if she felt guilty about it.

Gordon chuckled. "Dear, ain't nothing to be shy about. Exuberate confidence. That's how you're going to be a successful lawyer."

She nodded as if his father had given her the secret of how to win at life. "Thank you. I'll keep that in mind."

His father looked at Max and then at Josie. "How did you meet my son, Josie?"

"Our best friends got married. I saw him around previously, but not until Noel and Clara's wedding day did we actually speak."

Gordon nodded along. "Had I not had an important case, I would have been there. Always adored that Clara Parker. So you saw Max before the wedding?"

"Yes, Mr Sheridan—"

"Please, call me Gordon," his father interrupted.

Gordon.

Not once had his father ever wanted someone, let alone a complete stranger, call him by his first name. Not unless they were lifelong friends.

Max didn't miss her fluttering eyelids. She was just as surprised as he was. She smiled and then continued. "Max has been to the bakery a few times. Never noticed me until we got partnered up at the wedding."

Never noticed her?

If only she knew how wrong she was.

Gordon pursed his lips and then made a humming sound. "Typical of my son to miss such a good thing. Maxwell, you must have Josie over for dinner with your mother and me."

"Umm." Josie looked at him and gave him a tight and unsure smile.

"Dad—"

"I need to get to a meeting in the conference room. Maxwell, make sure to set up a dinner with Josie soon." Then his father turned and smiled at her. "It was lovely meeting you, Josie. I'll see you again soon."

"And it was an honour to meet you, Gordon."

Max watched the smile on his father's face deepen and his eyes glimmer. His father liked Josie, liked she was studying law, and no doubt loved the look of her. If only Gordon Sheridan knew just how sweet she really was to Max. His father nodded, walked past Max, and headed for the elevators.

Josie blinked several times in disbelief. "I just met your father," she said in awe. "I just met Gordon Sheridan. *The* Gordon Sheridan. His cases are taught in my lectures and tutorials. How did I go from meeting your father to him urging that I attend a dinner with you, him, and your mother? How does that even happen?"

"Honestly, I have no idea. My father has never warmed to someone as quickly as he has with you," Max revealed. Then something she had said had him curious. "You told him that I never noticed you before."

"Yeah. The first time we met was at the bakery. I had black hair and was kind of pretentious. Now, I have brown hair, struggle with contracts, and am about to ask you to tutor me," she said.

Max took in her chestnut coloured locks. "Brunette suits you much better than the black. And *Josephine* ..."

"Yes, *Maxwell*?"

He took a step closer to her, so his body was almost touching her body. Max reached up and tucked her loose hair behind her ear and said softly, "I definitely noticed you."

Her breathing hitched.

He hadn't missed it, though he wished he had. It would make being around her more bearable and give him a little room to breathe a little easier.

Friends.

You're both friends.

Max dropped his hand and cleared his throat. "You still gonna ask me to be your tutor?"

"Maxwell Sheridan, will you please tutor me in contracts?" Josie asked sweetly.

Max nodded. "Josephine Falkner, I thought you'd never ask."

Josie

"And was he mentally capable of comprehending right from wrong?" Jason Silverman, Josie's Legal Practice and Ethics tutor, asked. Jason was not only Josie's favourite tutor at Deakin University, but he was also working on his PhD between lectures and tutorials. Soon enough, he'd have the title of 'Doctor' before Josie could even say she had graduated from law school. Jason's dark brown eyes scanned the room and caused Josie to sink lower in her seat. When his eyes landed on her, he let out a sigh and trained his focus on another student. "Matt, what do you think?"

Josie let out a relieved sigh and picked up her pen to write Matt's answer and Jason's upcoming explanation in her notebook.

"From all the evidence, Jas, it sounds like he was completely sane when he killed his wife," Matt stated as Josie began to write.

Jason's lips pursed as he nodded. Then he pushed off the table he leant on and made his way to Matt's. Upon reaching it, he set his palms on the edge and looked down at Matt. "And what makes you think he was sane?"

"He *planned* the murder of his wife the moment he found out she was cheating on him. Hell, the guy even googled 'how to get away with murder' for tips."

The entire class laughed with Matt.

Josie only smiled as she flipped the page of her notebook over. Then she set pen to paper and craned her neck to find Jason looking her way.

"And what do you think, Josie?" her tutor asked.

It had been weeks since she had even answered in class, when she used to challenge Matt and his answers all the time. But now, now Josie wrote what she heard and counted the minutes until she could race out of the room and take the tram back into the city to be by her mother's bedside.

She pressed her lips into a tight smile and shrugged. What Josie really thought was that the murderous husband was sane but could use the circumstances for his bloodlust for an insanity defence. But she knew Jason well, and he'd ask her if it was an ethical practice. It wasn't. She knew right from wrong, and the husband was guilty. But as a hypothetical defence lawyer, it was about winning the case. Morally, it was completely unethical, but it was a legal practice. It was what won a lot of cases, this one included.

"I don't have anything to add to what Matt just said," she answered.

Jason pushed off the table and stood straight. "That's disappointing to hear, Josie." Then he glanced at the watch on his left wrist, and a smile spread across his face. "All right, everyone, that's time for us this week. I'll see you all at the lecture next week. I'll be taking over for Professor Ibrahim. I'll be cutting into the usual structure and adding a discussion, so be prepared."

"Anything else, Jas?" one of the mature students in the back of the classroom asked.

"Just the required reading in your textbook. Also, I'd like you all to think of an argument to counter or strengthen Matt's for our next tutorial. Have a great week."

Josie had quickly scribbled her thoughts on the case before she closed her notebook and shoved it, her pen, and the textbook into her satchel. Just as she was about to stand from her chair, she heard Jason clear his throat and say, "Josie, could you please stay back for a moment?"

She winced at her tutor's rigid stance. Then she pulled her phone from the leather jacket pocket and checked the time. There was no way she'd make her tram now that her tutor wanted her to stay back. She had been cutting it close before, but now she would definitely miss it.

Sighing, she set her satchel on the table. "Sure. What's up?"

Her tutor turned to face her, and she saw the disappointment in his eyes. It was hard to look away from him, and it made her uncomfortable and sick inside. Jason Silverman was cute for his late twenties. His short brown hair was combed perfectly. And as always, his button-down shirt was tucked into his black skinny jeans, and his brown dress shoes completed his tutor outfit. Sometimes, when he was running late or had been writing all night, he wore loafers, jeans, and a T-shirt. He was one of a few who treated her nicely and overlooked her previously wild and edgy attire when she had tested her father. When she had given up on that lifestyle, he had a smile on his lips and welcomed the real her back. He'd seen through her bullshit from the get-go.

"What's going on with you, Josie?" He sounded tired and fed up. She didn't blame him. She felt that, too. She was sick and tired of the world. But she had to brave it for her mother.

"Nothing," she lied.

"Don't, Josie. Don't lie to me."

She wasn't going to deny it. She was indeed lying to her favourite tutor who had always respected her and commented on how well she'd do as a lawyer someday.

"I just didn't feel like talking in class today," she explained lamely as she picked up her satchel's strap. She dropped it the moment Jason made his way towards her. The disappointment in his eyes faded, and instead, she saw sadness and understanding in them. It confused her. Then she gazed down to see something in his hand. Her heart hammered in her chest at the thought of what it could be. "What's that?"

Jason held the paper to her, and Josie took it. He took a deep breath and said, "I've taught you for a few years now, Josie. I can't write any form of recommendation with the work you've handed in. What happened to you, Josie? Your assignments were my favourite to mark. Your mind and approach to legal situations were always fascinating. You always led me through your answers with a uniqueness I've never seen before. Your critical thinking abilities are beyond your youth."

It was half a compliment and half a talking-to.

She had no response. All she could do was keep her mouth

shut and hope that Jason would take a hint and speed up his takedown of her.

"Have you got a placement for next year? You're required to complete a traineeship before you can practice."

"I don't have a placement."

Jason's disappointment made a return. "I can make some calls and —"

Lie, Josie.

"It's fine," she said, cutting him off. "I have a few interviews. I'm sure I'll have it cemented before exams."

Relief consumed his eyes. "That's good to hear. I've worried about you, Josie. You know you can come talk to me. I don't want to fail you, but if you keep handing in work as you have … You're lucky your arguments got you through this assignment. You have to contribute in class — at least try to. Don't let a guy ruin the makings of your career, Josie."

Shame filled her.

Of course, he would think it was a guy.

It had always been about a guy.

Josie faked the smile on her lips and nodded. She picked up the satchel strap and set it on her shoulder. "I won't let a guy ruin this. I promise to do better."

He didn't believe her.

It was so clear on his face.

No smile.

No hint of anything in his eyes.

Her words held no meaning to him.

So she would just have to prove it.

"Honey, I'm home!" West Montgomery sang as he entered the apartment Josie shared with his girlfriend, Stella Weller.

Josie didn't bother to look up from her legal practice and ethics textbook. She was catching up on last week's required reading before she read this week's and next. She had a lot of catching up to do. Visiting her mother meant more, but she was also determined to finish her degree. It also meant losing herself in the ethical side of being a lawyer. In fact, she had learnt that a lot of things lawyers did were, according to the theory, unethical.

"See, I told you she was alive," she heard West whisper.

Josie rolled her eyes and stated, "You owe me twenty dollars."

"She's most definitely herself," West added.

"Shut up, West, and get the groceries in the fridge," Stella ordered.

Moments later, her best friend placed something on the table. Josie set the textbook down to find a pint of Ben and Jerry's on the dining table she had used as her desk.

"Your favourite. Chocolate fudge brownie," Stella said with a smile.

Letting out a sigh, Josie reached for the pint of ice cream and worked at getting the plastic seal off the lid. "Is this your idea of cooking dinner?"

Stella let out a laugh as she got to work untying her blonde locks from her bun. "No. You know I can't cook. That's why I'm with West. Isn't that right, honey?"

A groan came from the kitchen. "I'm not your honey! I'm Josie's. Didn't you hear me call her that moments ago?"

"We can fight over her later. Get to cooking!"

"Yeah, yeah."

"You're both really annoying," Josie commented as she removed the lid and set it on the wooden table.

Out of nowhere, Stella produced a silver spoon from behind her back and handed it to Josie. "You love us. We weren't expecting to see you at home."

Stabbing the utensil into the pint of ice cream, she spooned an enormous amount out and set the tub down. She brought the spoon to her lips and shovelled the ice cream into her mouth. Instant regret filled her as the cold treat took over and caused her to cringe. Her temples felt that familiar cool ache, and she slapped her palm against the tabletop. It took some time before she could swallow it down.

"Want some water?" Stella asked with a laugh, glittering green eyes on her.

Josie shook her head. "No. I'm good. Thanks."

"No hospital tonight?"

Another shake of her head. "Doc told me to go home. Mum's on some heavy stuff tonight to help her sleep. They were meant to do the scans but couldn't. She wasn't feeling okay, but he assured me that she's next in line."

Stella's chin dipped. Her best friend had always seen Emily Faulkner as a second mother to her. "Do you think it could …?"

Josie hated the question Stella couldn't finish.

But the reality was, she did. She did think her mother's cancer could be terminal this time. She was a lot frailer now than during her first battle. The cancer took away her strong and healthy mother and left a shell behind. Her warmth was no longer hers to exuberate and for Josie to be in awe of.

"Yeah," she whispered, scraping more ice cream into the spoon. "I don't want it to be, but they keep telling me to prepare myself."

She raised her chin to find tears slipping down Stella's cheeks. "Em's a fighter. She's never lost a battle yet."

That's a lie.

The thought had Josie feeling disgusted with herself. It was horrible to think so ill of her mother. But she had lost one fight. And that had been to keep the love of Josie's father. She knew her mother still loved her father. Emily had defended him for being a selfish father and husband. Chose to leave them so he could be an ambassador. To serve his country rather than his family. And to rub salt in the wounds he'd inflicted, he even had a new German family.

"Honey, do you want apricot chicken or satay for dinner?" West asked from the kitchen.

Josie glanced over to see the smirk on Stella's face. "He means you, Josie," her best friend whispered.

"Seriously?"

Stella nodded.

"Apricot chicken!" Josie yelled out.

"I thought so," West answered. "Too bad it's gonna cost you twenty dollars for my apricot chicken, Josie."

"Do you take uncollected debts? Because you owe me that very amount."

The apartment went quiet.

Then her best friend's boyfriend screamed, "I'm Josie-debt free!"

Max: Josephine, it's been a few days. Do you still need tutoring?

Josie glanced down at her phone on the steel bench and tied the icing stained apron around her. Once she'd fastened it tightly, she picked up her phone and smiled at Max's message. It had been a hectic few days of classes, the hospital, her mother, and her roommate. Catching up on her legal practice and ethics readings meant forgetting about contracts altogether—especially since that class wasn't until next week. She'd neglected to schedule a free timeslot to acquire Max's legal mind. She felt guilty that he was waiting on her when he was a busy practising lawyer at one of the best law firms in the country.

Josie: I'm so sorry. I've been so busy catching up with a few of my readings. When are you free?

She watched the dots on her phone move, indicating he was already typing a reply.

Max: Question is, when are you free?

Josie: I have the morning shift today at the bakery then I have an afternoon lecture. Tonight?

Max: Can't do tonight. I'm sorry.

She couldn't help but feel slightly disappointed that he wasn't free to tutor her tonight. It was Friday. He probably had plans or even a date. The latter caused her to frown as a weird pang consumed her chest. It was strange. She hadn't felt that pang since she was eight and her mother told her that her father was having another daughter with another woman. She was jealous to share her father with another daughter.

Am I jealous of Max going on a date?
She shook her head. She couldn't be jealous.
In fact, she should encourage Max.
They were friends.
Friends weren't jealous of such petty things like the idea of Max dating other women.

> **Josie:** That's all right. I have the shorter shifts this weekend and a few errands. But besides that, I'm free in the afternoons. Whenever you're free and want to tutor, I'm at your disposal.

Josie watched Max begin a reply before it immediately stopped. The anxiety of watching someone write a text message was a form of torture. Her last message sounded desperate for his time. Well, she was technically desperate for it and his expertise in contracts.

"Josie, I'd like you to meet someone," Nadia, her boss and the head baker, said.

Setting her phone back on the bench, she turned to find Ally Moors standing at the kitchen entry with a smile. Her hazel eyes held an excited gleam in them. Josie glanced down to see Ally in a long floral skirt and a white off-the-shoulder top. She was stunning. Not an inch of the former life lived on her. Ally amazed Josie and made her proud of the person she had become since she had recovered from her kidney transplant and moved to Melbourne almost four months ago.

"Ally, it's so good to see you," Josie said.

It was. It was so good to see her with a smile and some colour on her face rather than the paleness Josie saw after her transplant.

"I'll leave you two to catch up," Nadia said as she left them alone in the kitchen.

The former socialite made her way towards her and instantly pulled Josie into a hug the moment she reached her. "You, too, Josie," she said once she ended their embrace. That was when Josie noticed the ring on Ally's left hand.

The sapphire and diamond gold wedding ring was beautiful.
It wasn't obnoxious.
Or flashy.

It was refined and stunning.

A lot like the woman who wore the ring so proudly.

"So you married the rower?" Josie said, biting back a smile.

A blush consumed Ally's cheeks. "Don't think we didn't invite you to the wedding. We eloped in New York. We're going to have an engagement party and an actual wedding soon, and you'll definitely be invited. Enough about me. How are you?"

Josie shrugged a shoulder. "Still working here when I'm not at uni. I actually want to keep talking about you. I saw Rob on TV!"

Ally's hazel eyes gleamed. "I'm so proud of him. We just got back last night, and he's had calls for interviews. He's turned them all down except for the ones for *Rowing World* magazine, Rowing Australia, and Rowing Victoria. They're the ones he's required to do."

"That's so amaz—"

Josie's phone chiming had her sentence ending. She glanced down to see that Max had replied to her. Her heart galloped at the sight of his name.

A stupid name evoked such reactions from her.

It was as surprising as it was annoying.

He was just her friend.

"Max?" Ally questioned. Josie didn't have to look at her to know she wore a smile. It was clear in her voice.

Josie swiped her phone off the steel counter. "Ah, yeah."

"This couldn't possibly be the same Max who's also my husband's best friend, is it?"

"Ah ..." It wasn't a secret that she and Max had seen each other while their friends were in France. It wasn't as if they were hiding their friendship. Yet Josie felt the need to.

"It so is!" Ally let out a laugh. "Max Sheridan is texting Josie Faulkner. How did that even happen?"

Josie was at a loss for words.

How did it happen?

The wedding.

That moment on that bridge had connected them.

Her failed dinner with her father had given them more than just the wedding.

Everything else seemed to come next for them.

As if they were meant to be in each other's lives ...

57

As friends.

"We saw each other one night at a restaurant and … numbers were exchanged and …"

"You like Max," Ally stated rather than asked.

Josie let out an unbelievable laugh. "Me? Like Max?"

Ally nodded with a large grin on her face. "I saw the way your eyes lit up when you saw his name. You like him."

"Umm, no! I just saw a glimpse of the cupcakes that Nadia was making, and they just so happen to be near my phone. That's it. Cupcakes light up my eyes."

Lame.

So very lame.

Josie watched as Ally glanced down at her phone and then her eyes had roamed the bench before she returned her gaze to Josie. Eyebrow raised and all. "There are no cupcakes." Ally giggled as she set her hand on Josie's shoulder. "I won't say a word, I promise. But I didn't come here to be your boss."

"You didn't?"

Ally dropped her hand with a shake of her head. "I came to see how you were and ask if you wanted to come to PJ's tonight? We're celebrating Robbie being world champion. So will you please come celebrate with us? Stevie will be there. And where Stevie is … Julian is, too."

"You mean your brother-in-law?"

Her new boss' shoulders sagged. "Yeah. The title has gone to his head. So what do you say? See you at PJ's at seven?"

Josie opened her mouth to oppose. She had a ton of reading to do and cases to start making notes on for her final assignments. "I would love to but—"

"Max will be there."

"Ally, Max is my tutor," she stated, downplaying whatever romantic notions Ally had in mind. "Nothing's going on between us. We're friends. Nothing more."

Ally's grin faded into a slanted smile. "Well, if you just wanna hang out with me and Stevie, you should come. No pressure. And I'm sorry if I made you uncomfortable with my 'you like Max' accusations. I just think if you did, there's nothing to be ashamed of. He's a great guy. I actually like the idea of you and Max."

"Ally, you ready to talk paperwork?" a man interrupted as

he entered the kitchen.

The former socialite glanced over her shoulder. "Sure. I'm ready, Adam." Her focus returned to Josie. "No pressure about tonight. But I know Stevie is looking forward to seeing you."

"Thanks for the invite," Josie said, not wanting to commit her attendance. She didn't want Max to think she was stalking him, and she didn't want him to feel uncomfortable with her presence.

"I'll be back. I'll finalise this ownership transfer, and then we can catch up." Ally spun around and made her way to the door.

When Josie was alone in the kitchen, she unlocked her phone and read Max's message.

> **Max:** Josephine, I promise, your education is a priority of mine. So please don't think I'm avoiding you tonight. As I said, you're important to me. But so is Rob. He and Ally, as well as Stevie and Julian, are back. They're celebrating tonight at PJ's. You should come, too. Be my plus one, Josie. I promise, this weekend I'll tutor you until you get bored of me.

"You don't play fair, Max," she whispered to herself, unsure of where she'd be tonight.

Chapter FIVE

Max

"I'm going to kill you!" Julian Moors yelled loud enough to have the indie band stop playing. Letting out a sigh, Max set his pint of Guinness down and faced his best friend.

"Okay?"

"Where is she?"

"Where is who?"

"Orchid!" Julian growled.

Rob's burst of laughter boomed behind him, and Max couldn't help but join along. He quickly cleared his throat and composed himself. "Orchid?"

"Yes. Where is she?"

"Your plant?"

Julian nodded, annoyance flared in his light blue eyes. "Where is Orchid the orchid?"

"Maybe she got plant-napped?"

Julian straightened his spine and then shook his head. "I didn't find a ransom note."

Max chuckled as he picked up his beer and let out a breath

of air. "Maybe you didn't look hard enough."

"Seriously, Max, I won't be able to convince Stephanie that I can take care of a dog if you've killed ... Did you *kill* Orchid?"

After a sip from his pint, Max set the glass down and turned to face his best friend. "I didn't kill your plant child."

"Then what did you do with her?"

"How do we even know your orchid is a girl?"

"Because I couldn't tell if it was either. Apparently, orchids can be both or something, so I chose a girl. If Orchid turns out to be a boy, I'll still be a proud mother," Julian said.

"*Mother?*" That was when Max burst out laughing.

"What?"

Rob's loud sigh caught his attention. "Julian, Max didn't kidnap your plant."

"Then who did, Rob? Who did? We need to report this!" Julian pointed at Max. "We need to know what Max did."

"I didn't do anything," Max said, defending himself from his best friend's accusation.

Max was no longer a lawyer. Instead, he was a suspected plant-napper.

"Stevie, can you please put a stop to this?" Rob pleaded.

Julian set a palm to his chest. "Blondie, no. No. I love you, remember? I was just joking when I said I didn't love you. Please don't tell me you did it."

Stevie pushed past Rob and covered the hand on her fiancé's chest with hers. "I go to the bathroom for one minute, and you're accusing Max of murdering your plant. Julian, you overreact so easily. I put Orchid in Clara's room because there was no decent sunlight on the balcony. It's on her window seat."

Max watched as Julian cupped the side of Stevie's face with his free hand. "Why didn't you tell me?"

"You've been sleeping all day. You're terrible with jet lag. Now, apologise to Max for calling him a kidnapper and a murderer." Stevie pulled away from Julian, turned, and offered Max an apologetic smile.

Julian rubbed the back of his neck with his palm. "Sorry, Max. It's just when you're a mother, you—"

"Apology accepted," Max said, interrupting Julian before he could give Max a speech about maternal instincts.

"Julian, you're such an idiot," Rob muttered.

Julian's lips spread into a large grin. "Ever since you became world champion, you've been even more gracious with your compliments, Robbie."

"Speaking of celebrations," Ally said, adding herself to the conversation. "Can we celebrate?"

Max peeked over to see the smile on Rob's face. He had never seen his best friend so happy, so content before. After everything he and Ally went through, and everything they were both about to sacrifice, it had worked out in the end for them.

Rob became the Men's Single Scull World Champion.

Ally got a new kidney and was no longer a socialite.

They were now happily married.

"Hey, Max," Ally said.

Max pushed off the bench, leant over, and kissed her cheek. "Hey, Ally. And congratulations on marrying my best friend over here. Now, let me buy you both a drink."

"Max, you don't have to—" Ally started.

"No, I insist. So when is this actual wedding?" Max spotted Mitch, the bartender, and waved him over.

When Mitch reached them, he nodded at everyone but smiled at Ally, his former employee. "Hey, Max. Tiff pour your beer all right?"

"She did," he confirmed. "Can we please get Rob a Guinness and a Sprite for Ally?"

"No worries," Mitch said as he reached for a glass.

"Say, Mitchy," Julian said.

Max turned his head to find Julian leaning on the oak counter staring at the bartender. Mitch had been the bartender at PJ's on Southbank for years, so Mitch was very familiar with Julian's antics.

"Yes, Julian?" Mitch didn't even look up as he poured the beer.

"How come Rob is allowed back in this pub? Did you or did you not ban him?"

Mitch set Rob's Guinness on the bar and grabbed another glass for Ally's Sprite. "I did ban Rob," he confirmed as he added ice to the glass and brought the soft drink dispenser nozzle to Ally's glass.

"So why is he allowed back in? I stood on the counter and

wasn't allowed within two metres of it. I had to shout my orders at you until you got tired of me yelling."

Once Mitch filled the glass with Sprite and dropped a slice of lemon in it, he handed the glass to Ally with a smile. Not one of the usual smiles Mitch gave to other female patrons. Instead, it was a friendly smile. "I love Ally like a sister. So if she's happy, I'm happy. As much as Rob pissed me off, he came to his damn senses and married her. But that doesn't mean I'm not afraid to punch him in the face again if he hurts her. Kidney or not."

Ally's kidney transplant was kept from the media. In fact, she only allowed a small few to know. She didn't want the attention to fall back on her, and she knew Rob didn't need it either.

"Max, want me to put it on your tab?" Mitch asked him.

He nodded and sculled back the rest of his Guinness. "Thanks, Mitch." Once Max set the glass down, he spun around and faced the newly married couple. "Congrats again, World Champ." Then he smiled at Ally. "Mrs World Champ."

"You're leaving," Ally said, sadly. Almost as if she was disappointed.

Max shook his head. "Just gotta step outside for a minute. I'll be back. Your husband may be the single scull world champion, but I think Julian and I could scull back a beer faster than he can."

Rob shook his head. "Can't drink like I used to now, Max." He winced. "The kidney?"

Ally's eyes fell to her drink.

Her husband wrapped an arm around her and brought her to his side. "The kidney," he confirmed proudly as he pressed a kiss to his wife's temple.

"Save all the lovely sentiment till I get back."

"Will do," Julian said over his shoulder. Then he returned his attention to Mitch. "But seriously, why isn't he still banned?"

"Julian, stop trying to get your brother banned from PJ's!" Stevie scolded.

Laughing, Max made his way away from his group of friends. He loved them all like family. They had all grown up together. But Max was the only single one left. It used to be the five of them, but it had dwindled to just him.

Alex Lawrence was engaged to Keira Perkins and had a

baby with her in New York.

Noel Parker married Alex's little sister, Clara Lawrence, and they lived together in Boston.

Julian Moors returned after years of living in Sydney and was reunited with Stevie Appleton. They had spent years apart after their spontaneous romance in Thailand. Now they were engaged and lived together.

And Rob Moors recently eloped with Ally O'Connor in New York when they had visited her specialist before the Rowing World Championships.

Max Sheridan was the last one standing.

He had wanted love more than some of his friends.

But Max knew he didn't deserve love.

Not after everything he had done to Alex and Noel behind their backs.

Someday soon, he had to tell them.

He should have told them at Noel's wedding.

Face to face.

But Max was too much of a coward.

Just like right now, he was escaping the Moors brothers and their perfect relationships to go sit outside for fresh air. He wanted what they had too much to stay exposed to it for too long. They both deserved it. They had both faced their darkest fears to keep the ones they loved.

He had to continue to be happy for them rather than envious.

Once Max made it out of PJ's, he found a free table and sat down at it. The night air was slightly warm for September, but he enjoyed it. The sun had already set, and the city lights reflected off the Yarra River. In all the cities he had visited, Melbourne was still his favourite. It was home. And he had been close to saying goodbye to it when he almost went to Boston to be with Andrea.

Letting out a sigh, Max reached into his pocket and pulled out his phone. To his disappointment, out of all the missed calls and messages he had received, none had been from Josie.

"Thought I'd find you here," he heard behind him. Max set his phone down and glanced over his shoulder to find Ally Moors behind him with two drinks in her hands. She shouldn't be doing that much work for him. Not after her stint in the hospital. Just as he was about to stand, she shook her head. "If you stand, Max, and try to help me, I will never talk to you again."

Max laughed at her determination and turned his attention back to the glittering river as Ally sat down. He peeked over to find her smiling up at him.

"You okay there, princess?" he asked, knowing she'd cringe at the nickname she hated.

And tonight was no different as she muttered, "I hate when you call me that."

"I know," he said with a laugh and craned his neck to give her his undivided attention. "Shouldn't you be inside with your husband?"

Ally let out a sigh and leant forward in her seat. He and Ally had things in common. Though they had never really vocalised their struggles with the pressures of a rich, better-off life, they had silently understood each other. "And you should be inside with us, Max."

"Just needed a minute to myself."

"You've been outside for almost a half-hour. Is everything okay with you?" She sounded worried. The last thing he wanted was for her to worry over his self-pity. Allison Moors had done a lot of worrying in her short lifetime. She was still practically a kid who had too much burden on her shoulders. Max would not add any pressure.

So he smiled.

Long and almost true.

A smile just for Ally.

"Just work, Ally."

The concern in her hazel eyes didn't leave her. "Then come inside and celebrate with us. It'd mean a lot if you did."

Ally was far too sweet to him.

He'd always found her attractive.

But she had always hidden a lot from him and everyone.

It had taken his best friend, a better man, for her to open up.

But something had bugged him since he visited her in the hospital almost four months ago. It had to do with the guilt in her eyes and the burden he was sure she still had resting on her shoulders. "Can I ask you a question?"

She blinked at him as her hand slipped away from her drink. "Umm … okay?"

"Why did Liam leave after you were in the hospital? It was as if he never wanted to be alone with you or anyone."

Ally flinched. "You noticed that, huh?"

He offered her a reassuring smile. "I didn't want to bring it up. But seeing how happy you are, that little bit of guilt in your eyes tarnishes it. You deserve to be happy, Ally. So I feel compelled to ask, but are you okay?"

At that moment, Josie's question that day on the bridge erupted an uncomfortable sensation in his chest. It felt as if flames were searing his heart. The thought of Josie resurrected a form of missing in him he hadn't known.

It was pointless.

They were friends.

He missed having someone to talk to.

He liked talking to Josie.

But all he got was silence from her since he sent that stupid message for her to be his plus one tonight.

"I'm okay, Max, honestly," she assured. And Max believed her. Then she let out a sigh. "The thing with Liam and four months ago was because of several things. He left Melbourne. I was trying to be a better person for Rob, but I couldn't escape the family company with Liam stepping down. He wanted to find himself. And I think he did … or almost did. He got a tattoo. And the moment my kidneys failed, he felt guilty about that because he couldn't give me his kidney." Tears brimmed her eyes, and Max felt like an asshole for making her cry. "And now I have Rob's and I am so grateful that I do because it means I get to love him for more days than I should have had, but I never wanted him to give up an organ for me."

"Hey," Max said in a soft voice. "He loves you, Ally. You're his world. His *entire* world. I've never seen him so content with his life."

Ally wiped her tears away, and that smile of hers returned. "Sorry. I didn't mean to unload all that on you."

"Does Rob know how you feel?"

She nodded. "Yeah. He knows all this."

"Even the Liam stuff?"

Another nod. "Yeah. He isn't a big fan of Liam's right now — especially when they had a screaming match in our apartment. It was after Clara went back to Boston, and it was the reason I had to go back to the hospital for a few days as a precaution."

"I didn't know you—"

"No one but us did. Nothing serious came out of it, I promise."

"What happened?"

Her eyes fell to her hands. "Please don't judge Liam. He made a mistake."

"What did he do, Ally?"

"He pushed her out of the way, and she fell into the glass coffee table," Rob said, surprising them.

"Robbie," Ally breathed.

Then Rob was kneeling by his wife's side. "I'm sorry about that day, Allison. I'm so sorry. I shouldn't have brought up Clara. I shouldn't ..."

"It's okay, Robbie," she assured. "You have to understand he's my brother. And I married someone who reminds him of the man who he lost her to. He wants to move on, and reminders of and seeing Clara isn't helping him. That's why I signed the bakery ownership transfer today. The burden of that bakery and what it symbolised for him is no longer his to bear."

Max flinched in shock. "You own the Little Bakery on Little Collins Street?"

Ally faced him and nodded. "Yeah, I do. I was there today. I saw Josie, too."

"You did?" he blurted out.

A smile returned to Ally's lips as Rob stood and sat in the seat next to her. "Josie?" Rob asked, confused. "Max, why are you so interested in Josie?"

"I ... uh ... I'm not," he said, instantly hating the fact he had lied. No one had interested him the way Josie had. And he hated himself for denying it. "I mean … It's…"

Rob squinted at him. "You haven't stuttered like this since we were teenagers. Max, do you *like* her?"

Max could see hope in Rob's eyes—as well as Ally's.

They wanted him to confirm it.

He knew that Rob would approve of his interest in Josie more than Andrea or Sarah.

But so much had happened while Rob and Ally were in France.

Max had done a whole lot of growing.

He had let go of so much of his past.

So instead of confirming he was interested in Josephine Faulkner and all her mystery, Max stood from his chair and said, "I don't know."

He hoped it was enough to satisfy Rob and Ally.

Just as he lifted his chin, he noticed her standing nearby with a small smile on her face. "*Josie*," he breathed. "You came."

She nodded. "Yeah, Ally invited me this morning. I hope that's okay?"

It was Max's turn to nod, ignoring the two who sat at the table with him. "It's okay."

But his heart and its needy beats.

That was not okay.

Josie

I don't know.

Josie smiled at Rob and Ally who were staring at her. She had missed much of their conversation except for the part where Robert Moors had asked Maxwell Sheridan if he liked her. And Max's answer had her heart dropping. It shouldn't have, it made no sense to, but she felt horrible that he didn't know.

She didn't know the context.

If he liked her as more than a friend?

If he liked her as just a friend?

If he liked her just as his tutee?

If he liked her at all?

He doesn't know.

"Hey, Rob," Josie said, "Congratulations, World Champion."

Rob was one of the first of Max's group of friends she had met. He had been a fan of Clara's peanut brittle cupcakes. It was one of the first cupcakes she had ever created. It was also the first time she had met Clara's brother, Alex.

"Thanks, Josie," Rob said.

Ally got out of her chair, walked over to her, and wrapped her arms around Josie. Then she whispered, "Did you hear everything?" in her ear.

When Ally had ended the hug, Josie shot her a tight smile and shook her head.

"I'll give you the proper context later," Ally said in a hushed tone.

"Okay," Josie said, a little unsure if she even wanted to hear what Max really meant.

She had talked herself in and out of attending tonight. But Ally had asked her as a friend, and she couldn't disappoint her. Josie had had enough of disappointing the people she cared about. It wasn't just her desire to see Max again. He was only half the problem.

She felt like she imposed.

Like she wasn't meant to infiltrate this group of tightknit friends.

She was the outsider.

Just as she was in her father's life.

Ally stepped back and spun around. "Robbie, can you bring my drink inside? I let it go flat."

Rob's brows furrowed as he looked at his wife. Then his mouth made an 'O' shape, and he got out of his seat.

"You did, too," Rob said in a very mechanical and fake voice. Robert Moors was certainly a better rower than he was an actor. In a matter of moments, Mr and Mrs Moors had hurried into the pub, leaving behind the bubbling lemonade drink on the table.

"What was that?" she wondered out loud.

Max chuckled. She took her eyes off the pub doors and to the man standing to her left. Maxwell Sheridan was a sight that she was sure took many women's breaths away. The way he'd styled his brown hair back and the way his brown eyes softened was beautiful.

Yeah, if she wasn't so sure she was attracted to him before,

69

she was now.

The way he looked at her gave her hope that maybe he could be sure of his feelings towards her someday.

No one had ever been sure of her before.

And she was kidding herself if she thought Max would be that someone who would.

He was her friend.

Her tutor.

And she would not take advantage of him by letting her heart hope.

"That was marriage."

His joke had her letting out a laugh.

"But they look happy," she added.

Max nodded. "I think now they can be."

"That sounds very ominous, Max."

"I guess it did. You wanna sit for a bit? It's loud in there."

Just as she was about to agree, she felt her phone vibrate in the back pocket of her black skinny jeans. As she made her way towards Max's table, she pulled her phone out to find a message from her absent father. Once she sat down in front of Max, she unlocked her phone and pulled up the message.

> **Ambassador for abandonment:** Josephine, I'm sorry about dinner. I couldn't leave the Chancellor in Canberra. I'll be back in Australia in a few months. We can have dinner then. If you need anything, please don't hesitate to contact me.

The phone almost slipped out of her hand and onto the table.

"If I need anything," she mumbled.

She was insulted.

Completely and utterly insulted by her father's message.

She shouldn't have expected anything new.

Or anything that resembled a meaningful apology.

Her father had no idea how close she was to crumbling.

For now, until she could tell him what a useless father he was in person, a text message would have to do.

Josie: You're not sorry. And I won't have dinner with you the next time you decide to come back to Australia. To be honest, Jeff, I have a better relationship with your assistant than my supposed father. Don't worry about me. I won't be contacting you for anything. I've done all right without you for all these years. I can keep going.

"Everything okay?" Max asked.

Josie glanced up from her phone to see the concern on his face. Then she turned the screen over to show him. "It's just my dad."

Max had glared at the screen before a smirk plastered his face. "Ambassador for abandonment. Creative."

Josie brought her phone back to her so she could see if her father would reply to her rather blunt message. "I would much rather a more explicit contact name for him, but from what I remember, the eight years we did have together were amazing." She peeked up from her phone to offer him her apologetic smile. "I'm sorry. I have father issues."

To her surprise, he laughed. "I knew that from the moment I talked to you. And it's okay to feel hurt, but you shouldn't hold onto it forever, Josephine. Trust me, I know this person who did, and they became a horrible, vindictive person."

Her lips parted, and all that came out of her was air.

She wanted to say more.

But she wasn't sure what to say.

She was curious to know who this person was.

What they meant to Max.

Her father's reply quickly squashed her need to ask questions.

Ambassador for abandonment: Josephine, that's not fair. You know how important my job is. Someday you might understand.

Tears of anger filled her eyes.

She didn't want to feel such powerful emotions.

But they had surprised her.

What her father didn't understand was that her mother's

cancer was not only killing the woman who had loved her unconditionally, but it was also killing Josie inside. No matter how much love her mother gave her, Josie had never felt more alone in her life.

> **Josie:** Every day for the past fourteen years, I have tried. You have no idea how much I have tried. But I don't. I don't understand. The minute you left for Berlin gave you no right to take your love and affections away from me. And you had no right to make me your third daughter when I was your first. I had a right to know them. To know my half-sisters. But you never gave me the chance.

Josie stared at the message.
It was too raw.
Too honest.
Her father wasn't deserving of it.
So instead, Josie deleted the message and went for a shorter version.

> **Josie:** For fourteen years, I have tried to. I will never understand you.

Once she had sent the message, she set her phone down and took a deep breath, satisfied that her reply would mean her father wouldn't go seek out her mother. Her last message would have. And her father would go to extreme lengths to make sure her mother knew how frustrating Josie was. And she had to avoid it. From now on, she would think through her interactions with her father.

To spare her mother.

To protect her from her father knowing that his ex-wife had cancer.

"Josie," Max said in a low voice.

For a moment, she had forgotten he was sitting across from her. She didn't force a smile to assure him she was fine. She wasn't. A lot of factors in her life were against her. And tonight, she thought she'd be able to forget her problems and celebrate with her friends. She had promised herself that she would try to be a better friend to Stevie and Ally. And she was already failing.

"I feel compelled to ask this, but are you okay?" He asked it so sincerely that her chest tightened.

No man had asked about her well-being quite like Maxwell Sheridan.

And it was a shame he was completely out of her league.

She wouldn't even know how to make someone like him happy.

She couldn't even make herself happy, let alone him.

But she could be his friend.

Josie would respect him and be someone he could depend on when and if he ever needed someone to listen to him.

Her smile was honest and grateful.

She appreciated whoever had her path cross Max's.

She knew it was a mistake.

But she would never undervalue it or him.

So she would be honest with him.

"My best friend used to tell me that I was self-destructive," she confessed. "She wasn't wrong. I punish my father because it's easier than admitting I'm not the perfect daughter he needs. He has two. And I guess I've just held this resentment because he's this public figure who shares his perfect life with his perfect family, and I'm … I'm not important enough."

Max reached out, wrapped his fingers around her phone, and set it next to him and away from her. That small distance was all she needed to feel. It was as if she could breathe a little easier. She had no idea how Max did it. He knew what she needed before she did.

Right now, it was just them.

She and Max.

No one else.

Friends.

Just two friends sitting across from each other.

"Why do you think you're not important enough?" he asked.

The question stung her.

Sliced across her chest for salt to find.

A simple question that made it hard for her to breathe.

A question that exposed her black and blue.

"Because if I was, he would have been there," she said in a small voice. "All those milestones in my life since I was eight—he should have been there for at least one of them. I thought when I graduated from high school, he'd be there. I thought when I got accepted into Deakin Law, he'd somehow congratulate me and be proud. I give him an inch, and he takes my heart every time. I've already saved all this disappointment for when—*if*—I graduate with my law degree and not find him there. There's no point in inviting him when he's only going to let me down."

Josie watched as Max corrected his posture, back straight and shoulders squared. He took a deep breath and exhaled it seconds later. "Then invite me."

She flinched. "What?"

"Invite me, Josie."

"Why?"

"If I'm gonna tutor you, then you gotta let me watch you walk across that stage to get that bachelor," he explained. His facial expression was all serious and taut.

"Max," she began.

"No, Josie. You gotta trust that not every man will let you down. Some will, and some won't. I've done a lot of that. I was that guy. I might still be that guy," he confessed. Then he reached over and grasped her left hand in his. "I just don't want to disappoint anyone anymore. And if you'd let me be honest for a single moment, you'd know you're the person I'm scared to let down the most."

She swallowed hard at his confession.

Is Max drunk?

He had to be. No sober guy had ever expressed his feelings towards her before. To admit he was scared to disappoint her. And she certainly didn't think Maxwell Sheridan would. Truth be told, she didn't think she deserved to be thought so highly of.

"Why me?" she asked, completely confused. "What have I done?"

Max squeezed her hand. Then he glanced down at where they joined, and a small smile spread across his lips. "You were the first person to ask me if I was okay in a long time," he revealed. His focus remained on their hands. "You have no idea

74

what really meeting you has done to my life. You bettered it. You made me look at myself and realise I made poor choices."

"How did I do that?"

Finally, he lifted his chin so his brown eyes gazed into hers. "You gave me the chance to be your friend."

Friend.

The 'F' word.

For a selfish moment, she was miserable at the word.

At the idea.

At the notion.

But it fled her quickly.

Because she was honoured to be his friend.

She would rather him as a friend and a tutor than as nothing at all.

Stella had been right.

Josie was self-destructive.

And she wouldn't be if it meant she could be Max's friend.

No more talk of her father.

Of all her worries.

Not when it hurt her and could hurt her mother.

"I have to go," she whispered and pulled her hand free from Max's. Suddenly, she felt hurt all over. She wasn't sure why, but she did. But she knew she was the reason for this pain. For letting herself believe for one single moment that she could have been Max's. She had read it so wrong. She let her fickle mind believe in insatiable fantasies. "I have work in the morning, and it's getting late."

Max pressed his lips into a fine line and picked up her phone. He held it out to her, and Josie took it from him. "You still want me to stop by tomorrow afternoon?"

To save herself, she should say no.

She didn't want to let him down.

And she definitely didn't want him to feel as if he had let her down.

But she knew all she could do to keep him in her life was to agree.

To pretend.

To make someone other than herself happy.

To make Maxwell Sheridan happy because she knew that no woman had treated him fairly. And she would be the first, but she knew the truth her heart hated to acknowledge.

She certainly wasn't the last.

"Yeah, I still need you and the knowledge you have on contracts if I wanna pass this prerequisite class and finish this degree. I need contracts to be able to get into civil procedure and dispute resolution next semester."

"Message me after you've finished work?" he asked, and the hope and excitement that twinkled in his eyes could have killed her.

So Josie nodded. "I'll message you. Could you tell the others goodbye for me? I don't want to disrupt the celebrations inside."

"Sure thing, Josephine. I'll see you tomorrow."

I was Josephine.

Just not his Josephine.

He's not my Napoléon.

And Max won't be gifting me forever in his lifetime.

Opening the bakery on a Saturday morning wasn't the same as it used to be. Clara Parker made Saturday tolerable. Josie would even come to work hungover and still managed to get through the shift, but now that Clara had moved to Boston, Josie was in charge of prepping the bakery and putting in the first batches of cupcakes.

She used to whine about how early she'd have to get up and be at the bakery. Making sure cupcakes were in the ovens by six a.m. used to be so dismal. But now, Josie had found herself in a routine. It kept her mind off all the other issues and hardships she faced. It meant three hours of being alone and busy before the rest of the Saturday crew began work. Josie was glad to walk into the store to find that she didn't have to make a single batch for the morning's service. Nadia and Taylor had spent last night making each mix for Josie to put into the ovens.

Just as the morning radio presenter told her that Melbourne would have a sunny day, the bell rang, and she glanced over at the door to find her new boss walking in with her sister-in-law or soon-to-be sister-in-law.

"Morning, Josie," Ally greeted as she began to pull off her orange woollen coat. Though it was now spring, it was still chilly in the morning.

"Morning," she said, confused as to why they were both at the store so early. Josie picked up the next chair, flipped it, and then set it on the ground. "You both realise that it's not even six in the morning, and you both have really hot significant others you could be with rather than here" — she raised her brow at them — "with me?"

Stevie Appleton covered her mouth with her hand and yawned. "Trust me, I know," she mumbled. "The six o'clock thing, not the hot significant other thing. I love Julian, but after our trip to France and him meeting my mother, I need a day away from him."

Josie laughed as she made her way to the next table and began to flip the chairs over. "So you decided to come here?"

"Ally, the new owner is … will be … who cares about technicalities at almost six in the morning? Anyway, my sister-in-law asked if I could help out. And since I haven't seen you in forever, I thought why not?"

"Seriously?" Josie asked, relieved because Taylor had messaged her last night saying she wouldn't be in.

Ally nodded. "Of course. My dad isn't letting me do a whole lot of O'Connor Investments stuff since he wants me to sort out this new wedding. So my focus is on making sure this bakery is well looked after."

"And …" Stevie added.

"OH! That's right," Ally said as she pulled an iPad from her bag. Then she held it up so Josie could see the device. "Clara wants to FaceTime if that's okay with you."

Josie smiled. "You're my boss now. I do what you say."

Ally grinned. "I say Stevie can make us some hot beverages. We'll FaceTime with Clara while the cupcakes are in the oven. And when we're done, we can all ice them together."

There was a groan from Stevie. "I hate that coffee machine."

"Fine," Ally said as she handed her best friend the iPad. "You clear these chairs from the tables and get Clara on. I'll get Josie to show me how to use it."

"I agree to this plan." Stevie then pulled her straight blonde hair into a ponytail and fastened it with the hair tie she had around her wrist. Then she frowned and pulled her phone from her jeans pocket. She sighed as she answered it. "Julian, go back to bed. No, I don't care what I said about getting your jet lag under control. You're undoubtedly and extremely hungover from last night."

Josie laughed as she watched Stevie put the phone on speaker, warned her fiancé that everyone could hear him, and made her way towards the rest of the tables.

"Josie, wanna teach me how to use it?" Ally asked as she pointed at the Gaggia Deco D espresso machine.

"Sure," Josie said and then led Ally behind the counter to the red and silver machine. She watched as Ally pressed her fingers to the machine, and her eyes widened in astonishment. "How much does one of these cost?"

Josie knew at that moment that Ally would be a more hands-on boss than her brother had been. She wanted to learn, and Josie was proud to see that determination and wonder in her eyes. "I think this one cost Danny almost fifteen thousand dollars."

"Wow," her boss breathed. "And how does one get a new one if it breaks?"

"Don't worry. I can ask Danny for you."

Ally turned and smiled. "Thanks, Josie. I know you're a lot closer to Clara than you are with me and Stevie, but we consider you our friend, too. And as my friend, I have to ask you about Max."

Josie winced.

Max.

It was too early in the morning to mention him.

When she had left him outside PJ's, she had taken a taxi home to find that Stella and West were already out for the night, and she had no one to unload to. So Josie had gone to her room, slipped off her heels, and crawled into bed. Then she lay on her back and stared at the ceiling, replaying Max's words over and over again. It had taken some time until she finally fell asleep in the outfit she'd worn to see him.

When Josie woke this morning, her chest felt heavy, and she knew that no matter what she felt, Max mattered more than her heart. He needed a friend, and she would be that friend. She wasn't going to let him down.

It was time someone looked after him.

"We're friends, Ally," Josie assured, and that smile on her boss' face faded.

"Julian, seriously, I don't care if you're awake. I'm busy," Stevie said in the distance.

"But, Blondie, I like this dog." Julian's voice echoed from Stevie's phone.

Josie glanced over to find Stevie sitting in one of the booths with her hands by the side of her face; her irritated expression had Josie chuckling.

"Fine," she breathed, sounding exhausted. "Send me a link, and I'll think about this dog. You said you liked a Dalmatian after we saw one in Paris. Once you're done with that, get some sleep, and then go get some greasy food and catch up on some of the paperwork you've neglected that Rogers wants by Monday. *Je t'aime.*"

"*Je t'aime*, Stephanie," Julian said in a low voice, and Josie could hear the love. She didn't have to be fluent in French to know that they had just said 'I love you' to each other.

"Josie," Ally said, getting her attention.

She returned her gaze to find her boss with that concerned expression on her face. "Yes, Ally?"

"Do you want to know the context of what you heard last night?"

Do I?

Knowing would only complicate it.

And she couldn't have any more complications in her life.

She needed a friend.

Max was there for her.

And she had to be there for him, too.

To be fair to her heart, she shook her head. "No, thank you, Ally. I don't want context. I just want to be the friend he deserves. Want me to show you how to use the espresso machine?"

Ally let out an exhale and nodded. "Sure. Show me how this works."

"And a chai latte for Stevie," Josie said as she set down Stevie's usual order.

She had taught Ally how to use the espresso machine, but the former socialite found it difficult. Josie had told her it was okay and it would take some time before she knew how to use it expertly. And the only way Josie could remove that helplessness on Ally's face was to tell her Danny's secret. And that was that Danny had broken the expensive espresso machine twenty minutes after it had been delivered to the bakery. He had to trade a year's supply of cupcakes to have one of his connections come in and fix the faulty machine. The problem was that Danny did not read the instructions and left the safety cap on one of the nozzles. It had been a very embarrassing day for her former boss.

"Thanks, Josie," Stevie said as she reached over and brought the glass closer to her. Then she patted the table. "I just messaged Clara, and it's like four thirty, and she's home from her classes. She wants to see you, too, since you didn't get to see her when she was last in Melbourne."

Guilt ravished her.

Besides Stella Weller, Clara Parker was one of the closest friends she had ever had. Clara had listened to all her whining when it came to her previous ex-boyfriends and her father. And Josie had almost thrown a party in the bakery when she found out Clara had left her cheating ex-boyfriend, Darren Porters. What Josie loved most about Clara was that she was always there for her. And when she had moved to Boston to live her happily ever after, it was hard not to miss her being in Josie's life every day.

"Here are your sugars," Ally said as she handed the packets over and climbed into the booth next to Stevie. Ally set down her cup of tea and peeked over at her. "Josie, do I have to play the boss card? I really don't want to. But we haven't hung out together since before Clara got married. You just checked on the cupcakes, and the shop floor looks good. You need a break."

No way would Josie win against Ally. The almost twenty-year-old had found a backbone, and it was inspiring to see. Since her transplant, she was living the life she had always dreamed of, and Josie was honoured to be part of it. She had always liked Ally. She had always liked all of Clara's friends. And when Clara had asked her to be a bridesmaid, it surprised Josie to see how accepting her friends were of her. They had made her feel as if she was their friend, too.

Without another word, Josie slid into the booth and sat next to Ally as Stevie picked up the iPad and swiped at the screen to unlock it. Then she typed in the code and pressed on Clara's name. It took a few minutes for Clara to accept the video chat and her face to appear on the screen.

Before she had even said hello, Josie watched Clara flinch in surprise, and a beautiful smile appeared on the screen. In all the years she had known Clara Parker, she had no idea just how beautiful she was and how envious Josie was that she didn't have her golden brown eyes.

"Josie!"

She smiled. "Hey, Clara."

"How are you?" her ex-co-worker asked.

"Good. Just opening the store. Sorry I didn't get a chance to see you while you were here."

Clara shook her head. "Don't even apologise. I see those two managed to get to the store early."

Stevie groaned. "Ally practically stormed the apartment and pulled me out of bed."

"I'm just glad Julian wasn't naked," Ally mumbled next to Josie, causing her to laugh. A naked Julian Moors wouldn't be a horrible way to start the day. With his boyish charms and those light blues, she wasn't surprised tough Stevie Appleton had fallen in love with him.

"Trust me, Ally, he would have loved it because then he would've used it against you. Like, 'my sister-in-law is a big perve, Robbie. She saw my — insert some sort of euphemism for his penis.'"

Ally shivered. "I don't think I could handle that for the rest of my life."

"Too bad you married his brother," Clara commented from the iPad.

"Mrs P!" shouted from Clara's end.

"Mrs P?" Josie asked, eyebrow raised.

"Sorry, give me a sec. I'll be right back. Kyle left his baseball bat in my car." Clara had raised her index finger to indicate she would be a second and disappeared out of the camera's focus.

Josie then got a view of Clara's huge kitchen. It was an absolute dream. Josie wasn't one for interior decorating or features of a house, but when you worked with Clara Parker, who dreamed of being a dessert chef, you were bound to hear about her dream kitchen. And that was what Josie saw. She could see the white marble tops and the large white cabinets with glass panels. The huge stainless-steel stove that almost took up half of one side of the kitchen and all the counter space. It appeared as if Clara's husband had chosen well and fulfilled her kitchen dreams.

"Have you both been to Clara's house?" Josie asked as she turned her attention to Stevie and Ally.

They shook their heads.

"We're headed out there in a few months. We're gonna go see Keira, too. The boys want to meet Will," Ally said.

Josie had received many pictures from Keira, Clara's future sister-in-law, who Josie had spent time with while she was in Melbourne. Keira and Alex's son, William Archibald Lawrence, was by far the cutest kid Josie had ever seen.

Just as Josie was about to comment on how adorable Clara's nephew was, a suit-clad Noel Parker appeared on the screen as he entered the kitchen and set his briefcase down on the counter.

"Wow," Josie said appreciatively as she watched Noel loosen his grey tie. "I feel like such a pervert right now."

Stevie laughed. "She's traded up since Darren, huh?"

Nodding, Josie watched as Noel began to peel off his jacket and then set it on the bench. "Oh, she definitely did."

When his fingers reached for the top button of his business shirt, it was as if all three of them had held their breaths.

Suddenly, they heard, "Noel, wait!"

Noel stilled as he turned in the direction of Clara's voice, who was still out of frame. "Kyle's gone, right? God, I couldn't stop thinking about how much I've wanted to —"

"I'm FaceTiming," Clara quickly interrupted.

Josie watched as Noel turned in their direction, and she could just see the blush on Noel's face as he lowered his hands from his shirt button. "Hey, everyone," he said, slightly embarrassed.

"Hi, Noel," Ally greeted with a hint of humour in her voice.

Clara's husband waved and then cleared his throat. "Baby, I'm gonna go change in the bedroom. It was good to see you, Stevie, Ally, and Josie."

"Not as good as it was to see almost all of you," Stevie teased. After Noel had kissed his wife, he left the kitchen. Stevie peered over Ally and smirked at Josie. "It was so nice living with him for a while."

Josie laughed, knowing exactly what she meant. "You saw?"

"Sadly, no, but I saw that chest a few times. And I heard them at it. He definitely knows how to please Clara —"

"Stevie!" Clara gasped. "Really?"

Josie had been expecting to see a pissed-off Clara Parker on the screen. Instead, Clara had an amused expression on her face.

"As much as you wanna see my husband naked, it's not gonna happen, Stevie. Now, I feel like I talk to you both every day, so I wanna talk to Josie for a minute." Clara's eyes darted over to Josie, and she felt as if she was about to be interrogated. "How are you, Josie?"

"Good," was all Josie could reply with without actually lying to Clara.

"Anything new?"

"Nope."

"No new DJs?"

That had Josie laughing. "None at all."

"Any new guy you're seeing?"

From the corner of her eye, she could see Ally staring at her, which made her uncomfortable. So Josie's lips made a fine line as she shook her head. "No. No new guy, Parker." The oven bell ringing came to her rescue as Josie slipped out of the booth. "I've gotta check on the cupcakes. I'll be right back."

"I'll be right here," Clara said, and then Josie made her way behind the counter and into the kitchen.

Once inside, she breathed out a sigh of relief and stood still for a moment to get her bearings. Since the bakery was quiet, she could hear the girls out on the shop floor talking as Josie made her way towards the oven.

"Is Josie okay?" Clara asked.

"She's okay," Ally answered.

Josie was thankful that Ally quickly changed the subject and spoke about Clara attending Boston University. With a heavy exhale, Josie wrapped her hand around the oven handle and pulled it open. She stepped back as the heat escaped and reached for an oven mitt. Once it was on, she pulled out the first tray to see that the raspberry and lemon cupcakes still needed another five minutes to get that golden colour to them. It was one of Clara's recipes that was still beloved by so many customers.

Josie pushed the tray back inside and closed the oven door. She reset the timer for another five minutes and made her way to the bench. She would have to start prepping the icing bags for the lemon curd icing. Deciding to let Stevie and Ally speak to Clara for a little while longer, she headed towards the large pantry for the lemons. Just as she reached the door, she felt her phone vibrate in her jeans pocket. Once she opened the pantry door, she pulled out her phone and then flicked the light on.

When she unlocked her phone, a message from Max greeted her. She hated that she felt butterflies at just the sight of his name. But everything he had said last night, and the way he had said it, only added to her confusion. No man had treated her so sincerely. It was a nice change, but she knew he only valued her as a friend.

She had to value him just the same.

And that meant not ignoring his message like she had the last.

> **Max:** Morning, Josephine. I've got a few cases my dad wants my help on. We still on for this afternoon?
>
> **Josie:** If you need to help your dad, Max, seriously, help your dad. We can reschedule.
>
> **Max:** Josephine, I don't think you realise it, but you're my first and only priority. Trust me; he

doesn't need me around for the whole day. What time do you finish work?

The thought of her as his priority had her smiling. She knew it had to do with his promise of not letting her down. That was the thing about priorities — they would always change, and she knew that her being his would, too. But for now, she'd revel in it and believe it meant more than she knew it should.

Josie: I have a few things to do after work, and my books are at my place.

Max: You need a hand?

Those 'things' she had to do was visit her mother in the hospital.

There was no way she'd let Max into that part of her life, no matter how friendly they were.

Josie: I'm good, thanks. I'll text you my address later if you wanna meet at my place?

Max: Sounds good to me. I'll see you later.

Chapter
SIX

Max

Josie: I'm running late. So late. I'm so sorry, Max. Are you already outside my apartment building?

*M*ax let out an amused laugh. He was tempted to call her after he'd been standing outside her building for ten minutes. Josie's apartment building appeared to be a renovated warehouse in Collingwood. It was in an impressive area that most university students couldn't afford, but then again, Josie's father was a diplomat. Though Josie was very headstrong, he knew she might have taken money from her absent father to pay for her livelihood. Shaking his head, he ignored the topic of Josie's finances and texted her back.

Max: I am outside. You're lucky I'm not charging you a fortune.

Josie: I'm so sorry. I promise I'm on my way. The code to get into the building is 3662. Once inside, go straight until you see the elevator. Use it to get to the

3rd floor. My apartment number is four. Just knock on the door. Stella's home.

Max: Stella's your best friend?

Josie: And my roommate. She's sceptical but means well. If she doesn't offer you a drink, there are plenty in the fridge. She doesn't play happy host very well.

Max: All right. I'll see you soon.

Josie: I'm so sorry, Max.

Her apology only had him laughing.

Max: It's seriously fine, Josie.

Once Max had pressed send, he shoved his phone back into his jacket pocket and headed towards the large industrial warehouse doors. When he glanced over to his left, he saw the keypad. After he had typed in the security code, he pressed the green button. A loud beep sounded, and he knew the doors had unlocked. Max pressed his palm against the steel door and pushed on it, opening it easily. When he stepped inside, he was surprised to see that he was standing in an indoor garden. Tropical trees and flowers lined either side of the path, and a small pond was there with a stone bench by it. From the outside, Josie's apartment building appeared boring and run-down. But he was surprised to see it so decorated. It was definitely a hidden treasure.

Noticing the elevator at the end of the path, he made his way towards it, up some small steps, and past the reception desk with the smiling man behind it until he reached the steel doors. Max stretched out his arm and pressed the up button on the keypad and waited. Moments later, the doors opened, and he stepped inside and pressed Josie's floor. When the doors closed and the elevator began to rise, he heard soft, tranquil music rather than jazz. It was strange. He'd never come across an apartment building as unique as Josie's. When he reached Josie's floor, he stepped off the elevator and headed for her apartment. Once he stopped in front of the door with the large number four on it, he knocked.

Max waited some time for no answer.

Then he knocked again.

This time, he heard footsteps then some mumbling. When the door opened, a frowning blonde woman greeted him. Her hair was tied into a top knot, and she wore a blue dressing gown.

"Oh," she said, disappointed. "Should have known you weren't West."

"Are you Stella?" Max asked.

The woman before him crossed her arms over her chest, squinting at him. "I might be a Stella."

"Josephine didn't tell you?"

"*Josephine?* I haven't heard someone call her Josephine besides her mother." She lowered her arms, and her lips parted as if she were in awe. Then she dug a hand into her dressing gown pocket and pulled out her phone. After she had read the messages Max assumed Josie had sent her, she stepped away from the door and welcomed him into the apartment. "And yes, I'm Stella, by the way," she confirmed once Max was inside.

"I'm Max," he said, introducing himself once the front door closed behind him. Max followed her down the hall and into the large living room. It looked like a penthouse rather than a third-floor apartment. Two designer leather couches faced the TV, and on either side of it were shelves built into the exposed brickwork. It was stylish and stunning. He recognised the books stacked on the shelves from when he went to law school.

Stella smiled as he took in the rest of the apartment, but the scepticism didn't disappear. She didn't appear to trust him completely. "Can I get you a drink? Josie's text says I have to ask."

"No, I'm all right."

"Great. So are you one of the mature students in her class? You know you don't have to wear a suit to a tutoring session, right?"

Max chuckled. He was twenty-five, and although he would technically be considered a mature age student, he wasn't. "Not a law student."

Confusion swept over Stella's face as her green eyes

88

clouded, trying to figure out who Max was. "Then what is Josie doing hanging out with you if you're not in her class, not a DJ, and definitely don't look like someone who would piss off her father?"

To save Stella from guessing, he revealed, "I'm a lawyer."

"Oh," she breathed. "Are you here to ...?" Her brows furrowed, and she shut her mouth immediately.

"To what?"

"Never mind. I'll let you finish telling me who you are. So go on, Max."

Suddenly, he felt nervous. Palms sweating kind of nervous. This was Josie's best friend. Normally, he didn't care who liked him, but he did with Stella. He wanted her to see him as someone fitting of Josie's time. He hoped she couldn't see the man he had been trying to hide and be better off. To be rid of. The man who had loved Sarah and pursued Andrea. He prayed she didn't.

He wanted to be the man Josie saw the good in.

Last night, when Rob asked him if he liked Josie, he had answered that he didn't know. The truth was, he did. He enjoyed her company and her smiles. He enjoyed the way she looked at him as if he was a good man rather than a man who had done such horrible things to the people he cared about.

"Our friends got married at the start of the year. We got paired up, and we're just catching up. I offered to tutor her after her dad didn't show up at the restaurant I was at with my work colleagues." Max explained everything he thought she'd need to know while keeping all the raw and honest moments he shared with Josie to himself. It seemed more meaningful to keep the moment on the bridge just for them and no one else.

"Oh," Stella breathed. He noticed her green eyes flickered with pain, and that had confused him. "I had no idea you've known Josie that long. She normally tells me everything."

Max flinched. This time, the pain that found and clawed at his chest was a unique kind. He'd felt many different versions throughout his years with Sarah and then Andrea. But this pain felt new. "I didn't know I was a secret. I'm sorry," he said in a small voice.

Her eyes now gleamed as she shook her head. "No, don't be. You're not a secret, Max, and I definitely know who you are now." Stella pressed her lips together and swallowed hard. "I'm still in my pjs, and I'll have to go meet my boyfriend soon. Make yourself at home. Josie shouldn't be too long."

"Thanks, Stella."

This time, Josie's best friend's face softened as did her eyes. "No, Max. Thank you."

"I'm so sorry I'm so late," Josie blurted out as she ran into the living room, small beads of sweat lining her forehead.

Max smiled as he got off the couch. "Don't worry about it."

She let out a sigh as she wiped her forehead with the back of her hand. "Traffic was a nightmare. Have you been waiting long?"

Almost an hour.

But Max knew she'd feel worse if he told her. In fact, he didn't mind. Stella had come out of her bedroom after her shower to chat with him. She had even asked him his opinion on what colour lipstick she should wear. Max had decided on the dark plum lipstick because it suited her more than the bright red lipstick she said was her usual colour.

"Not very long."

"Good," she breathed as she walked over to the couch to his right and dropped her bag on it. "Is Stella still home?"

He nodded. "Yeah, she's getting ready to go out for dinner with West."

"She told you about West?"

"Stella gave me a history of them and of you and her."

"Of course, she did." Josie pulled her phone from her jeans pocket and then frowned at the screen.

"Your dad?"

Josie lowered her phone and shook her head at him. "I just saw the time. Max, it's almost five. You waited for ages, you liar."

He shrugged. "It's no big deal, Josephine."

"It is —"

"Josie, you're home," Stella interrupted as she walked out

of her bedroom. "You took ages."

"See! Even Stella is honest that I took ages. Wait, Stella, you're not wearing red lipstick? To go out?" Josie appeared surprised.

Stella tilted her head, and her lips spread into a large smile. "Your tutor chose my colour. All right, kids, have fun with the law. I'm gonna go. And no, Josie, I can walk myself to the door. Offer your guest a drink and don't be rude." Then Stella shot Max a wink and made her way to the front door.

When the door slammed shut, Josie let out a sigh. "She did offer you a drink, right?"

"She did," Max confirmed. "But I didn't want one when she asked."

"Do you want one now?" she asked.

"Sure."

She smiled, and it was the first time her smile hurt him. The way her lips spread so flawlessly was mesmerising. Josie was absolutely beautiful. But her smile, rare as it was, was his favourite part of her. Every smile she made. Ones full of guilt and sorrow. The ones full of gratitude. And this one, one he couldn't describe, hurt him.

Hurt him in the way he adored it and her.

It was so wrong to adore her when he was a mess of a man, and she undoubtedly wanted to be friends.

"My textbooks are in the dining room. I'll grab the drinks and meet you there," she said as she made her way out of the living room and into the kitchen.

The open plan layout made it easy for him to walk from the living room to the dining room on the other side of the apartment. When Max approached the oak table, he took in Josie's books, notes, and laptop all sprawled out. It wasn't just contracts that he could see; there were other units. She had a lot of classes. And from where Max stood, he could see she might be struggling with her workload.

"How many units are you doing?" he asked, raising his voice so she could hear.

"Full course," she answered.

"Over trimesters?"

He had heard some rustling before she said, "Over two trimesters."

When Josie approached him with their drinks, he frowned at her. "Why aren't you taking advantage of Deakin's three trimesters?"

She handed him a can of Coke, and her eyes fell to her can in her hand. "I have my reasons. Two trimesters just work better for me than three."

"But it spreads your workload out. You have a lot going on," he pointed out.

Sighing, Josie approached the table and set her can of soft drink down. "I'm quite aware I have a lot going on, Max. You did law. What did you do?" Annoyance boomed in her voice.

He had her there.

He was in no position to judge.

But he didn't have a choice.

She did.

"I had semesters. I would have much rather done trimesters."

"But you managed just fine with twelve-week periods. Look at you, Max. You're a successful lawyer, working at the top firm in Victoria, if not, Australia," Josie pointed out. "Even if you had trimesters, you would have aced every unit. I can't even get through contracts, and it's a pre-req. I fail this, and I'm screwed for the rest of my degree. I can't afford to fail and repeat these classes."

Max set his can down and closed the distance between them. He set his hands on her shoulders and turned her so that her sad blue eyes focused on him. "You're not going to fail, Josie. I promise. This is why I'm here."

She let out an unbelievable laugh. "Giving up your Saturday night to tutor a clueless law student. Surely, you have better things to do."

She was dismissing him.

A surge of desperation shot through him.

He hated when she belittled herself.

"You're my better thing, Josephine. Why can't you see that?"

Bewilderment consumed her face. Those lips of hers parted ever so slightly. It was a stunning sight to see Josephine Faulkner in awe before his very eyes.

"I'm ...?" she whispered.

"Yeah," he confirmed breathlessly. "Now can I please tutor

you?"

She didn't answer vocally.

Instead, Josie nodded and pulled away.

"When is your assignment due?" Max asked as he watched her take a seat at the table and pull her laptop closer.

Josie searched the table until she picked up a piece of paper, read it, and tilted her chin up at him. "Three weeks. It's a memo of advice, and it's two thousand words."

Max had slipped off his jacket and hung it behind the chair next to Josie's before he sat down. "And it's worth?"

She glanced back down at the unit handbook. "Thirty percent."

"Any other assignments for contracts?"

"Nope. Just the final two-hour exam."

Then she looked his way, and he smiled at her.

The determination in her eyes.

The hope.

The desire to succeed.

At that moment, he was sure she'd make him proud when he watched her walk across that stage to receive her law degree.

The chatter around him had Max internally groaning.

It was Sunday.

He was at family lunch with his parents and the rest of the Sheridan family at Max's parents' grand Toorak mansion. Quite different to the suburban house Max had grown up in back in the South Eastern suburbs. When Gordon Sheridan began winning cases and became a highly sought-after lawyer, he left one of the best law firms in the state to create his own.

The only plus side to family lunches was spending it with his younger cousin Katie. Out of all his cousins, she was his favourite. He thought of her as a little sister. And when her drink had been spiked a few years ago, he had acted quickly and got her out of the club and away from the bastard who had tried to drug her.

"Max," Katie whispered next to him.

He craned his neck to see her frowning at him. "Yes?"

Katie held up her silver fork. "I will give you my entire inheritance if you stab me in the eye with this fork and end my suffering."

Max stifled his laugh and forced a serious expression on his face. "If I have to suffer, then you do, too."

Katie glared at him, dissatisfied with his answer. "Our fathers hate each other, and we have to sit here and pretend it's sibling banter."

"I know, but I only come over for the indoor heated pool after lunch."

"I like your selfishness," Katie remarked as she brushed her light brown hair behind her ear. "You've got a message, by the way."

"What?"

She smirked as she held up his phone. She must have swiped it from the table when he wasn't looking, and she was begging him to stab her in the eye with the utensil they had been using for their garden salad.

Katie's brow arched as she glanced at him. "Who's *Josie*?"

"Give me my phone, Katie!" he hissed and tried to grab it from her.

"I swear to God, Maxwell, if you changed Sarah's number to 'Josie,' I will kill you!" she promised with passion and irritation in her voice.

"I didn't! Now give me my phone before I throw you in the pool."

It was war.

Katie pulled her arm as far away from him as possible, and Max couldn't reach her without making a scene. Then she pressed her thumbs to his screen, and before he knew it, the phone was to her ear.

Then her nostrils flared. "Stay away from him, you bitch! I swear, I will ruin you. Max was the best thing to ever happen to you, and you fucked him over!"

"Katie! Give your cousin back his phone," Uncle Simon demanded.

His little cousin ignored her father. "Yeah, I bet you have nothing to say, and that's why you're silent." Then Katie's face paled. "Oh, I'm so sorry. I-I …" She didn't finish her sentence.

Instead, she quickly handed him the phone and mouthed another apology.

Max's heart pounded in his chest as he looked at the screen, confirming his worst nightmare.

Josie.

Katie had called Josie thinking she was a code name for Sarah.

"I told you what I had with Sarah was over," he growled as he got out of his chair, ignored his family, and made his way out of the dining room and to the kitchen. When he was sure that he was alone, he set his phone to his ear. "Josephine, are you still there?"

"I'm still here," Josie said in a small voice.

"That was—"

"Forget it," she said, cutting him off. "Thanks for explaining my contracts assignment and for pretty much telling me what to write. I did the extra reading you suggested for contractual capacity, and I'm getting there. Seriously, thanks. I think I have everything. I'll stay away now."

What?

"No, Josephine, that's not—"

"It's fine, Max. I'll see you around."

And then she ended the call.

Josie

*M*onday was the worst day of the week.

It consisted of a whole day of contracts.

Four hours of class and a one-hour seminar.

It didn't help that it was always so hard for her to understand her monotone professor when he delivered his seminars. But having done this week's reading and the extra reading Max had suggested, she'd understood today's content. Interpretations confused her, but she was sure she'd understand it more once she got home and read the tutorial work. But she had skipped the last two hours of class to be by her mother's side.

Today was finally the day her mother could have her body scan. Soon enough, they'd know if her cancer had spread to other parts of her body. When Josie had arrived to greet her mother, she was barely conscious. All she could do was hope that her mother understood she was there to support her. It wasn't easy to see, but the only way they could treat her mother properly was to know the extent of her cancer.

While her mother had her scans, Josie sat in the visitor's chair next to her bed and set her laptop on her lap. She'd have to write her contracts tutor an email to explain her absence. When her emails had loaded, she noticed one in her inbox from Max.

Yesterday, the phone call she received from some woman had been demoralising. The verbal strike so out of the blue. When the woman had finished with her warning for Josie to stay away, Josie told her that she didn't mean to get in the way and to thank him for tutoring her for four hours on Saturday night. Then, to her surprise, Max was on the phone, and she had repeated her appreciation before she promised to stay away and ended the call.

That call had been over twenty-four hours ago.

She had promised to do whatever it took to make sure Max was happy. And it was evident their friendship didn't make him and the new woman in his life happy.

Curious, Josie clicked on his email and read it.

To: Josie.Faulkner@hotmail.com
From: MaxwellSheridan@GordonSheridan.com.au
Subject: My apology and feedback.

Josephine,
    I am incredibly sorry for yesterday. I swear, Katie, my cousin, is dead to me for how she spoke to you. She thought you were someone else during our family lunch and believed it was her cousin right to stand up for me. She feels terrible.
    I feel even worse.
    I profusely apologise for my cousin.
    And I'm so sorry you had to experience something like that.
    You don't have to accept my apology.

You don't even have to reply to me.
I read your interpretation of the case
you were given. You took an approach I
was honestly not expecting. That doesn't
mean what you wrote was wrong; it was
actually refreshing. You have a talent
for writing something exciting out of a
boring topic. I've attached my feedback
in the word document. It's not much,
but you did a great job. I can see you
spent a lot of time thinking through
your interpretation of the issues in
that contract. I think my notes might
get you that higher mark you're looking
for.
I'll see you around.
If you ever need me, you have my number.
Please use it, Josie.
Max.

Her heart was torn.

Josie did want to see and talk to him. The four hours they spent together on Saturday were amazing. But that didn't warrant more time together. She understood stuff about contracts that her professor and tutor neglected to teach her. Max gave her real-life teachings. He told her of his experiences and how he approached each problem. Unlike the lawyers who had come to her tutorials to give talks, Max was different. He was a compassionate lawyer who cared more about his clients than the money. He wanted what was best for them. She wanted to be the kind of lawyer Max was.

Thoughtful, compassionate, and dedicated.

He wasn't about trying to eclipse his father in any way. Max wanted to be his own lawyer. To represent his clients his way. It wasn't about the money, and she could sense that when he spoke about each client by their names rather than titles.

Josie closed her laptop and sighed.

He had nothing to be sorry about.

Josie was the one who had let her emotions get the better of her.

As his friend, she had no right to feel hurt by him.

Now she felt stupid because the supposed other woman in his life was his cousin and not a potential lover.

Jealousy was an emotion Josie had never handled well.

Setting her laptop on the table by her mother's bed, Josie reached down and picked up her bag from the floor. After she had set it on her lap, she rummaged inside, pushing aside pens, papers, and books to find her phone. She noticed she had several missed messages from her father, Stella, and to her surprise, Stevie. Josie ignored them as she unlocked her phone and began to type a new message.

> **Josie:** Max, you have nothing to be sorry about. I'm sorry; I guess I just took what your cousin said to heart. She had a lot of passion in her voice, so when she told me to stay away, I thought I had done something that really warranted it. Like waste your time. So know that I'm sorry, too. I haven't had the chance to read your notes, but just know that I appreciate them. I'll see you around.

Just as she was about to lock her phone, she saw that he was already typing a reply.

> **Max:** I told you, you're the better thing in my life, Josephine. Whenever you need me, just call me.

And that, the sudden lightness in her chest, was her heart wanting Maxwell Sheridan for all the selfish reasons that would end with Josie losing him.

"Knock, knock."

Josie glanced up from her taxation assignment to find her best friend at the hospital room door with a bouquet of pink roses in her hand. "Don't you have class?"

Stella shook her head as she entered the room and made her

way to Josie's side. "Told them I had a family emergency and I wanted to be by your side."

"Family emergency?" she questioned with a teasing tone. Josie saved the document with her problem-based research assignment and then closed her laptop. She set it on her mother's bed and watched as Stella grabbed the chair from the other side of the bed and brought it to Josie's side.

"Em's family, Josie. You both are," Stella said as she sat down with a huff.

"How was school today?"

Stella craned her neck and let out a huff. "Year nines are the worst, but I like the school. They said they'd call me up if they need more CRTs. So that's nice."

"Are you ever going to find a school you want to teach at?"

Her best friend hummed. "I haven't found one I really like just yet. Plus, the casual pay of being a CRT is really good right now, especially since we don't pay rent."

Josie groaned. "Don't remind me it's dirty money that pays for where we live."

Stella reached over and squeezed her arm. "You know I'm thankful, right? I hope you don't think I'm taking advantage of you and your strained relationship with your father for free housing."

"I know," Josie said with a laugh. "Your conscience is clean because I took advantage of it when I realised all we could afford were horrible studio apartments. Trust me; I felt terrible when I asked his assistant to ask him. But then he let me down by not showing up for my birthday to go on holiday to Monaco with his family, and all was right with the world."

"Josie," Stella said in a small voice. The curiosity in her green eyes mixed with a gleam of concern.

"Yeah?"

Her best friend squeezed her arm once more in reassurance. "Why didn't you tell me about Max?"

She blinked at Stella, unsure why something as small as Josie knowing Maxwell Sheridan would concern her.

"What's there to tell?" Josie asked, hoping her nonchalance was enough not to spark Stella's interest. But from the way her nostrils flared, it was clear it had the opposite effect.

"The fact you didn't tell me. Josie, you've told me about

meeting every single guy who has ever caught your eye. Hell, you even told me that if Danny wasn't your boss, you'd have tried to sleep with him. You've told me about that guy who lasted thirty seconds with you. You've told me everything *except* Max."

"He's just a friend."

Stella sighed as she pulled her hand away from Josie's arm, twisted in her seat to properly face her, and set the roses on her lap. "He's not just a friend to you, Josie. I see it. Does he feel the same way about you?"

"I don't know."

What Max had said to Rob resurfaced.

She knew the reality of her relationship with Max. Katie had thought she was someone else and told her to stay away. She had heard things about Max and other women, and Josie knew she treated him better than the last had.

But her feelings would go unreciprocated.

She couldn't and shouldn't hope for more.

A small smile touched her lips as she made a small nod. "We're just friends."

"That's a shame."

"It's not," Josie assured. "I think he might still be in love with someone else or hoping for someone else. I think he needs someone to understand him rather than love him."

"You could be both ..."

Josie let out a light laugh. "I'm the last person someone is going to want to fall in love with."

"That's not true," Stella stated.

"It's true."

Her best friend shot out of her chair as tears consumed her green eyes. She threw the roses onto Josie's mother's bed. They landed with a thud, and several petals fell from the flower. "It's not!"

"I'm not someone's first choice, Stella. I'll never —"

"Josie," Dr Frederickson said as he walked into the room, only to stop when he saw Stella with her. "Oh, I'm so sorry. Is this a bad time?"

Josie jumped out of her chair and shook her head. "No." She swallowed hard as her palms began to sweat. "Is my ...? Has the cancer ...?"

She couldn't.

For the life of her, she couldn't finish any of those questions.

A slow smile developed on the doctor's face as the relief consumed his eyes. "It hasn't spread. The fever's down, and your mother is doing well. She wanted me to tell you the news while she gets some fresh air with the nurse."

This.

This was what she needed to relieve the pressure and strain on her heart and head.

Not caring that Stella would see her cry, Josie let her tears fall as she stepped forward and wrapped her arms around the senior doctor. "Thank you," she whispered into his chest as his arms circled around her. "Thank you, Doc."

"Your mother is a fighter, Josie," the doctor said.

Josie cried even harder, proud of her mother. "I'm sorry I'm ruining your shirt."

The doctor chuckled as he unlocked his arms from around her and set his palms on her shoulders. He took a deep breath as he pulled her back and serious Dr Frederickson had returned. The same expression on his face as when he confirmed the cancer had returned.

"Josie, I don't care about my shirt. In fact, that's probably the best way to ruin it. But you have to understand that this *will* take its toll on your mother. She's already suffered a great deal over the past two weeks. We can't be sure the chemotherapy will work until she goes through several rounds and scans."

Josie nodded. "I understand."

"She needs your love and support most of all. We'll keep her in the hospital for a little while longer just to make sure the neutropenia fever hasn't affected her other systems."

Again, she nodded.

"The nurse will help your mother back to the room. Have a good afternoon, Josie," the doctor said then left the room.

Josie spun around to see Stella crying. Her best friend quickly closed the space between them and wrapped her arms around Josie in a tight embrace.

There was nothing more to say.

Not about Max.

Or what Max meant to Josie.
Because this was what mattered.
Her mother's second cancer battle.

Chapter
SEVEN

Max

It had been over a week since he last messaged Josie. Not that Max was counting. Texting her was all he wanted to do. Every moment he thought of her had him reaching for his phone, but he had to refrain. He suspected Katie's words had really affected her. His cousin had said some horrible things to the wrong person. If it had been to Sarah, he wouldn't have cared at all.

But it was to Josie.

Sweet, innocent Josie.

He'd never had someone as sweet as her in his life.

Someone who was nice to him because they wanted to be.

It had been a long time.

The last?

When he and Sarah were kids.

Before they became teenagers, and she had chosen Alex.

It was right that Max had ruined something as good and as pure as Josie's friendship before it could even really develop.

"Max?" He heard Stevie call his name. Blinking, he lifted his chin to shift his gaze to his best friend's fiancée. Her brows furrowed as she stared at him. Then she turned her head and shrugged her shoulder at Julian. "I tried. You're right. He's broken."

"See. I told you I wasn't overexaggerating," Julian said.

Stevie rolled her eyes as she set her palms on Julian's cheeks. "I'll never doubt you again."

Max watched as Julian leant closer and said in a low voice, "You always doubt me."

"Yeah, and I still seem to love you, *mon soleil rayonnant.*" She pressed her lips to Julian's and kissed him.

That.

That love in their eyes.

That connection.

That smile they made.

That was what he wanted.

What he had with Sarah Collins never looked like that. What Stevie and Julian had was what Max wanted more than anything. His want for that had him getting up from his chair and creating a loud, scraping sound.

Julian pulled away from his fiancée's kiss and yelled, "He's alive!"

Stevie laughed as her hands left Julian's face, and she glanced up at Max. "You've been out of it since you got to PJ's," she pointed out. "What's going on with you, Max? Did something happen while we were in France?"

Too many questions, Stevie.

But instead, he asked, "Have you seen Ally?"

Stevie blinked at him and then nodded towards the bar. "She's with Rob at the counter."

"All right. I'll be back." Max stepped away from the table.

"Can you get me another—" Julian yelled out.

"No," Max said, cutting off his best friend. He wasn't going to return to the table. Not with what he planned to do.

Max searched the counter to find Ally sitting on a barstool with her husband by her side. Since Ally had worked at PJ O'Brien's when she was first cut off, she was untouchable by all the regulars. It meant that no trouble would find her. And now that she had married his best friend, Robert Moors, the row club and its members had her back. She was now a world champion's wife. And it didn't take much convincing for them to love Ally.

When he reached the married couple, they both turned to him.

"Hey, Ally, can I talk to you for a second?" Max asked, almost afraid to.

"Everything okay?"

He nodded.

"You need me to go?" Rob asked.

If it had been anyone else, Max would have said yes, but Rob had always supported him and his decisions. He had been the one who told him that everything would be all right when he'd eventually come clean with his past sins. And Max would. He promised he would. And to be a better man worthy of having Josephine Faulkner in his life, even as a friend, meant asking for forgiveness from his past.

"No, that's all right," Max answered.

Rob stayed put, wrapping his arm around his wife.

"Are you okay, Max?" Ally asked, her hazel eyes shimmered at him.

Taking a deep breath, Max straightened his spine and squared his shoulders. "You're the new boss of the bakery, right?"

"Correct," she said with a nod.

His mouth suddenly became dry.

The organ in his chest doubled in size.

The beats it was supposed to make were anxious clenches.

But he was desperate beyond words.

Ally's smile faded. "I've already signed the contract my family's lawyer drafted. I'm sorry, Max. I didn't even think of asking you to have a look at it."

He chuckled. "No, that's not what I was going to ask."

"Oh?"

Max licked his lips and sucked in a deep breath. "Do you know if Josie's working tonight?"

His best friend's wife flinched in surprise. "You wanna know if Josie's working?"

"That's right."

The shock turned to excitement and relief on Ally's face. "She is. She's closing tonight."

"Great. Thanks, Ally," he said appreciatively.

Just as he was about to turn around and make his way out of the pub, Ally got off the barstool and lifted her chin at him. "What happened when we were in France?"

Max glanced over to see the intrigue on Rob's face.

"Nothing."

Ally's brows met. "*Nothing?*" She sounded disappointed.

"Nothing," he confirmed. Then he balled his hands into tight fists. "But I wanted something to happen."

"You did?"

Max grinned. "I did. And I'm gonna go do something about it. I'll see you later."

"Wait," Rob said, grasping his arm. "Does that mean you're over Andrea?"

Glancing over at Ally, he saw that hope in her eyes dwindle. Max wanted to say yes. Start fresh with whatever it was he had with Josie and see where his attraction towards her led.

But Andrea Wallace was almost it.

The woman was almost his.

Max pulled his arm free from Rob's grasp and said, "I'm going to be."

Noel: Hey, Max. When you're free, can you give me a call?

Max entered the bakery with his phone in his hand and reread the message his best friend in Boston had sent while he had driven to the cupcake bakery to see Josie.

He knew he might not be able to have what he wanted with Josie. His affection for her didn't make sense. But she understood him in ways no other woman had. She understood he held guilt, and she saw it clearer than anyone else had.

If all she wanted was a tutor and friend, then Max would be that for her.

His attraction towards her would be the unrequited kind.

Locking his phone, he decided that right now, he wasn't

free. As much as it pained him not to be there for his best friend, his focus and priority were Josie.

"Max?"

He tucked his phone into his black leather jacket pocket to find her with a tray of dirty dishes in her hand. Her hair was a mess, brown curls falling out of her bun, and she had what looked like a coffee stain on the white sleeves of her uniform.

"What are you doing here?"

Max cleared his throat and shoved his hands into his jacket pockets as he shifted his weight from the balls of his feet to the tips of his toes. "I was in the neighbourhood ..."

She let out a sweet laugh, and he knew she didn't believe him. "Seriously?"

"Nah," he confirmed as he made his way across the shop floor to stand before her. "Came to see you."

Josie shifted the tray to hold it in both hands. Max watched her cheeks colour a soft pink shade.

Did he make her nervous?

Did he make her heart beat as newly as she did with his?

Could she ever see him as anyone worth caring about?

Especially after she knew the things he had done?

"Why?"

Max removed his hands from his pockets and took the tray from her. He stepped towards the counter and set it down. Then he faced her and asked, "Any customers?"

She shook her head. "It gets really quiet on Wednesday nights. So why are you here, Max?"

He let out an exhale. Right here, he should just tell her. That in the eight months since they shared that conversation on the bridge, he had been a better man. Through her compassion, he had changed for the better. But as he watched her eyes search his, he knew there was a small chance he could disappoint her. His feelings for Andrea hindered the truth of his desires.

So Max made a decision.

For him.

For her.

For the sake of their friendship.

"My pride has been a little shot for over a week."

She appeared amused as she tilted her head at him. Those big blue eyes of hers were remarkable. He knew two other sets, and they were nowhere close to matching Josie's. Her eyes showed him that she knew pain he didn't know. And it only made him in awe of her.

"Your pride?"

He nodded. "You haven't told me what you thought of my notes on what you emailed me."

Josie chuckled. She turned, and he watched as she made her way behind the counter and reached for a cup. "What's your drink, Sheridan?"

Max approached the counter. "Just coffee."

She nodded then spun around and began to press some buttons on the espresso machine. He watched as she spooned coffee into a scoop and then connected it to the machine.

"Any milk?"

"Just straight black for me," he said.

Josie glanced over her shoulder. "Any sugar?"

"No, thank you."

As Josie made his beverage, the smell of fresh coffee filled the bakery. It was a rich aroma he knew was quality coffee and not the cheap kind his father's law firm had in the staff room. When she finished, she spun around and held the saucer the cup was on and smiled at him.

"I've gotta make sure this order for tomorrow morning is doing okay in the oven. Grab a booth, and I'll be a minute," she instructed and handed the hot beverage over.

Max took the cup of coffee, careful not to spill it, and nodded. Then he slowly turned towards the booths and made his way to the nearest one. Unlike the tables next to the windows, the lights wrapped around the rafters and built into the back wall of the bakery brightened the booths. Upon reaching the booth, he set his coffee down and slid onto the cushion.

Reaching for the handle, he grasped it and took a sip of the coffee. It was perfect—smooth but with the perfect hint of bitterness from the roasted coffee bean. He couldn't remember a better cup of coffee. As Max set the cup down, Josie slipped into the booth across from him and set a cupcake in front of him.

"I'm pretty sure you were always a fan of the banana and Walnut Whip cupcake," Josie said as she pushed it towards him.

"You remembered?" He was bewildered that she did. The banana and Walnut Whip cupcakes were one of the rare cupcakes. He never knew when they were going to be the cupcake special. He had once begged Clara to make a batch, but she didn't know the recipe.

"I did."

"Can I ask you a question about this cupcake?"

Josie crossed her arms on the table and nodded. "All right."

"Who makes this cupcake? Because the only person I know who can make any tasty cupcake is Clara, and she swears she doesn't know how to make this one." He pointed at the cupcake for emphasis.

Josie bit down the smile that peeked through. "*I* make these. They're only the rare cupcakes because I can't be bothered making them. That, and we also have to import all the Walnut Whips from the UK."

"Marry me," he breathed as he picked up the dessert and peeled the paper down. His mouth watered as he took a big bite. The vanilla whipped icing hit his tongue, and he groaned. "Seriously, marry me."

"You should be proposing to Danny."

"What?" he said, a mouthful of dessert hindering his ability to be coherent.

"I know how to make them because he gave me the recipe before he left for San Francisco. I didn't create it. I'm sorry to be the bearer of bad news." That smile of hers hadn't retreated. In fact, it only stretched wider.

Max swallowed down the cupcake with a sip of coffee. "You were almost too perfect, Josephine."

He had meant for it to sound like a tease.

But it was more of a confession *and* a lie.

The truth and a lie.

Too perfect and Josephine Faulkner would be completely out of his reach.

It was selfish.

Completely and truthfully selfish.

The colour of her cheeks brightened as she turned her head away, breaking their eye contact.

Max pushed the coffee and cupcake to the side and reached out to grasp her hand. Josie slowly turned and glanced down at their contact. After a few silent moments, she lifted her gaze to his, and for a brief second, he believed his feelings could be requited. He allowed himself to believe it.

To give him hope at being truly adored by someone who wasn't vindictive.

To be adored by her would make his life meaningful.

To be adored by her, he'd go through every hellish task.

I want her to adore me.

To want me.

Because he knew worst things in the world existed than being adored by Josephine Faulkner.

In fact, she was the better thing in the world.

His world.

And at that moment, he adored the way her blue eyes glittered up at him.

"Another question," he requested.

She answered him with a nod.

"Why do you want to be a lawyer?"

Josie blinked at him. Seconds later, she sucked in a deep breath through her nose and said, "I wasn't expecting that."

Max squeezed her hand. "What were you expecting?"

"Honestly?"

He nodded.

"I kind of expected you to ask about my father."

"You did?"

"Yeah," she said in a small voice. "I guess my answer kind of involves my father. Actually, I want to be a lawyer in spite of him. My dad divorced my mother when I was eight, and her lawyer ended up getting her nothing out of the divorce. Growing up, I was so angry because I watched my mother work hard while he had the life of a diplomat. Then, when I found out that his new wife—who he married months after meeting her and the divorce only just finalised—was pregnant, I wanted her to have nothing from my father. I thought for so long she was a gold digger. But then she had a second kid two years later, and his affections were no longer meant for me. I wanted to be a lawyer so that when the abandoned partner needed representation, I would be there and get them what they deserved."

Her eyes shone with unshed tears.

"You must think I'm so selfish. But it drove my need to get into law school. Before my parents divorced, I actually wanted to be a dancer. My first dance was when I was four, and it was for my parents in our living room to this music box that played my mother's favourite song. The next day, my dad signed me up for lessons. I used to dance for them. When he left, I danced in hopes of getting his attention. It took many recitals, many no-shows and empty reserved seats for me to realise he would never show up for them. Not even my last recital. Disappointment just came complimentary. I decided to be a lawyer so I could fight for those who were left behind."

His thumb softly brushed the back of her hand. "I don't think you're selfish, Josephine."

Her soft smile was all the reassurance he would ever need. "Thank you, but my reason for becoming a lawyer started off as selfish. Now, I just want to help people. I don't know what my speciality will be just yet. But don't worry, you can be the contracts expert."

The way she eased the conversation into a tease at his expense was a ride he was in awe of. She could convince him of things he never did, and he'd plead guilty in a court of law for them. He had no doubt that she'd excel at whatever kind of lawyer she decided to be. She'd be a sought-after lawyer before she knew it. And for Max, he had to ensure she graduated and realised her potential.

In spite of her father or not, she'd have that bachelor in the end. She'd know that when she had it, she had done it all for herself and not for him.

Josie surprised him by covering their joined hands with her free palm, trapping him in the best way possible.

"Can I ask you a question?" she asked in a soft voice as if she were afraid. The fear in her eyes was a beacon, luring him to her.

"Yes," he breathed.

Josie had run her teeth across her bottom lip before she released it with a short exhale. "Your cousin. She thought I was someone else. Was she ... Was she someone you loved?"

Sarah.

Memories of when they were kids collided with the struggling beats of his heart.

He thought he was clean of her.

But the emerging pain that intensified throughout him was proof he wasn't. She had been the first person he had ever promised never to let down. That day on the step outside her front door, he had promised to be there for her. She was eight. Then, eight years later, on that very doorstep, he promised that it would only ever be her after her mother revealed she was leaving her father.

That was when Sarah Collins had gone from the little girl he would always protect to the teenager with a chip on her shoulder. She hated everyone in her path—Max included. He had wanted to stop her abnormal behaviour, but he couldn't. She had pushed him away only to find the arms of his best friend, Alex Lawrence. But not even Alex could bring back that lost little girl she had been. Max had thought he had when she appeared on his doorstep telling him it was over with Alex.

But that had been a lie.

She had cheated on Alex with Max that night.

And it was a devastation Max had lived with for seven years.

Realising he had been quiet for some time, Max began to pull away from Josie's touch. He needed air. He needed to be away from someone as pure as Josie. She couldn't know what he had done.

But Josephine Faulkner did something surprising. She latched onto his hand with hers and made him stay. The first woman who, in her smallest actions, ever wanted him to.

That revelation wounded him in the very best ways.

With her hands clutching his, he wanted to be clean of every past sin for her.

And that meant being honest.

"I did," he confessed in a tiny voice. The weight on his shoulders neither heavied nor lightened. Instead, he became comfortable. Max knew he wouldn't be free until he told Alex the truth. Seven years was a long time to withhold it.

Josie's lips pressed into a tight smile. "But?"

"Why do you assume there's a 'but'?"

"Because I can see it on your face. When we stood on that bridge, the guilt in your eyes was one I couldn't look away from. Just like right now. You hold a lot of guilt because of her."

It was a statement rather than a question.

Max nodded.

He had never come clean to anyone. His best friends assumed or had figured it out. No one outside his close circle knew. He had never wanted anyone to judge him. And at that moment, out of all the people he had ever met and come across, Josie was the one he didn't want to think so little of him.

He wanted to be the hero in her story.

Her ending entwined with his.

Max wanted to be Josie's hero.

But he knew, just by looking at her and revelling in that soft gaze of hers, that she would be his hero.

And maybe he was looking for that all this time.

Saving.

Redemption.

Respect.

Someone to understand him.

"I've never told anyone this," he said in a small voice.

"I would never judge you. I hope you know that."

He smiled at her. "I know. And even if you did, I would never hold that against you."

"But I won't," she insisted.

And he believed her.

Taking a deep breath, Max knew it was time. The first step to a better, cleaner future. "I used to believe in love with this woman named Sarah. We grew up together. I saw all this good in her that people seemed to have forgotten she had. I understood her. I understood why she was so angry with everyone and the world. I thought she realised I was the one on her side. One day, I just kissed her, and that was that. I knew I had put myself out there. The next day, she was Alex Lawrence's girlfriend."

"Clara's brother?"

Max nodded. "Yeah. But don't think Alex stole her from me or anything. It was never like that. He just never knew how I felt about her. He was always the better guy—always will be the better guy. I think she was just scared to have someone understand the real her. She didn't want to feel, and with Alex, she could pretend. With me, I knew all her scars and her pain. I knew the real her."

He paused to see if Josie was still with him or if she needed him to stop, but Max noticed her nod, so he continued.

"So I stayed away. I thought I could handle seeing them together, but I couldn't. I let my best friend have the girl because I knew he could make her feel better. But then one night, she just appeared at my house. Told me it was over and that I was the one she really loved. That night, I told her I loved her. I thought I showed her that … but the next morning, I walked into school to see her in Alex's arms. She had cheated on him with me. She ripped my heart out when our eyes met, and she had this vindictive smile on her face. I knew then it wasn't real."

"I'm so sorry," Josie whispered.

"That's not the worst part," he warned.

"Okay."

"I went back to her," Max said, ashamed of his secret. "I confronted her, and before I knew it, I was getting dressed. I slept with her again and again. I couldn't stop even though I tried so hard to. But she knew how much I loved her, and she used it against me. I begged her to leave Alex, but she didn't. When he broke up with her, I thought it meant we could finally be together, but she moved on to some other guy."

"You never deserved what she did to you."

"*Alex* didn't deserve what we did to him," he corrected. "I still haven't told him."

Josie's thumb circled the back of his hand. It was as if she were soothing his past transgressions away and making way for the better Max Sheridan he was capable of.

"Last time I saw Alex, he looked at Keira with a love that could never be broken by something like the past. Trust me; I don't think it'll hurt him the way you think it will. I think it hurts you more," she pointed out.

"I have to tell him."

"I know you will."

"I have to apologise to Noel, too," he announced.

Josie's thumb stopped its turns. "Noel?"

Max let out a sigh. "This is where I think you'll actually be disgusted in me, Josephine."

"I can honestly say I won't. I'm your friend, Max," she assured.

Friend.

God, it hurt him to hear that.

114

He knew he was the hopeful one for wanting more than just to be a mere friend to her. It wasn't fair to her if he presumed anything more would come out of their mutual friendship.

He hoped.

And if Max was going to be the hero in her story, he had to be what she needed and not just act on his selfishness.

"The moment I met his girlfriend, I was already starting to fall for her. I thought this time she'd understand me. She must have known Noel was in love with Clara. She's a corporate lawyer just like me, and when we got to talking, she understood my work problems. One stupid bet and I pushed her against the closest tree and kissed her. Right under Noel's nose, I stole his girlfriend's kiss."

Josie pulled her hands from him. It was slow. Agonisingly slow. And it was also painful to see her take her touch away from him.

"You think I'm a terrible person," he said, the hurt he couldn't hide from his voice.

She shook her head. "I told you; I will never judge you— especially for something you did in the past. You might not have made the right choices, but you feel guilty, so that means you know what you did was wrong. I would judge you if you felt any pleasure or sense of rightness. You made a mistake, Max. You're human. You're a man who let your emotions and affections guide you. People out there have done a lot worse, and you, Max, are not the worst kind of man out there. You're one of the good ones who didn't get the chance to be loved right."

"You think so highly of me."

"I do," she said with a smile. "You taught me clauses in contracts that I didn't get in my lecture. Your notes on my draft assignment were great. And I think that should put your pride back in its place."

And there it was.

That ease that came with being with Josie.

She made him better.

She accepted and understood the wrongs of his past.

Sarah understood his personal life.

Andrea understood his career.

But Josie?

Josie understood both.

"Thank you," he said as he felt his phone vibrate in his jacket pocket.

"Don't thank me. I can't let my tutor's confidence take a hit, or I'll never pass contracts," she teased.

Max reached into his pocket and let out a dry laugh at Josie's jab. He glanced at his screen, unlocked his phone, and read the message he had just received.

Julian: Maxie, you've been gone a loooooooong time. Can you please come back? I mish you. OVAH!

"Gotta run?"

He glanced up from his screen to see Josie's big blue eyes on him. "It's Julian. He gets a little needy when he's had a few."

She laughed. "Needy for you and not Stevie?"

"Yeah, he's always been strange like that." Max slid out of the booth and glanced down at Josie. "You okay if I go? Trust me; I'd never hear the end of it if I didn't show up."

"Go. Julian didn't leave that table by the window once when I told him I'd give him a free cupcake if he delivered Stevie's order for her exam cramming. He said he needed another free one because the first one magically disappeared. I had to give him one just to get him out of the store. So yeah, I get it."

"Do you want me to stop by and go over any of your work with you? It doesn't have to just be contracts, you know. I can help you with your other classes."

Her lips pursed as she mulled over his offer. "How is Friday afternoon?"

"Perfect. I'll text you," he promised.

"Great. I'll see you later."

He nodded, but as he was about to take a step towards the bakery doors, he stilled. "Josie?"

"Yes, Max?"

He hoped she saw the sincerity in his smile and the honesty in his eyes. "Thank you."

"No, I should be thanking you for tutor—"

He shook his head, interrupting her. "No, thank you for letting me be honest with you … about Sarah and Andrea. Thank you for not judging who I was."

That teasing grin on her face transformed into a small smile. Josie slid out of the booth and stood in front of him, her hand settling on his arm as she tilted her head back to look at him. "You don't have to be afraid to be who you are around me. There's no shame in the man who you are. I quite like Maxwell Sheridan. Nothing I have learnt about you has changed how I look at you. I'm honoured you trust me enough to reveal parts of yourself that you haven't before."

Max's eyes fell to her pink lips.

It'd be so easy.

So right to just cup her face and have her mouth touch his.

The need outweighed the want.

And watching her lips part was torture.

Max tore his eyes from her beautiful mouth to land on her curious blue eyes. He saw it. The hint of desire. Maybe it was lust or attraction.

He could kiss her to find out.

But you can't ruin this, Max.

Not with Josie.

The small voice in his head was right.

He couldn't.

Instead of giving in to his needy wants, Max smiled and said, "I'll see you on Friday, Josephine," before he pulled away from her touch. He needed to get the hell out of the bakery before he did something stupid.

Like kiss her.

Josie

Feeling any better? I'm sure it's just the forty-eight-hour flu that's going around. Which means only twenty-four more to go.

I called Nadia, and you have the weekend off.

Please don't hate me if it lasts longer. I'm going into quarantine so I don't get sick since West is feeling better.

*J*osie groaned as she scrunched up the sticky note she found on her bedroom door. Then she read the one behind the note she had just peeled off.

> West just messaged.
> He says he's sorry for making you sick by staying over.
> Seriously, stay in bed I will check on Em for you and tell her. While I'm there, I'll call so you can talk to her.
> I love you, Josie.
> STAY THE HELL IN BED!
> Stella—the best roommate and best friend in the world.

This time she rolled her eyes and peeled the square piece of paper from her door to find, unsurprisingly, another note.

> How to cure the flu?
> Watch Gilmore Girls
> As recommended by Dr Stella Weller
> (DVDs are on the coffee table. Episode of Rory graduating high school is on pause because I know how much you love that episode)

Josie smiled.

Her best friend was a lot of things.

And thoughtful was definitely one of them.

But as Josie stared at the small writing on the note, she wondered, "How did she manage to fit it all on such tiny square pieces of paper?"

When she pulled the note down, she found another.

> To answer your question,
> I had to rewrite all these notes about a trillion times before they could fit.

And then she found the last note.

118

No, I can't read your mind
I just knew you'd ask.

LOVE YOU
Stella xo

Because the last note made her laugh, Josie left it on her bedroom door and held the stack of sticky notes until she made it to the large kitchen. When she agreed to her father's terms of where she would live, it meant the apartment being refurbished to appease her father. It was before her mother's very first cancer diagnosis. When her father's assistant told him of her need for help, Josie had been embarrassed and never returned his calls. Her mother had played middleman and was able to get them both to agree to conditions.

It meant a new car.

It meant expenses paid for.

Until Josie had gotten so mad at her father for not calling for her birthday that she cancelled the apartment's amenities and put them under her name instead of her father's. Bills began to stack up, and she had worked extra to pay them off—never telling Stella what she had done and never asking her roommate for any money.

Josie wasn't ashamed to admit she had a lot of pride.

Her father was the only person who ever tested it.

She had been scorned and abandoned by the man far too many times.

Upon reaching the kitchen counter, she set Stella's sticky notes down and let out another groan. The fogginess in her head and the heaviness in her eyes made it hard for her to stay awake. Her best friend was right. She should stay in bed, but she had an appointment with a doctor to get a medical certificate for her tutors and lecturers. She was sure whatever she had wasn't going to go away in a day's time. Josie would kill Stella's boyfriend for infecting the apartment with his sickness.

Suddenly, she felt something vibrate against her rear. Josie swung a hand around to find the cause of her vibrating bottom. It was several messages from Max. When she glanced at the time on her phone, she saw it was 10 a.m. and her 'Do Not Disturb' function had ceased for the day.

Smiling through the heat that consumed her body—which she blamed on her sickness rather than seeing Max's name—she unlocked her phone and read his texts.

Max: Do you think I'm a bad friend and tutor if I tried to persuade you not to be a divorce attorney?

Max: Seriously, will you hate me?

She laughed at his questions.

Josie: You're a lawyer. Convince me that your arguments are valid.

Max: Well, for one, you'd have to deal with Sully. He's the lawyer who's going through a divorce with his cheating ex-wife and is about to lose everything. Plus, I'm sitting in on this meeting with him and his new client. I feel horrible for finding it so entertaining to watch two people belittle each other after having vowed to love each other through thick and thin.

Josie: You're only convincing me that it's my field. The higher the marriage rate, the higher the divorce rate.

Max: Or you could be a prosecutor? But you'd have to face my father in a courtroom.

She bit back a grin as she climbed up onto the barstool by the bench and sat down. Her body felt almost too light to trust it to keep her vertical.

Josie: I'm sure by the time I'm a lawyer—wait, scratch that. IF I become a lawyer—I might have the confidence to prosecute your father's clients. But right now, I haven't chosen what kind of lawyer I really want to be.

Max: My father would not stand a chance with you

in a courtroom. You already charmed him. Trust me; I hear it when he steps into my office wondering how I met a woman like you. We can discuss your field of practice when I come over to tutor you.

Her heart swelled in her chest.
She loved that his father wondered about her.
That Max spoke about her to others.
But Josie knew his heart was not hers to claim. Not when it was divided into two—maybe not-so-equal parts. One part belonged to Sarah and another to Andrea. Josie knew she couldn't own a part.
Not romantically.
Whatever space he had left, she hoped it housed a spot for their friendship.
Because she was sure that was all he'd ever give her.
And to be fair to him meant being honest.
So she began her honest text about cancelling today's tutoring.

Josie: Today's not a good day for tutoring, which sucks because I had a question about equities that I've been meaning to ask you. I'll email it later.

Max: How about during the weekend? Josie, I told you to message me at any time when it comes to your classes.

Josie: Max, you deal with all this legal stuff every day. You must get tired of it. Surely, tutoring me is painful. But this weekend is not gonna work.

Max: Are you avoiding me? Was Wednesday night too much? I don't know if I've crossed a line.

Oh, Max.
He surely didn't play fair.

Josie: Max, I'm sick. Have been since yesterday morning. I'm seeing a doctor to get a medical certificate in an hour, and I really don't want to get you sick, too. I don't think the companies who pay you will appreciate you being unable to work. And I definitely don't want to be invoiced their legal fees. I'm not avoiding you. I like you, remember?

To her horror, she had pressed send.
"I *like* you?" she said in disbelief. "Shit, shit, shit!"
There was no way to cover it.
No way to take it back.
So she sent him a retraction.

> **Josie:** Don't let it get to your head. I like you, yes. As a friend, yes. I should have clarified, but I'm sick. Please don't judge me.

One minute.
Two.
Five minutes.
Ten.

> **Max:** Sorry, had a client drop by for a quick chat. I don't judge you. I will never judge you. Message me when you get home from the doctor's so I know you made it back.

Just as relief poured over her stressful heart, Max sent her another message.

> **Max:** And, Josie, to be very honest and real with you, I like you. In whatever way you want me to like you back.

And that message became a problem for her heart.
Her mind.
Her sanity.
Her hopes.
And her supposed friendship with Maxwell Sheridan.

"Bed rest, Miss Faulkner," her doctor prescribed. He was a young doctor in his late twenties. He had jet black hair and a smile that could make any woman swoon. If she hadn't known the effects of Max's smile, he might have affected her. "The cold and flu medicine you're taking is sufficient, but make sure you drink plenty of fluids. I also recommend electrolyte supplements. I can see the sweat dotting your forehead. I'm sorry, but it's only going to get worse. You'll need the electrolytes replaced in your system."

Josie nodded and raised her arm to wipe the sweat off her forehead with the sleeve of her hoodie. She wasn't sure if her heated cheeks were from embarrassment that the cute doctor was seeing her at her very worst or from the stupid flu she had.

"How come my roommate's boyfriend only had this for like two days?" she whined rather than asked.

Dr Ryder chuckled.

And Ryder?

Of course, his name would be 'Ryder'?

More like ride-her.

Josie bit the inside of her cheek to stop herself from smiling. Jokes like those were wasted on her own ears. Stella would have found it hilarious and agree. She allowed her eyes that moment to take in his arms as he began to type notes into her file.

Doctors shouldn't wear such tight shirts.

"I've been doing some training for a charity run," Dr Ryder said as he removed his focus from his computer screen to smile at her.

"I said that out loud?"

"You did," he confirmed.

She sank into her seat in embarrassment.

She decided then that Dr Jennings, her usual doctor, was not getting a Christmas card this year for being away when Josie was sick.

"Sorry," she quickly apologised. His laughter threw her off. Normally, she was so sure of herself with men, but this very attractive doctor was a rarity. Especially since she wasn't expecting him. "You won't ever see me again. I promise no more emergency doctor visits from me. I just really needed that medical certificate."

Ryder swivelled his chair to look at her properly. His eyes fell to her chest. And oh, did she love that his eyes remained there.

Oh, Josie, you are a pervert.

Lack of sex + the flu = undeniably sexually starved.

"Deakin, huh?"

"Yep," she confirmed as she glanced down at the university hoodie she had worn.

"What are you studying?"

"Law."

"You're going to be a lawyer. That's impressive."

"Not as impressive as a doctor."

Stop it.

Stop flirting with the very cute doctor.

Ryder's cheeks flared with the colour red. "Well, I'm glad you're impressed. I'll sign this certificate, and you'll be on your way."

Josie smiled. She was sure she looked delirious because she began to feel it.

The doctor returned to his computer, pressed a button, and then after several minutes, retrieved her medical certificate from the printer. He signed the paper flawlessly and then handed it to her. "I mean it, Miss Faulkner, plenty of rest."

"I'll rest when I get my law degree." She folded the evidence her tutors and lecturers would need.

"Thought you'd be a determined one. So that medical certificate is until Tuesday. Not sure if you have classes on Monday, but I'd assume so. Though I'm not your regular doctor, I'd highly suggest you get a blood test so we can see how your iron levels are. I can see how tired you are, and it isn't from the flu."

You have no idea.

"I can't make promises, but if you tell Dr Jennings, she'll call me relentlessly to make it happen."

He grinned at her. "I'll be sure to let her know."

"Thanks," Josie said as she picked up her bag from the floor and stood from the chair where she'd been sitting.

"Miss Faulkner, before you go," Ryder said.

"Yes?"

He got out of the leather chair and towered over her. Those grey eyes were pretty, but they didn't make her feel as if she were lost in them like Max's.

"Now that I'm officially not your doctor, and I hope you don't find this inappropriate, but would you like to grab dinner sometime? When you're feeling better, of course." He asked so politely that a yes almost fell out of her mouth.

Ryder wasn't like the typical men she dated.

He was the complete opposite.

And to her disappointment, her father would approve of him.

The realisation had her frowning.

"I know I'm a lot older than the guys you probably date. But I find you attractive and funny. I'd kick myself if I didn't at least ask," he said.

A smile tugged at her lips, but she forced it back. "I have a lot going on at the moment."

The disappointment reached his eyes. "Of course. You're a busy woman. I'll let you continue with your day."

She nodded then spun around and made her way towards the door. When she reached it, she paused and let out a heavy exhale. Her father might approve of a doctor, but her mother would be thrilled that she'd possibly date someone like Ryder. She returned to the doctor in a matter of seconds.

"Dr Ryder, you seem nice. If you were my regular doctor, I'd tell you that this is completely inappropriate. But since you're not, then there's nothing wrong here. Right?"

"Right," he agreed.

"I'm not going to make you a promise for dinner. I have a lot going on in my life. I probably won't ever see you again—"

"I'll take that chance," he cut her off.

"Just please don't hold your breath. I have a year left with my law degree. If by some chance in a year's time you're free, then sure."

He laughed. "A year, Miss Faulkner?"

"More like a year and a half. I have this semester and then next year."

"So when you're done, you're saying we could possibly go for dinner?"

"If you're free," she added.

"All right," Ryder agreed and reached out and took the medical certificate from her. Then he scribbled something on the back of it and handed it back to her. "In case you have free time before you finish your degree."

That had her heart fluttering.

Not as strong as she had felt before.

But it was there.

She said nothing as she made her way out of his office and down the hall. Once she reached the end, she heard a door open behind her and someone calling, "Miss Faulkner," behind her.

Josie spun around to find the doctor wrapping a stethoscope around his neck. "It's just Zac."

"And it's just Josie," she said and then spun back around and headed out of the medical centre, feeling oddly satisfied and ashamed of herself.

Chapter
EIGHT

Max

"Takeaway order for Max," the woman behind the counter said in a flirty voice.

Max got up from the bench he was sitting on and headed to the counter. He smiled at the waitress. She had served him several times before, but he had never stuck around long enough to get her name.

"Thanks," he said as he collected the soup from her. "I'm sorry. I never got your name."

Her lashes fluttered as surprise consumed her pale hazel eyes, brightening the line of yellow around her iris. "It's Fel."

"Fel?"

She nodded. A blush succumbed her cheeks, and it was the perfect backdrop for her freckles. She was pretty, but her young girlish features weren't for him. "Short for Felicity."

"Well, it's nice to meet you, Fel. I'll see you next time."

"You, too, Max," she said as Max spun around and made his way out of the restaurant and to his car.

When he reached his car, he pulled the key out of his pocket and unlocked it. Careful not to spill the soup, he opened the passenger side door and set the takeout food on the seat. As he closed the door, his phone vibrated in his jacket pocket. He pulled it out to find Noel calling him.

Guilt doubled in his chest. He had been avoiding Nolan Parker's text message for two days. His priority was Josie. After that, he simply wanted to forget it was there. Realising what a shit friend Max had been, he answered the call and made his way to the driver's side.

"Hello," Max greeted as he opened the car door and slipped inside. He shoved the key into the ignition and turned his Porsche to life. Then he got to work getting his phone connected to his car.

Seconds passed, and he heard Noel say, "Hey, Max. How are you?" through the speakers.

"Not bad," he replied as he put his seat belt on. He had indicated right, checked that he was clear to pull out, and drove towards Collingwood.

"That's good. Your father not pressuring you to take on more clients?"

Max shook his head, aware that his best friend couldn't see it. "He's got me shadowing other lawyers in the firm. Seeing how they all work. He takes time away from my current clients, but besides that, he has eased off a little."

"That's good, mate."

A sense of accomplishment washed over him as he heard the proudness in Noel's voice. When he finally told him what he had done behind his back, he knew that would be gone. He just hoped Noel would still consider him his friend afterwards.

"How are you and Clara doing?"

Noel sighed. "Good. I feel like I barely see her anymore. Her classes and assignments have her preoccupied. Honestly, her doing this degree is pointless. I don't mind paying for it, but that's just it. I'm not paying for it. She's using some of her trust fund money, and it's hard to watch her waste it. She doesn't need to finish her business degree to be a dessert chef. She had promised to use the money to open her own bakery."

"Have you spoken to her about this?"

"Yeah. It's actually what we fight about."

"You guys are fighting over money? Do you need some help ... financially?"

128

His best friend sighed again. "No, that's not why I called or sent that text. Honestly, we're good. I don't make a lawyer's salary each year, but I make enough where we're both comfortable. We fight because I know she's delaying her dreams. She's scared of another setback like at the last restaurant where she worked. The head chef really destroyed her confidence."

Max pressed on the brakes and came to a slow stop behind traffic. "Clara's not happy?"

"No," Noel confirmed in a sad tone. "It doesn't help that she knows Andrea is coming back from the Florida office soon."

Andrea.

Max's heart stalled at the sound of her name.

The woman he'd kissed under a tree in New York.

The woman he dared.

The woman who had left him scorned with her confusing emails demanding space.

"Max? Max, are you still there?"

He swallowed hard. The pain in his chest radiated, but he was fine. Two days ago, he thought he had let her go. But hearing Noel say her name was the latch breaking. The hurt she inflicted came back to him, stronger than ever, repeating its assault on his heart.

"Still here."

Noel went silent.

Max continued to drive as he waited for Noel to speak again.

"I know what I have to do, but she won't like it."

"What are you thinking?" Max asked, curious.

"I've got to get in touch with a few of the restaurants back in Melbourne to see if they'd still be open to having her work there."

Max turned onto Josie's street and parked his car outside her apartment. He cut the ignition and stared at his phone in the slot next to the brake handle. "How is that going to work?"

"It's not," Noel stated. "We're not working right now, Max. She keeps hiding her true feelings because she feels like she owes it to me to be in Boston. But she matters more than my job does. And she shouldn't have to sacrifice her dreams after she's worked so hard for them. I've still gotta work out how to do this without it affecting our marriage. She needs kitchen experience and a confidence boost. She doesn't need to be stressed over

129

management statistic assignments and all that."

"I agree," Max found himself saying. He knew how hard Josie was working for her bachelor and for her dream career. It was only fair that Max encouraged Noel to support Clara achieving hers. "Look at Rob; he's now the world champion. Clara worked hard to become a chef. She already went to culinary school. Whatever you think is right, encourage her not to give up."

"Thanks, Max. I knew you'd understand."

He grinned as he removed his belt, reached over, and picked up the soup he had ordered. Then he picked up his phone and disconnected the Bluetooth so that the call went back through his phone. When it successfully disconnected from the car's speakers, he pulled the key from the ignition and got out of the car.

"Hey, Noel, I've gotta run. Anything else you want to discuss?"

Noel hummed. "Oh, it was nothing important. Just wanted to see if you wanted to do some *pro bono* work here in Boston— off the record, you'll be receiving a gratitude package, and it'll be all expenses paid."

Max closed his car door and blinked at Josie's apartment building, surprised at the offer his best friend was expressing. "What?"

"As I said before, Andrea's coming back to Boston soon after she took over the Florida office for eight months. She finally got the senior lawyer position, and she's coming back with a lot of work. Gregson asked me if I knew any corporate lawyers willing to help out for a month or two. And well, besides Andrea, you're the only other lawyer I know. Thought since the whole Sarah thing and your dad's firm pressuring you, you might want to get away. You're welcome to stay with us if you'd like. I ran it past Clara, and she insists."

Boston.

Working with Andrea.

Seeing Andrea.

"Noel ..."

"I know, but maybe you being here and Clara cooking for you can boost her confidence, too—"

"Noel."

"And I'd like seeing you around more often. We could make weekend trips to see Alex, Keira, and Will. It'd be nice to have you in the US, Max."

He let out a bothered sigh as he made his way towards the gate of Josie's apartment. Typing in the security code, he let himself in. As Max made it into the elevator and up to Josie's floor and then apartment, he listened to Noel discuss how good of an idea it was to have Max in Boston working pro bono. The money wasn't the problem.

It was seeing Andrea.

She had humiliated him with her silence.

With her short messages.

With her need for space.

When he reached Josie's front door, Noel had suggested, "At least think about it?"

"I'll think about it," he promised as he said goodbye and hung up on his best friend. Juggling everything in his right hand, he balled his left into a fist and tapped his knuckles against the door.

His answer was silence.

He knew she was home.

She had texted him two hours ago to say she had seen her doctor.

Max knocked once again.

He finally heard footsteps and Josie saying, "Hang on a sec!" before her door opened and he was presented with a pale, sweaty version of her.

"Max?" She squinted at him. "What are you doing here?"

He lifted his right hand higher, and her eyes darted to the plastic bag.

"What is that?"

"Soup," he stated.

The annoyance didn't leave her face, but he noticed her sway and the increase of sweat that dotted her forehead. "Why did you bring soup to my door?"

His lips curved into a smile. "Because you're sick."

"So that requires soup delivered to my door?"

He gave her a nod and pushed past her to enter her apartment. "I'm looking after you," he said once he reached her kitchen bench.

Josie was slow to catch up, and she stood on the other side, glaring at him. "Max, you don't have to look after me."

Max untied the plastic bag and pulled out the still hot chicken soup. He pushed aside the wet plastic bag and pulled off the lid.

"Josephine, I'm your friend. Go back to bed, and I'll bring it to you."

"No," she whined.

He stepped around the counter, gently wrapped his fingers around her arm, and ushered her out of the kitchen. "Come on. Bed, please."

"But … but …" Then she sighed. "Fine, but don't expect me to be happy."

Josie grumbled as she made her way to her bedroom while Max laughed at her. He spun back around and went to the top cupboards in search of a bowl. After opening several, he pulled out a black bowl and set it on the counter. Out of the corner of his eye, he noticed a folded piece of paper with something scribbled on it.

Curious, he set his fingertips on the paper and brought it closer. Then he picked it up and unfolded it to read what was written down.

Josie,
In case you wanted dinner in the meantime.
0423 540 535.
Zac.

Max frowned at the message.

Then he turned the page over to find that the dinner invite and phone number from a man named 'Zac' was written on Josie's medical certificate. The discovery had him frowning as a sense of urgency filled him. He had no right to feel possessive.

She wasn't his.

He was her friend.

His need to make sure this 'Zac' never went to dinner with Josie was unwarranted. If she wanted to date him, Max had to let her. He had no say in her personal life whatsoever.

At the bottom of the medical certificate, just below the signature, he noticed her doctor's name.

132

Dr Zachary Ryder.
Zac was her doctor.
She had met him today.
Gotten his number today.
Max folded the certificate and set it back on the bench. He had no right to pry into Josie's love life. If she wanted to date a doctor, she had his blessing. He wanted what was in her best interests.
And if that was her dating a man in the medical profession, then so be it.
But no doctor could ever understand her future career better than a lawyer.
No.
No one would understand her better than Max did.
He knew the pressure of law school.
Of placement.
And of actually being a practising lawyer.
He decided then to ignore what he saw. Be oblivious to her getting another man's number. Max picked up the bowl and spun around. He reached over the bench and picked up the takeaway container filled with chicken soup. Carefully, he poured the hot contents into the black bowl and then set the plastic container down. Max took in the kitchen to find the drawer housing the utensils. When he made his way towards the skinny drawer, he pulled it opened. He took out a spoon, closed it, and headed to Josie's room.
Upon reaching her door, he noticed the yellow sticky note on the door. He squinted at the note and read it.

No, I can't read your mind.
I just knew you'd ask

LOVE YOU
Stella xo

He found that quirk between Josie and her roommate, Stella, was sweet and sentimental. Knocking lightly on the door, he grasped the handle and twisted it. He peeked into the room to find it dark. The curtains covered the windows, and he could just see Josie lying on her side. He tiptoed towards her and sat on the empty side of her bed.

"Josephine, I have your ..." He reached over and set his free hand on her shoulder. He peered over to find her eyes closed. "And you're asleep."

Max pulled back and set the bowl of soup on her bedside table. Then he got off the bed and made his way to her. He bent his knees and set his hand on her forehead.

Heat met his palm.

She was burning up.

She wasn't kidding when she said she was sick.

Josie had a fever, and to ensure that she would get better, he let her sleep.

Josie

"You're okay, Josephine," a sweet voice whispered. "Sleep. Your fever's gone down."

She groaned as something cool touched her forehead.

He let out a deep chuckle. "Stop moving. You're making the cloth fall off."

Josie waved her arms to try to swipe away the hands on her. She kept her eyes closed, unable to open them. Her eyelids were still heavy and hot. "Too cold."

"Too bad."

She recognised that voice.

Her arms fell to rest on the bed. "Max?"

"Right here," he confirmed. "I'm just gonna sit down next to you."

"How long have I been asleep?"

"Soup's gone cold. It's just after four. Stella's home."

Stella ...

Josie jerked up to a sitting position. Her head quickly succumbed to heat, but she pushed through the aches.

Stella was meant to call so she could speak to her mother, but she had fallen asleep. The room was still dark, and she tried to focus on her surroundings. The first thing her eyes landed on was Max staring at her.

"I've been asleep for four hours?"

Max nodded. "You have. I stayed for a bit but had to take a phone call, so I let you sleep. Changed the cloth several times when it warmed."

She glanced down to find the wet cloth next to her on the bed. "I'm so sorry I fell asleep." She reached over and flicked on the bedside lamp, illuminating his face and her room. The worry on his face mixed with the relieved gleam in his eyes.

Her heart swelled knowing he worried about her health.

That he looked after her.

Whatever spontaneous feelings she had towards the doctor she had met earlier today meant nothing.

Her heart wanted this man who pressed his palm to her forehead.

Her heart now beat his name.

Max.

Max, Max.

Max.

Doctors were nice, but lawyers, they were her weakness.

Actually, Maxwell Sheridan had become her weakness.

"Yep, the fever's going down," he announced with glee tinting his voice.

Josie let out a soft moan once he set the cold, wet cloth back on her forehead. It was relief.

The cold mixing and extinguishing the hot.

Closing her eyes, she melted into his touch the moment he used his free hand to cup her jaw.

He was definitely her saviour in her time of need.

Max.

Max, Max, Max, her heart sang.

A soft moan escaped her lips and boomed loudly in her ears. But at that moment, she didn't care.

"I like you, Max," she whispered.

His thumb pressed just below her bottom lip. Relieved her eyes were closed, she memorised his touch and what it did to her. Tomorrow, she'd blame it on her sickness. Take it back to save her pride and her heart.

"As a friend?"

She felt as if his words caressed her lips with how close she suspected he was. That thumb of his gently moved to the corner of her mouth.

135

She hummed and shook her head lightly.

"Max," she breathed as the cloth fell away from her forehead and another hand steadied her jaw.

"Yes, Josephine."

God, the way he says my name.

"To be very honest and real with you ..."

"Yes?"

"I like you ..." She lifted her eyelids to find his light brown eyes staring at her. Wide and beautiful. She dragged her teeth on her bottom lip before saying in a low voice, "In whatever way you want me to like you."

Those beautiful eyes of his softened as he leant forward and pressed his forehead to hers. Just for a moment, he held her there. Then he whispered, "*Honestly.* Like me honestly, Josephine."

When he pulled back slightly, she asked, "Will you like me honestly?"

"I will," he vowed as he brought her closer to him, this time pressing his warm lips against her forehead. The searing heat between her fever and his lips caused the jolt in her chest and the heaviness in her eyelids to take over and forced them to fall closed.

And she didn't care that she began to hum her mother's favourite song.

It felt perfect for this moment.

For him.

For them.

La

Vie

En

Rose.

The room was dark when she woke up.

Josie was alone.

Raising her hand up, she grasped the dry cloth and removed it from her forehead. She let it fall to the bed as she sat herself up. The last thing she remembered was humming to Max before her body succumbed to sleep. Josie slowly swung her legs over her bed so that her feet lay flat on the carpet. She was about to get up off the bed when she noticed her phone. She picked it up to find her mother had sent her a message.

> **Mamma:** Josephine, Stella stopped by to visit. She told me you're sick. Drink plenty of fluids. Take care of yourself. We tried to call, but you must have been resting. I will be out of hospital soon. Dr Frederickson says I'm recovering from the fever, and we can start chemo in a week. I love you, my sweet Josephine.

Tears began to well.

She knew her mother must be feeling a lot better if she was able to send a text message. Josie read the message once more, and those tears that formed slid down her cheeks. She reached up and brushed them away because they were tears of relief. Her mother still had strength in her to continue fighting.

And Josie believed in her.

Just like she had always believed in her mother.

Josie glanced at the time on her phone to see that it was 9:26 p.m. She had slept for another five hours. But unlike when she woke up this afternoon, she felt better. Her body didn't feel as hot. Didn't feel as heavy or sluggish. She had needed the additional five hours.

Now the only problem she had was that she'd be awake all night, and she was hungry. She knew the chance of Max saving the soup was highly unlikely, but she knew bread and peanut butter were in the kitchen waiting for her. After quickly texting her mother that she was feeling a little better and that she loved her, she got up from the bed and made her way out of her bedroom. Closing the door behind her, she noticed a sticky note next to the one Stella had stuck on her door. The dim light wasn't enough for her to read it properly. She lifted her phone so that the brightness illuminated the note.

Josie,
Stella said I could join in on the note sharing.
Hope you're feeling better.
Max.

She couldn't stop the smile that splayed on her lips. And she couldn't help the way her heart sped up at the memories of him on her bed, holding her so intimately.

Honestly.

He wanted her to like him honestly.

And he had promised he'd like her honestly, too.

However, that could still mean platonically, and that little reminder brought reality back to sprinkle its "come back to the real world, Josie" dust all over her. But tonight, she would let her foolish heart hope for more.

The sounds of women talking caught her attention. Josie spun around and made her way down the short hallway and into the living room to find the TV on. Then she heard the theme song and noticed Max sitting on the couch. He hadn't heard her. She leant against the corner of the entryway and watched as he nodded his head along to the *Gilmore Girls* theme song. She recognised the episode. It was when Rory moved into her Yale dorm to discover that Paris was her roommate. When she had watched that episode with Stella, they would always fight over who was Paris.

To end every *Gilmore Girls* fight they had, they both conceded that neither were Paris or Rory. And that fight would turn into who Rory should have ended up with.

Jess or Logan.

Stella was Jess all the way.

Josie was still torn between the two.

She had her reasons.

But she sided with Jess. She just never admitted it to Stella so she could avoid the 'I told you she has to be with Jess!' talk.

Josie smiled when Max let out an 'ahh' when Lorelai noticed the 'R.G.' sticky note on Rory's bedroom door. He had made the connection. It had been what sparked Josie and Stella's sticky note messages. Pushing off the wall, she made her way towards him and smiled when he swung his gaze to her. Josie didn't say anything as she sat down on the couch next to him.

She had made sure to leave space between them, but it seemed Max didn't want space as he wrapped his arm around her and pulled her close.

"You sleep okay?" he asked, looking down at her. That softness in his eyes from hours ago was still there.

Soft and sweet.

His arm remained wrapped around her, and Josie rested the side of her head on his shoulder.

There had been a shift in their relationship.

Honestly could be in the makings.

It felt as if it were happening right now.

But then she pulled back. Not because she wanted to, but because she remembered she was still sick. There would be no more bodily contact with him until she was better and had a clearer, non-flu-fogged mind.

"I slept great," she confirmed with a small smile.

"You feeling any better?"

"A little."

"That's good," he said, his arm still wrapped around her shoulder.

Josie glanced over at the screen to see Lorelai telling Rory to do a re-walk-in of her dorm room since she had missed it. "You're watching *Gilmore Girls*."

Max gently squeezed her arm. "Yeah, I hope you don't mind. Stella and I were talking, and she noticed that you hadn't watched it. She asked if she could play the episode where Rory graduates in the background while she made you fresh soup. It's still on the stove. I can heat you up some if you want?"

"Hmm, not just yet. I can't believe Stella made me soup."

"I told her about your soup going cold when she came home, and I had walked out of your room ready to throw it. She went down to the shops to get everything."

She loved her roommate more than she could possibly love another nonrelated human being. Tomorrow, she'd have to thank her. Josie would write the corniest *Gilmore Girls* pun note Stella had ever read.

Josie's brows furrowed when she realised exactly where Max was at on the *Gilmore Girls* timeline. "Wait. You've watched Rory graduate, right?" She craned her neck to see Max nodding at her. "This is season four."

Another nod from Max. "Stella changed it before she went to bed."

Josie's jaw dropped. "And you've been watching it since?"

"I have. You don't mind that I'm ahead?"

She laughed as Max removed his arm from around her, and he turned to face her.

"I've seen every episode at least three times," she explained. "Have you ever seen *Gilmore Girls*?"

"Nah. I was too busy chasing girls, which is a shame because I really should have. I cannot take my eyes off Lorelai Gilmore." He then frowned. "Who is Jess?"

There was a gasp behind them, and they both noticed Stella in her pjs with her palm to her chest. "You *don't* know who Jess is?"

"He's going to meet Logan first, Stella," Josie teased.

Her best friend shook her head. "No. That cannot happen. You have to watch this from the start, Max." Then Stella scurried over to the cabinet where all the DVDs called home. She pressed her foot on the switch of the tall lamp next to the cabinet and searched inside. Seconds later, she pulled out handfuls of *Gilmore Girls* DVDs. "You don't have plans for this weekend, do you, Max?"

"Stella," Josie hissed.

"What?" her best friend asked as she walked over and set the DVDs on the glass table. "He can't just ask who Jess is right before he meets Logan. That's not fair, and you know it."

Max chuckled next to her. "I'm guessing she's a Jess fan?"

"She is. Now, you have to be prepared if you want to start a *Gilmore Girls* marathon. Once you start, you can't stop—especially if Stella is watching, too. And trust me, she hates the first season because it drags and because of Dean."

"Dean?"

And on cue, Stella groaned as she lowered herself onto the other leather couch. "I can't stand Dean. It's torture watching the first season."

Josie watched as Max nodded along with Stella. "But we like Luke, right?"

Her heart had all but given up the absurd fight it was having.

Max had said *we*.

Not just her and him.

140

But we as in her, him, and Stella.

And that had her falling for him quicker than Lorelai convincing Luke for a cup of coffee with her wit and charm.

Stella looked over at Josie and gave her that squinted look. The "he's too perfect" look. It was the same look she had given her when she had first started dating West and had introduced Josie to him. Josie hoped the expression she was giving back was the "Don't get any ideas. We're friends!" look.

Stella jumped off the couch and nodded as she picked up the first season of *Gilmore Girls*. "Oh, we are so Luke for Lorelai."

Max leant back on the couch. "Good. I like Luke."

"Then you're going to love Jess," Stella remarked as she opened the DVD and got to work introducing Max to the first season of one of TV's finest shows.

It was just after 1:30 a.m. when episode four and the first disc ended.

Max hadn't said much during the four episodes they watched with Stella. He had his little remarks. Stella's favourite had been, "This Dean kid has a hidden agenda. Yeah, I don't like him." She had also shot Josie that "you have to be with him" look when he had excused himself to go to the bathroom. Then halfway through the second episode, he had heated Josie and Stella a bowl of Stella's—but actually Stella's mother's—perfect every time chicken soup. Stella had practically forced Max back into the kitchen to make himself a bowl.

And when she asked him for his opinion, he had told her that the title of "perfect every time" was justified. If he was lying to impress her best friend, Max did so flawlessly.

"She's asleep," Max pointed out.

Josie glanced over to find Stella sprawled out on the leather couch. She smiled at the peaceful-looking, Jess-loving best friend of hers.

"Should we wake her up?"

She got up off the couch, flinching when the aches in her head returned. They weren't as painful as earlier in the day, but they were still troublesome.

"You feeling okay?" Max asked.

She glanced down and gave him a reassuring smile. "I am. I'll get her a blanket from the linen closet. Helpful hint—never wake up a sleeping Stella Weller."

"Wait," Max said between stifled chuckles. "Stella's last name is *Weller?*"

"Yeah. You didn't know that?"

"No." More laughter from him. "I would have remembered. Julian is going to piss himself. He's gonna wanna meet her."

Josie rolled her eyes. "Of course, he does. Her father was the one to name her Stella. He thought it would be adorable. She got teased a lot, apparently. But it never hurt her because, to this day, she loves that her name rhymes. She's already vowed never to take West's name if they ever get married."

"I like that," Max said as he got up off the couch. "I'll turn this off."

"Thanks. I'll be back in a second. I'll just grab the blanket." It took her a matter of minutes to grab the spare fluffy blanket from the linen closet in the hallway. She could have grabbed the thin blanket in the trunk by the window, but the fluffy mink blankets were Stella's favourite. When she returned, the TV was off, and Max took the blanket from her and gently covered her best friend with it.

It was sweet and unnecessary of him.

But she appreciated it wholeheartedly.

Josie had walked over to the lamp and turned it off before she led Max away from the lounge room and to the dimly lit hallway. Josie had left her phone on the couch she and Max had sat on, but she knew it was too late for him to drive.

"Do you want to stay the night?" she asked in a soft voice.

Max's eyes widened. "Is that okay?"

She lightly laughed. "We're adults, Max. If you want, you can sleep in my bed, and I'll sleep in Stella's. That way you won't catch what I've got."

Max stepped a fraction closer, stealing the little air between them as he set his hands on the nape of her neck, drawing her closer. "I've had a flu shot, Josie. I'm okay with sharing a bed with you."

"Like with a pillow between us?"

He nodded in agreement. "If that makes you feel more comfortable."

They were going to share a bed.

Her bed.

His body covered by the same blanket as hers.

The thought that his strong arms might wrap around her had her shivering.

"Josie, you all right?" His hand shot up and pressed against her forehead. "Okay, let's get you to bed. Your fever's still there."

His touch was soft and calculated.

Not too much pressure.

Enough to make tingles flutter over her skin.

Oh, she most definitely was delirious from him.

The thought had her correcting her softening posture. When she was sure she wouldn't fall over, she nodded. She was glad that the dimmed lights hid her heated cheeks.

Max's hands left her face, and he turned in the direction of the hallway that led to her bedroom. Taking a small breath of air, Josie began to lead him to her bedroom. It dawned on her that this was the first time a man would ever share her bed. She had a strict no-hookup-sleepover rule. Her apartment was too lavish to trust some of her previous boyfriends or casual flings to be left alone in. It also cheapened her wild persona to have a place bought by her father. Her rebelliousness would be questioned. And she didn't want Stella to see or have any contact with the men she had slept with. Nor did Josie want her to hear the lacklustre sex she was having.

When she stopped at her bedroom door, Max reached over and grasped the handle. It took him no trouble at all to open and hold the door for her. Josie stepped inside and stood at the foot of her queen-size bed. A flick of the light switch by Max had the room brightening.

Then she took in her bed.

It was a mess.

The blanket she had laid on top of was all wrinkled.

And the pillows no longer perfectly aligned.

"Right or left?" Max asked once he closed the door behind her and stood by her side.

Josie peeked up to find him staring down at her. "What?"

143

"Do you sleep on the left side or the right?"

Her lips made an 'O' as she understood his question. "I sleep in the middle most of the time."

"And the other times?"

"The side closest the window."

Max nodded as he walked around her and to the side of the bed she had just slept on. She watched in amazement as he flung the covers back and readjusted the pillow.

"Are you also gonna tuck me in?" she teased as she made her way to him.

"If you want me to," he said in a throaty voice.

Josie shook her head. "No, I can manage."

Max stepped back and gave her space to climb on the bed and lie down. Before she could even reach out for it, Max had covered her with the blanket.

"Not too warm?"

She shook her head as her eyes began to droop. "I'm good."

A yawn left her as she wiggled in the bed to get comfortable. "Can you turn off the light and get in here?"

A sweet smile spread across his perfect lips. The same lips that had pressed against her forehead. "No pillow between us?"

"We're both adults," she answered softer than she would have liked. Then she rolled onto her left side and tucked her hands under her cheek. Her eyes drifted closed seconds later.

Josie heard the light flick off and then Max's tepid footsteps. The bed dipped under his weight, and then he whispered, "Josephine?"

"Yes, Max?" Eyes still closed, she willed her lungs to commence a normal sequence of breaths.

"You don't mind if I take off my shirt, do you? My pants are fine once I take the belt off."

She bit the inside of her cheek, hating that she loved the idea of her *friend* — who had spent the day looking after her — being shirtless as they slept.

"I don't mind."

"Thanks," he said, and she heard him begin to undress.

Josie blinked her eyes open, only seeing the darkness of her room.

She waited.

Memorised each breath he took.

Cherished the way those small sounds made her heart beat his name.

She knew she was long past the fall.

She was currently spiralling out of control.

And there was no way to stop it.

Josie heard the belt buckle hit the carpet and then another sound. It was softer, and she assumed his shirt had joined the belt on the floor.

Then the bed dipped once more, and she felt the tug of the blanket.

She was tempted to see just how he slept. If he faced her or his back was turned to her. The urge to peek made her restless. Josie wiggled once more in the bed and finally found comfort.

"Josie," Max said into her dark room.

Josie had held her breath for a long moment before she released it. "Yes?"

She waited for him to speak, wondering if he was still awake or if he'd whispered her name in his sleep.

The covers moved, and she felt him turn next to her. "Can you face me for a second?"

Exhaling, she readjusted herself so that she now lay facing Max. She couldn't see the features of his face, but he had reached out and set his fingers on her jaw for a long moment. Josie said nothing, too afraid her voice would betray her and expose her feelings. All she could do was wait and be thankful the darkness around them hid her face.

Max's fingertips slowly made their way down her jaw and along her neck. Then his touch disappeared until his palm found her hip.

"I don't want to be Max," he whispered as his thumb circled her hip, causing the almost audible gasp to escape her. "Not to you, Josie. I don't want to be Max."

"What?" she asked once his thumb halted its movements.

"I watched the start of season four. I don't want to be the Max to your Lorelai. I want to be Luke," Max revealed. "*Your* Luke."

After that, Max said nothing more, his revelation met with silence, and his soft inhales.

And sleep took a long time to find Josie.

145

Chapter
NINE

Max

I want to be Luke.
  Your *Luke.*
  Maxwell Sheridan had said more than he should have last night. Last night, he had confessed his attraction to her, but he wasn't sure if Josie had heard him. She hadn't replied, and the room was too dark for him to see.

He had no reaction from her, and Max presumed she'd fallen asleep.

That his want for her to be his Lorelai fell on deaf ears.

And as Max took in the woman sleeping next to him, he realised how correct and true his attraction towards Josie was.

He would be her Luke.

And she, his Lorelai.

He had no idea if Luke and Lorelai ended up together at the end of *Gilmore Girls,* but they made sense and had a connection that was friendship, mutual respect, and more.

Just like he and Josie.

It wasn't hard to come to terms with the fact that he liked Josie.

He liked her honestly.

Completely true without a hint of hesitation.

Josie's brows furrowed, and a small groan escaped her lips. "What time is it?" she asked, voice still heavy with sleep.

Max smiled as he watched her eyelids flutter until her bright blue eyes greeted him. That right there. That moment her eyes found his was a moment worth keeping and replaying every day of his life. Josie waking up to him was one of those moments he knew would never leave him.

He had no idea how it happened.

How she could captivate him.

How she was able to soothe every wound others before her had inflicted on him.

Her lips broke into a beautiful smile. "Morning."

Not caring that their friendship and his heart was on the line, he reached up and brushed her brunette hair from her face. Josie wasn't as pale as she had been when he first appeared at her apartment with soup. Her colour had returned. But he did feel the warmth of her skin.

"Morning," he greeted as his fingers traced the side of her face, and her eyes softened.

She was claiming him without even knowing it.

And he realised—there lying in her bed with her—that he adored her.

Maxwell Sheridan adored Josephine Faulkner with a fondness he had never felt for any other woman he'd met, loved, or desired.

"Can I ask you something?"

She nodded.

"Last night ..."

Her eyes widened. "Y-yes?"

"You sang something to me," he revealed. It was when Max had come to change the cloth helping with her high fever. She had hummed a sweet melody that was familiar to him. He'd heard some words, but then she hummed the rest.

It was beautiful.

He had smiled and taken in every hum and note sung.

"I did?" she breathed as she sat up. Her cheeks reddened in a shade he loved seeing.

Max followed and sat up, too. "I think it was French?"

A sad gleamed consumed her bright blues. *"Oh."* The muscles in her neck tightened as she swallowed. "I remember now. I did."

"What song was it?"

Josie brushed her wavy hair behind her ears as she got off her bed. She made her way to a dresser and pulled open a drawer. She returned moments later and sat on the bed with something in her hand. Max glanced down to find a music box in her palms.

She opened the lid, and a ballerina emerged and began to spin. Then the music followed. Gentle and sweet and so familiar. He had heard it once before. It was enchanting as he watched the ballerina in a pink tutu continue to dance with the music. When the music stopped, so did the ballerina, and Josie closed the square box and set it on the bed.

"What song is that?"

A small, sad smile deepened on her lips. Her chin dipped, and her gaze fell on the box as she reached up and brush at her cheeks.

She was crying.

Max cupped her jaw and lifted her face so he could see her. The fragility and sadness in her eyes were heartbreaking. She was crying, and she had tried to hide it from him.

"La Vie En Rose," she answered in a small voice. "That's the song."

"It's beautiful," he admitted as his thumb brushed away the tears that escaped her.

"It's—" His phone beeping caused her to stop. "You should get that," she urged with a pleading smile.

Max dropped his hands from her face and nodded. He scrambled off her bed and bent down to pick up his phone that had rested on his white business shirt. When he unlocked it, the worst kind of message for a Saturday greeted him.

> **Dad:** Max, need you at the firm as soon as you can make it. It's very important.

He groaned and swiped his shirt from the floor. His suit jacket was folded over the leather couch in Josie's lounge room. He glanced over his shoulder to find Josie with a hairbrush in her hand, staring at him.

"Gotta go?" She didn't seem upset. It was refreshing to see the understanding gleam in her eyes. Sarah never got it. Never got why his career and his father's firm took him away from her. But Josie did. She wanted a career in the very same profession.

Max stood, spun around, and threaded his arms into the sleeves. He didn't miss her eyes dropping to his naked chest as he buttoned his shirt. He bit back a smile, afraid of embarrassing her if he noticed her staring. In fact, he loved that she could possibly find him attractive.

"I do," he confirmed as he shoved his phone into his pocket and picked up his belt. Max then passed the leather belt through the loops of his pants and fastened it. "It's my dad. I've gotta head down to the office. I'm sorry."

She smiled. "Don't apologise. I understand." She set her hairbrush on her bed. "I'll walk you out."

He shook his head, receiving a raised brow from her. "Stay in bed."

"Why?"

"You've still got a mild fever. You're sick, Josie. Back to bed."

"But ..."

"Seriously, get some sleep. I'll message you later to check on you."

She folded her arms over her chest, trying to evoke a stronger stance. The beads of sweat dotted her forehead once more. "I'm fine."

"You're not." He rounded the bed and set his hands on her shoulders then ushered her back into bed. When he flipped the blanket over her, her hairbrush fell to his side of the bed, and her glare accompanied the tight line her mouth made. "You'll thank me later."

"I will do no such thing."

He laughed at her defiance as he reached over and picked up her music box. He carefully set it on her bedside table then bent down and pressed his forehead to her warm forehead. "Then sleep for me."

The way her eyes softened stole the beat his heart had made and the air his lungs had just inhaled. She was beautiful. Succumbed to sickness and all, she was beautiful. And he hated knowing she was there all this time and he had missed her.

Missed her in his sickening love for Sarah.

Missed her in his fruitless chasing of Andrea.

She was there, and it took him a long time to appreciate what she was capable of. The influence she had in his life.

The coercion to make him a better man.

"No wonder you're a lawyer," she said with a huff and rolled onto her side.

"And why am I a lawyer?" he asked with a layer of humour in his voice.

Josie closed her eyes. "You just don't play fair," she mumbled. "You and your words don't play fair."

I affect her.

The thought had him smiling as he stood. "Sleep well, Josie."

She made a humming noise.

Max made his way towards her bedroom door and stopped when he heard her say, "Max ..."

He glanced over his shoulder to find her propped on her elbows. The fear in her eyes almost had him running to her, but he told his legs not to move. To wait for her to speak.

"Yes?"

"I think you need to watch the entire series ..." She took a deep breath. "Without me."

"Why?"

"To see if Luke gets Lorelai," she explained as she laid back down.

He wanted to say more.

Beg her just to tell him the ending.

All he wanted to know was if he got the girl.

If Max could have Josephine.

But it was a lot more complicated than just a TV show dictating their ending. Max still had a past. Still had sins he hadn't been forgiven for. He wasn't the man Josie deserved just yet, but he was working towards it.

Deciding to let her sleep rather than ask her more questions, Max spun around and opened her bedroom door. He stepped out and closed the door behind him. He was tempted to leave another note on her bedroom door but decided against it. He'd already written her one after Stella had suggested he take part in their tradition. Last night, Max had learnt where they had gotten the inspiration for their sticky note communication system.

Gilmore Girls.

When he made it down the short hallway—which was only really a wall that separated the rest of the apartment from Josie's room—he spotted his suit jacket hanging over the leather couch. Then he noticed Josie's best friend and roommate, Stella, sitting on the other couch with a cup in her hand. He walked to the couch and picked up his jacket.

"Morning," she greeted with a smirk on her face.

She knew something.

What? He didn't know.

But she knew something.

"Morning, Stella."

Her eyes had run down his body before that smirk faded and she raised her brow at him. "Your belt isn't done properly, and your shirt isn't tucked in."

He glanced down to find she was right.

"Do we need to have a talk, Max?" He heard both the teasing and warning tone in her voice.

Max would fix his belt once he got to his car. He had to go home, shower, and change before he headed to work. He shook his head at Josie's best friend.

"You were the perfect gentleman and didn't touch her?"

"I didn't touch her," he promised.

Stella let out an exhale, leant forward, and set her cup down on the coffee table. "Is Josie still asleep?"

"She's getting there. I told her to go back to sleep."

"Good." Then Stella's facial features hardened. "So …"

"So?"

"How do you like *Gilmore Girls*? Think your answer over carefully because it might get you on the no-visiting-this-apartment-again list."

He chuckled. "It's not a bad show."

"Thoughts about Dean so far."

"Not for Rory," he admitted—not to be in Stella's good graces, but because he honestly didn't like Dean.

"I like you," she declared. "You're allowed over with my blessing."

"Thanks, Stella. I've gotta get ready for work. I'll see you later."

Her grin returned. "Counting on it. If I miss you meeting Jess, can you tell me your thoughts the next time I see you? Or you can leave a sticky note on my door. I need to know your thoughts before you meet Logan."

Max laughed. "I promise I will." Then he waved goodbye and began to make his way towards the front door. He halted his steps, remembering what Josie had told him in her bedroom. Max let out a sigh and quickly spun around. "Stella?"

She tilted her head in his direction. "Yeah?"

He knew he would sound insecure if he asked, but he had to. It didn't matter that he suddenly began to feel hot and uncomfortable all over under her sceptical glare. "Does Luke end up with Lorelai?"

Stella's eyes widened as her lips slowly parted. She mulled his question over for a long while, and then her lips tugged into a small smile. "Do you want to ruin the journey of experiencing something like that by me telling you how it ends?"

The experience.

The journey.

He wanted that with Josie.

He needed to feel it and to witness it.

He didn't want a spoiler.

Max shook his head. "No, you're right. I don't want to ruin it."

Stella's smile deepened. "You deserve to experience every amazing thing about it."

"Thanks, Stella."

Just as he was about to turn, she said, "I just want *Lorelai* to be happy."

The way she said Lorelai, he knew she really meant Josie.

"I do too," he agreed.

I want Josie to be happy.

"What do you think, Maxwell?" his father asked from across

the boardroom table.

Max sighed as he glanced down at the file once more.

It was a new case his father was considering taking on.

But his father never rushed his decision to represent a client. He was careful in his consideration. Not that he ever represented the easy cases he'd win in court. His father loved a challenge.

And this murder case was a challenge.

It was a contract for hire case.

His potential client had claimed he was innocent the moment he was arrested and the media caught wind of the murder.

"It's going to be hard to convince a jury," Max pointed out. "The IP address doesn't lie. He was there, Dad. It puts him there as reading and sending those emails."

His father nodded. Then he picked up the case file and sighed. "I believe he's innocent. He could be my first loss in court, and it would severely hurt."

"Your ratio," Max deadpanned.

"No, it will hurt me morally because I know he's innocent. Some of the other clients I've represented have always had a speck of guilt on them. But with circumstantial evidence, I've been able to have the jury disregard it in order for us to win. But this one, I just know we're missing something."

Max was stunned.

His father always cared about his win-loss ratio. He was famous in the legal world because of it.

It was a supposed murder-for-hire case.

His wife had been shot in their house, and emails were found with their potential client agreeing to the terms and conditions of his wife's murder. It seemed too planted for Max.

He wasn't a criminal lawyer.

But he knew contracts.

And the one in the email was a standard exchange that seemed too simple and clear, begging to be spotted.

He pursed his lips as he picked up one of the printouts of an email from the client's deceased wife. It was an email she sent telling a friend that she had a great time at the party. But something in the middle of the email caught his eye.

Max reached for a highlighter and read what he spotted out loud.

"Exchange for a service. The shoes have to go."

It seemed strange for it to be in the middle of an email saying how much the wife had enjoyed the champagne.

"Dad, can you have all the emails the police seized brought to my office?"

His father's brown eyes darkened. "Did you find something?"

"Maybe," he said, not wanting to get his father's hopes up. "We need to obtain the wife's laptop and her emails if they haven't been submitted into evidence already. I think another contract is in her emails. I just have to filter through them to find it. It might clear him."

The proudness consumed his father's face. "So we should represent him?"

Max nodded. "I'll investigate these emails and let you know what I discover. I have a few contracts I can set aside this weekend. This is high priority."

"I'll have one of the interns bring them to your office and go through them with you," his father said.

"Thanks. I'll get on it," Max said as he collected the files his father had given him and headed out of the boardroom. He went down the hall to the last office on his right, pushed the glass door open, and made his way to his desk. He dumped the folders down on the desk once he had reached it. He knew he'd spend all weekend helping his father.

Gordon Sheridan wasn't one to ask for help from his son.

Max rounded his desk and pulled out his leather office chair. Once he sat down, he pulled his phone from his pants pocket and set it on his desk. Then he rolled up the sleeves of his white business shirt until they hit his elbows. Max opened his laptop and noticed an unread email.

He felt his heart hammer wildly in his chest when he noted the sender.

He was torn.

It was the first time she had emailed him back in over eight months.

The ones he had sent after she broke up with Noel went unanswered.

Never acknowledged.

He was supposed to be over her.

But seeing her name, it hurt him to remember what that kiss of hers had done to him. What he was prepared to give up for her.

Andrea.

To: MaxwellSheridan@GordonSheridan.com.au
From: AndreaWallace@GandMC.com
Subject: G&MC welcome package.

Dear Mr. Sheridan,
    As advised by Mr. Gregson at the recommendation from Mr. Parker, please find the G&MC welcome package. Inside, you will find information about our accounting company and history—as well as an overview of what you will be assisting with during your time with us. I have also been advised to attach the expense packet. It has your daily expenses budget, hotels of your choosing, and a list of the company approved airlines you may wish to use to fly to Boston, Massachusetts, from Melbourne, Victoria.
    We do hope this information helps with your decision in assisting our legal department. If you have any questions, please reply to this email or email me directly at: XenaDavenport@GandMC.com
Kind regards,
Xena Davenport
Executive assistant to Andrea Wallace.
Senior supervisor.
Legal Department.
G&MC accounting firm.

Max's heart dipped.
It wasn't Andrea.
It was her assistant using her email address.
If G&MC were playing games to get his interest, they had

done right by using Andrea's email account.

The hope that radiated from seeing an email from her sickened him.

She played and toyed with his emotions.

She had left him a wreck.

Max got out of his inbox and opened his sent folder.

He scrolled down until he found one of the emails he'd sent Andrea.

Taking a deep breath to ease his anxious heart, he clicked on the email and opened it.

```
To: AndreaWallace@GandMC.com
From: MaxwellSheridan@GordonSheridan.com.
au
Subject: Us.


Andrea,
    These games you play, they're killing
me.
    I just need you to be honest with me.
    You can't tell me you're confused when
we both know how right that kiss was.
    Yeah, I feel like a shit friend for
doing that to Noel. But you even said
it didn't feel like Noel loved you
anymore.
    That you felt DISCONNECTED from him.
    WE connected.
    We have to discuss this.
    You broke up with him and messaged ME
minutes later.
    Make a choice.
    I can fly to see you when you've made
it.
    But don't forget to tell me when you
do.
    I can wait, Andrea.
    But I don't think I could wait forever
if you keep throwing this 'it feels
right with you, Max, but I love him'
```

talk in my face.
Max.

He scrolled to find another he had sent her.

```
To: AndreaWallace@GandMC.com
From: MaxwellSheridan@GordonSheridan.com.
au
Subject: He's engaged.
```

Andrea,
    He proposed to her.
    They came back, and she had his ring on
    her finger.
    I'm not telling you this to hurt you.
    I'm telling you because you may love
    Noel, but he loves HER.
    And I know it's going to be hard for
    you when they return.
    But I just want to say that I hope
    you meant it when you said that you
    respected Noel's decision to be with
    her.
    Please don't hurt them.
    They belong together.
    Although I care about you, he's my best
    friend.
    I love Noel like a brother.
    And I've already hurt him and Clara
    enough.
    Please understand them.
Max.

Then he clicked on another.

```
To: AndreaWallace@GandMC.com
From: MaxwellSheridan@GordonSheridan.com.
au
Subject: They have a house together.
```

Andrea,
My emails are probably sitting unread
in your inbox, but I don't care.
Open one.
Any one of them.
Just reply and tell me you forgive me
for confusing you.
I kissed **YOU**.
I'm NOT sorry.
But you're making me feel horrible
things every time I look at him.
I look at him and want to confess and
rip his happiness away from him and
make him feel the pain you felt when he
told you it was Clara.
How fucked up is that?
I want to hurt MY best friend **FOR YOU**.
To make **YOU** feel better.
I want to kill him for making YOU weep.
For making **YOU** feel so little.
That **YOUR** love was never enough to him.
I don't want him to be happy if it
means **YOU'RE** unhappy.
This isn't fair, Andrea.
YOUR silence isn't fair.
Not when I confess my heart **TO YOU** and
betray him.
I PICK **YOU**, GODDAMMIT.
YOU.
YOU. YOU. YOU.
I FUCKING PICK **YOU**!
Max.

Pain.
It entered his chest, found his lungs, and burned them alive.
It was hard to read his desperation.
It was also hard to see how much he wanted her.
But you don't adore her.
Max flinched.
He didn't adore her.

That was true.

He adored Josie.

But adoration wasn't love.

Or it was, and he wasn't willing to accept it.

Shaking his head, he opened another.

To: AndreaWallace@GandMC.com
From: MaxwellSheridan@GordonSheridan.com.
au
Subject: He's married.

> Her name is now Clara Louise Lawrence
> Parker.
> Nolan James Parker's wife.
> And he loves her, Andrea.
>
> He.
> Chose.
> Her.
>
> Please don't forget that.
> You let him choose her.
> And I chose you instead of him.
> I'll stop waiting for something that
> will never happen.
> Goodbye, Andrea Wallace.

Unlike all his other emails, he hadn't signed off with his name.

At the time, he couldn't.

It had been just after Noel and Clara had been announced man and wife. He had slipped away long enough to send her one last email.

And like before, she had not replied.

She had only ever replied a few times to some of them.

Later that day, he had a moment on a bridge with a woman he adored through sickness and every assignment she had.

Max got out of his sent folder and returned to his inbox to find a surprising email.

To: MaxwellSheridan@GordonSheridan.com.au
From: Josie.Faulkner@hotmail.com
Subject: Thank you.

Max,
    Thank you for the soup.
    And for taking care of me.
    And for watching Gilmore Girls with not
    just me, but also with my roommate.
    I have more to be thankful for, but now
    I'm a little dizzy, and I'm trusting
    Siri to make sure this email doesn't
    embarrass me.
    Thank you for tutoring me and caring
    about my education space space enter
    crap oh my God this is so stupid enter
    no enter new ford it Max just not that
    I'm really thankful for you Jesse

Max laughed at the mess Josie had sent him.

The bliss that consumed his chest was what he wanted to feel when he read emails.

Not the anger and resentment he felt just now as he had read the emails he had sent to Andrea.

Reaching over, he picked up his phone, unlocked it, and brought up his messages.

He couldn't hide or even stop the smile on his face when he saw her name at the top of the screen.

Max knew this was right.

No matter how much his heart felt as if things with Andrea Wallace were unfinished.

Closure.

She never blessed him with it.

And this was him moving on without it.

Max: Jesse, please tell Josie that I will never use that email against her if she promises to never use Siri to email for her again. Also, I'm gonna have to discuss the importance of proofreading emails with her. It's a skill she'll need when she's a lawyer.

After a few minutes of him staring at the ellipses on his screen, she actually sent a message.

> **Josie:** She makes no promises about using Siri to write her emails to you ever again.

And that bliss overshadowed his guilt and reminded him that he was much happier being Josie's friend than Andrea's doormat.

Josie

Over a week later and feeling much better, Josie sat by her mother's side. Her mother should have been released from the hospital two days ago, but Dr Frederickson decided to keep her. The first round of chemo had been a success, but it made her mother incredibly ill. She had vomited to the point of dehydration. Every time Josie thought she might feel better, she actually looked worse. And just when she thought her mother could actually battle her cancer strongly, her slow heart rate told her another story.

Josie knew her mother was lying about how she really felt.

And Josie was lying about how accepting she was of her mother's health.

She was still furious with God and the universe for smiting her mother once more. And when she thought that way, she felt guilt blacken her heart. No one deserved cancer. And no one deserved it a second time.

"Josephine," her mother said in a weak voice.

She glanced up from her laptop to find her mother tilting her head to face her. The half-smile her mother made only made Josie miss her full ones more. The warm ones she'd wear when Josie spoke about her future outside university and in a law firm.

"What are you working on?"

"It's my contracts assignment. I'm writing a two-thousand-word memo of advice."

That half-smile of hers stretched a fraction wider. Not completely full, but Josie saw it reach her mother's eyes. "What is a memo of advice?"

"It's like a letter intended for someone in-house in a law firm or a client. It's supposed to address the issue one has with a contract. Right now, the issue I had to address was if the loophole in my case study could potentially cost my client millions. And the short answer is yes. I have to give him suggestions on how we can strengthen the client's position and be persuasive in my arguments. You know — that I'm right and he's wrong."

Her mother pressed her hands on to the mattress and sat herself up properly. "And how are your persuasive skills?"

"Improving," Josie said with a smile.

It was true.

Since Max had started tutoring her — well, through emails since he was busy actually practising law — she was able to juggle her workload and actually understand the content being taught. Max made it easier for her to understand what her professors neglected to properly teach. Her favourite tutor, Jason Silverman, complimented her on getting her act together. He asked if she'd heard back from any of the make-believe placement interviews she had, and Josie had told him no, rushing out of the tutorial to catch the tram from campus to the city. Then she ran to the hospital to be by her mother's side.

"That's good," her mother said as she stared at the lilacs West had dropped off on his way to work this morning. "How is everything else going?"

It was the first time her mother had been well enough to actually hold a conversation without succumbing to her exhaustion.

"Good. Ally's taken over at the bakery and is doing really well, so the pressure's off Nadia's shoulders. Ally approved Nadia's request for a few more employees," Josie commented.

"And how are Stella and West?"

Josie closed her laptop and set it on the table next to her. "Still love each other."

Her mother nodded. "And how is your father? You never told me how dinner was between the both of you."

She had hoped to avoid this because she knew she was about to disappoint her mother. She never meant to, but this time it wasn't her fault. Her father was the one who stood her up. Josie thought back to that night. She had sat at that restaurant for ages until she found out her father hadn't even left Canberra for Melbourne. She was about to leave when Maxwell Sheridan appeared and took her father's place.

Max.

Max who messaged her every day and answered her stupid questions. She knew she got in the way of his actual clients, but he never complained. Not once.

It was crazy how much she missed actually seeing him.

It had been almost a week and a half since he left her apartment.

He'd taken care of her when she was sick.

Sat up and watched *Gilmore Girls* with her and her best friend.

Maxwell Sheridan became her better thing in life.

Through the storm, he was the light.

He had no idea how much she cared for him.

She knew it was insane.

But there was no point in denying the truth.

I like him honestly.

It was hard to decide if telling him would become an issue for their friendship.

He had said he wanted to be her Luke.

For a moment, her heart had swelled.

But no one knew if Luke and Lorelai ended up together and happy.

The show was cancelled, and the truth was never revealed.

Maybe they could have what she thought Lorelai and Luke deserved outside the series being cancelled—a happily ever after.

Josie knew that right now, it wasn't a priority. Her mother's heath, university, and being Max's friend meant more.

"Josephine, did something happen with your father?" her mother asked.

She blinked several times and realised she hadn't answered her mother. Taking a deep breath, she knew she couldn't lie to her. She always knew when Josie lied about her absent father. "He never showed up for dinner, so I left."

Her mother winced. "He didn't?"

Anger flashed in her blue eyes, and Josie shot out of her chair. She captured her mother's cold left hand in hers and squeezed gently. "It's okay, Mamma."

Tears glazed over Emily Faulkner's eyes, wounding Josie more harshly than her father ever could. "It's not, Josephine."

"I'm used to it."

Her mother let out a struggled exhale. "But you shouldn't. I know I haven't been the best moth—"

"Stop that right now!" Josie demanded and pulled her hands free from her mother's. "Don't you say that."

"But—"

"No!" Anger suddenly consumed her as tears began to form. She didn't care that she had raised her voice at her mother or that the patients her mother shared a room with would hear. "Don't you dare finish that sentence."

"Josephine, it's true."

"It's not," she dismissed as those tears fell. She tried to hold back the next few, but they escaped. "You're the greatest mother in the world."

"I shouldn't have pushed you to have a relationship with your father when it only made you resent him more."

Josie shook her head as she reached up and brushed away her mother's tears. "He did that on his own with his lies and his incessant need to disappoint. He's actually quite good at it."

"But as your mother, I should have ..." She paused, and Josie noticed that she had balled her hands into tight fists. "I should have protected you from such disappointment."

"It's okay, Mamma."

"No. You shouldn't be this angry."

"It's not your fault."

Her mother wrapped her fingers around her wrist. "Josephine, I love your father. And I admit that I let my love for him hurt you when he left us. I gave him the benefit of the doubt. But you have to make amends with him."

Josie shook her head. "I can't," she cried. "I trust him for a second, and he'll... he'll let me down. And I don't want to feel stupid by giving him the satisfaction that I believed in him."

She tried to pull her arm free, but her mother tightened her grip. "You have to, Josephine."

"I don't want to! There's no point."

"There is!"

"THERE'S NOT!" she screamed and pulled her arm free.

Josie saw her mother flinch in shock at her outburst. "He lives in Berlin! Or have you forgotten that? He has two other daughters!"

Her mother's tears broke her heart. "You're his daughter, too."

"I'm not," she said, shaking her head. "Do you want to know what hurts the most about having a diplomat as a father?"

"No."

The heat that consumed her chest rose to burn her throat. "I have to see photos of him online. I have to see videos of him at his daughters' recitals. You couldn't have protected me from that. He watches them dance. Do you know how many times I invited him to see me dance? Do you have any idea how much it hurts to know that they have a dad? *My* dad. He was my dad first!"

Her mother's lip trembled as she reached out and grasped Josie's shaking hands. "They're your sisters, too." She tugged at Josie's hands, and she sat on the bed, allowing her mother to console her. "You always wanted to be a big sister."

Josie cried into her mother's chest. "He never invited me to Germany to meet them. I'd never be their big sister. They probably don't even know I exist."

"I'm sure that's not true," her mother whispered as she rubbed circles on Josie's back.

"I'm too scared to find out."

"Oh, my sweet Josephine," Emily whispered. "They're your family."

Josie shook her head. "No. You're my family. You're the only family I have ever needed," she sobbed as she wrapped her arms around her frail mother. "I love you so much."

She felt her mother's chest heave as she cried and inhaled. "I will always love you, Josephine, but I won't be around forever."

"Don't say that!" she begged. "Please don't say that."

"It's true. And if that time comes sooner than expected, you have to try to be a part of their lives."

"No," she breathed.

"Please, Josephine. Promise that you will try someday. At least meet them. And if your father ever changes, give him a chance. He might not show it, but he loves you so much."

"You're all I need, Mamma."

Her mother let out a low laugh that sounded as if it took so much energy to make. "No, Josephine, you need a lot more love in your life than just mine. You deserve more."

She wanted to argue further with her mother, but Josie was tired of crying. She couldn't imagine how much this confrontation took its toll on her mother's cancer-stricken body.

So for now, Josie let it go.

To give her mother peace.

But she knew no promises could be made if she never intended to fulfil them.

Max: I have officially not seen you in fifteen days.

Josie: You talk to me every day.

Max: It's actually not the same thing.

Josie: I'm in class right now.

Max: Which class is this? Legal practice and ethics or evidence.

Josie: Evidence.

Max: Did you get your contracts assignment handed in?

Josie: I did. Thank you for pointing out that my choice of wording in my argument needed to be a lot stronger. It definitely lacked a stronger stance. How is that case you were working on going?

Max: You need to be a bit more forceful in the tone you use in your memo of advices. You have another one coming up for evidence, right? Send me your draft, and I can look at it. And no, I won't give you the correct answer. I'll guide you through it.

"All right, everyone, don't forget to read the Uniform Evidence Act. Your assignment is based on it," Ruth, her evidence tutor, said. Just as Josie stood, Ruth walked over to her and handed her a piece of paper. "It's my letter of support."

She looked down at the paper and skimmed the page. "I didn't ask for a recommendation," Josie stated in shock as she looked up at her tutor.

Ruth smiled. "You're the only student who hasn't asked."

"I was?"

"You were. I don't know what's happened to you in the last three weeks, but the old Josie's back. The one who I put my money on as the next big lawyer in Melbourne. Have you applied for placements?"

Josie nodded. "I have a few interviews."

"Let me know how they go. I talked to Jason, and he's impressed with your progress. My door is always open if you need any help with your interviews or if you have any questions," her tutor said.

"I'll be sure to stop by if I do."

Highly unlikely since I haven't applied to any law firms.

Tucking the letter into her bag, she picked up her notebook and shoved it inside. She gave her tutor a smile of appreciation as she made her way out of the classroom. Once she was out in the hallway, her phone vibrated.

> **Max:** Realised I didn't update you on the case. The firm's representing him. I found the murder for hire contract in some carefully crafted emails. It took about eighty emails to find them. Some were harder than others. Some had only a few words or letters capitalised. We have some forensic accountants and cyber experts tracking down the money. This case is insane. It looks like she framed her husband. Not sure why people put so much effort into murder when divorce is quick these days.

Josie laughed as she made her way out of the law building. She finished her classes for the day and was excited to go home for a nap. She had visited her mother's hospital room early this morning before her evidence lecture. Her mother was moved into a different ward, but after a fall out of her hospital bed, she had a hairline fracture in her arm and would be staying in the hospital for a while longer. It was hard for Josie to keep her cool. She knew her mother was better off in the hospital than on her own, but it wasn't easy for Josie to watch her once brave and strong mother become a brittle version of the woman she had once admired.

Fuck cancer!

It was all Josie could do.

To curse cancer.

And to text Max back.

Josie: I have an essay for evidence. It's due next week. Everything seems to be due the week after each other. You found the terms of the contract in her emails? I can see why you work at one of the best law firms in the country.

Max: Nepotism has me working for the best law firm in the country, Josephine. I happen to be the founder's offspring.

Josie: Nepotism has its advantages.

Max: Not always. I had to prove I was a capable lawyer.

Josie: Speaking of being a capable lawyer, you shouldn't be texting me on the job.

Max: They won't fire me. I'd love to see them try. Is your class over?

Josie glanced up from her phone to find herself standing in the quad. She searched her surroundings and found a free bench. Approaching it, she sat down and continued her conversation with Max.

She missed him.

Their text messages and emails weren't enough.

Since the morning she had woken up to him in her bed, she knew she was attached. And not seeing him in person or seeing that smile of his was torture.

> **Josie:** Day at uni is over. I just have to read through some cases, and I'll be caught up with this week's readings. I worked on my evidence paper last night. I'll send it to you once I get home.

> **Max:** Are you working tonight?

> **Josie:** Taylor needed a few extra shifts, so I gave her mine since I have exams coming up.

> **Max:** So what you're saying is that you're free tonight?

She inhaled sharply at his text message.
Would she see him tonight?
It would be a 'friends' kind of activity.
Nothing her heart should get its hopes up for.

> **Josie:** I am.

She bit her lip as she waited for Max's reply. The bright sun warmed her skin as she sat on the steel bench and waited.

> **Max:** Good.

> **Josie:** Good?

The beats in her chest galloped in anticipation.

> **Max:** Because it's been fifteen days since I last saw you, Josephine. And to be honest and real with you, I miss you like crazy. Our texts and emails haven't been enough, and I should have told you that.

Her heart had all but stopped.

Max: It's been fifteen days too long, Josephine. Can I see you tonight?

And that message kick started that organ in her chest. Smiling, she wrote her reply.

Josie: I want to see you tonight, Max.

Max: Because you need help with your evidence paper?

Josie: No.

She took a deep breath and decided to like him honestly.

Josie: Because I've missed you, too.

Chapter
TEN

Max

Josie: Because I've missed you, too.

*M*ax stared at the last message Josie had sent him. It was risky admitting that he had missed her in the time they had spent apart. Max had been busy helping his father with his case, and Josie was recovering from the flu. Since she was out sick for almost a week, she had a lot of uni work to catch up on as well as classwork and assignments.

But the time away from Josie had really opened Max's eyes. It was the realisation he needed.

He missed her.

Adored her.

Wanted to be more than just her friend.

And hopefully tonight, when he took her back to the 'rain check' dinner she had completely forgotten about, he would ask. There was no mention of the doctor or any guy she was seeing in their daily text messages and emails. But then again, she had a right to privacy, and if she was seeing someone, he'd respect it. But that didn't mean Max would accept it.

Tonight, he'd just tell her.

He was sure Josie cared for him.

When she was sick and told him that she liked him, he believed her. He didn't believe it was the flu. He truly believed Josie was being honest with him. And after Max had read the messages he sent Andrea months ago, he realised that Josie had been the only woman who had ever put him first.

Above her.

She listened and supported him.

But more importantly, she understood him.

And when he looked into her eyes, he saw her compassion.

He saw her adoration.

He saw the little flecks of love blossoming.

Max hoped she was falling in love with him.

Because he was more than sure he was falling in love with her.

As he sat at his desk and stared at the message she had sent almost two hours ago, he knew it was right.

His feelings towards her were true and could be felt without guilt.

Max: Do you think you'll be free at around seven?

Josie: I don't think so.

Josie: That was a joke. A lame one. But yeah, seven sounds good.

Max: Okay, seven it is. It'll give me enough time to go home and change.

Josie: Can I ask where we're going?

Max: Can't I make it a surprise?

Josie: No, no, you can't. I'd like to know what I'm dressing up for.

He laughed at her sass.

Max: Dinner. You and me.

Josie: Like at my place?

Max: No. Like at a restaurant.

Josie: So we're talking …

Max: No pjs, Josephine.

Josie: Is the place fancy?

Max: Don't worry about what to wear. I'll see you at seven.

At five to seven, he stood outside Josie's apartment as nerves ravished his system. If he wasn't driving, he would have taken a shot of whiskey to calm his anxious body. But he knew the importance of tonight.

He couldn't let Josie walk around and not know just how important she was to him. Max had made so many mistakes in his life, but he wasn't going to let how much he adored her go unknown to her.

Max would fight harder than he had to keep her in his life.

He wouldn't be ashamed as he was with Sarah.

And he wouldn't be a coward as he had been with Andrea. With Josie, he was a better man.

A man she would be proud of.

It was strange how far he had come in nine months.

But being with Josie on that bridge had changed his life.

Sucking in a deep breath of air through his nostrils, he knocked on her door and waited. He felt hot as if he were sweating through his clothes. Max glanced down to see he didn't have sweat marks on the light grey long sleeve button shirt he wore. He glared at his tie and realised how stupid it was to be wearing one. It wasn't a meeting between a lawyer and a client.

It was a dinner with Josephine Faulkner.

The sound of footsteps had him straightening his spine and holding his breath as he waited. After a few long seconds, the door opened and that breath he had been holding disappeared.

His entire body lost its strength at the sight of her.

"*Wow*," he breathed.

A slow smile spread across her pink-lacquered lips. "You were vague on what to wear," she explained.

Max took in the tight black dress that hit just above her knee. It was simple but seductive with the added string above the bust, adding shape to the dress and her cleavage. It fit her perfectly. She was flawless. And he loved seeing her long brunette hair resting on her back, exposing her shoulders. Josie normally never wore any makeup except for mascara. But tonight, she wore lipstick, blush, mascara, and eyeliner on her eyelids. It wasn't too much, but that eyeliner made her eyes appear as if they were blue diamonds.

Her.

It's her.

His palms sweated as his heart sung her name again and again. "You look beautiful, Josephine."

Her eyelids fluttered as she glanced away, taken aback by his compliment. "Thank you."

"You ready to go?" he asked, unable to look away from those blue eyes of hers.

"I'll just grab my clutch," she said. Then she disappeared, and he let out a relieved sigh.

The pressure seemed as if it doubled.

He had to tell her.

He had to.

Josie sat across from him laughing.

"What?" he asked as he lowered his menu.

She ceased her laughter and grinned at him. "Is this that rain check dinner that I promised after you came to my disaster dinner date rescue and bailed on your friends before I ended up fleeing minutes later?"

Max smiled, closed his menu, and set it on the table. "It is," he confirmed.

Josie set her menu down. "I actually like this surprise."

"You do?"

She nodded. "It made me laugh, and then I realised we're replacing disappointment from a month ago with something …"

"Better?" he offered.

"Much better," she agreed.

Max sat up and gazed at that stunning smile of hers. During their twenty-minute drive to Pa La Blue, they updated each other on their day and all the things they had forgotten to tell each other in the fifteen days since they last saw each other. He hated that he had almost missed her in his infatuation with other women.

It took Noel and Clara's wedding for him to realise he had been pursuing the wrong women all this time.

It was Josie.

Her eyes widened as her lips parted. "I forgot to ask you something."

"What's up?" he asked as he picked up his glass of water and then took a long sip, quenching his thirst. The dryness in his throat was a constant pain. But Josie and that smile of hers caused it. That and her perfume that seemed to stain the breathable air in his Porsche.

God, she drove him crazy.

She affected him and his heart completely.

Max set the glass down and nodded for her to continue.

She picked up her phone, unlocked it, and then cleared her throat. "Stella wants to know if you've watched any other episodes of *Gilmore Girls*? And that I should ask you about spoilers or something? I don't know. She just texted me this stuff in the car."

"You don't mind if I tell her?"

She shook her head. "Go for it."

Chuckling, he reached over for her phone and took it from her. He knew what her best friend meant by 'spoilers.' He was tempted to find out through one of those articles about the "23 things we loved and hated about the last episode of *Gilmore Girls*" that included gifs and quotes. Max pressed his lips together as he began to reply to Stella.

> **Josie:** Stella, it's Max. Josie said I could reply to you personally. Don't worry; she asked the questions out loud. To answer your first question, I've been busy with a case, so I haven't watched any more episodes. But I did buy the series on my way home last week to experience it all. No spoilers. I want to experience Lorelai being happy. I want her to be happy, Stella.

Satisfied with his reply, he pressed send. Just as he was about to hand the phone back to Josie, Stella sent an immediate reply.

> **Stella:** She will be, so long as you experience the entire series. No spoilers, Max. Work for that ending. Also, if you wanna score some roommate brownie points, could you please bring home dessert?

> **Stella:** I presume you're going to be bringing Josie home since you picked her up. Please bring her home.

He laughed at her reply and playfully shook his head.

> **Josie:** I'll take her home. To ease your worries, I won't be drinking. And I will bring you back some dessert. Also, Stella, for added comfort, I just wanted to let you know that I'm in it for the ending and more.

He locked Josie's phone and handed it back to her. She had her brow raised as she took it from him and then set it back on the table next to her blue clutch.

"Let me guess; she wanted dessert?"

"How'd you know?"

Josie chuckled as she swept a loose curl behind her ear. "She's my best friend. I know her too well. Did you know she freaked out when she met Clara? Like she almost fainted.

Clara's like her hero."

"Are you serious?" he asked, amused by the glimmer in her eye.

She nodded. "I started working at the bakery before Clara did. It was doing well. Danny and I came up with a few cupcakes. Danny isn't a dessert chef by trade, but he saw an opportunity and took it. Clara applied to be a waitress. And one day, she tasted this batch of vanilla cupcakes that our boss had just made and said it was missing something. So he told her that the vanilla batch was her canvas and she should create her masterpiece. That's how the butterscotch surprise was made, which is Stella's favourite cupcake. Each time I finished work, I'd bring Clara's newest cupcake home and have her taste test them."

"Get out of here," he said, bewildered. He knew Clara's cupcakes were good, but he had no idea how she started baking.

"I'm serious. When Stella met Clara, she almost cried. Her cupcakes actually comforted Stella when she and West were fighting. So Clara's pretty special to a lot of people. It actually upsets me to know she's not baking anymore and is at uni. Seems like such a waste of her talents since she already went to culinary school," Josie said, the sadness clear in her voice.

"You miss her," he stated.

"Yeah, I do. It's not the same without her. But she has her happily ever after in Boston where I'm told things are better …" She paused, picked up her glass of water, and took a sip. "Oh, I know that this dinner is about us catching up and stuff, but I was wondering if I could get your advice?"

Max saw the nervousness consume her face. To reassure her that she could ask him anything, he reached over and covered her hand with his. "Josephine, you could ask me a million questions, and it still wouldn't be enough for me to feel like I've satisfied your curiosity. How can I help you?"

Her eyelids fluttered as if she were taken aback by his answer. Josie let out a sigh. "I feel like I'm taking advantage of you. I promised I would never use you for my own selfish gains."

He flinched. "Josephine, no. Don't think like that. I'm here for you. Whatever you need. Use me. Be selfish and use me."

She shook her head. "I can't. Now that I think about it, I've used you way too much. I've abused our friendship. You have a career as a lawyer, so you shouldn't be assisting me with my degree."

"I'm *tutoring* you."

"I feel like I'm wasting your time," she whispered.

Max stilled. She had no idea how wrong she was.

Her time was the most beautiful gift she could ever give him.

He was tempted to tell her that, but he held back.

One confession at a time, Max.

"What advice do you need, Josephine?"

She let out a sigh; her hand remained encased by his. "Okay, you don't have to answer, okay? It's stupid now that I think about it."

He squeezed her hand. "I won't think it's stupid."

"All right. Do you know what I could do to impress some law firms into agreeing to interview me for placements? I mean, were you as scared as I am to go for interviews?"

"I was scared," he enlightened. "But not for the reasons you think."

"Oh, then what—"

"Would you like to order?" their waitress asked, interrupting Josie.

Josie pulled her hand away from Max's and picked up her menu. Though she could shy away from his touch, she couldn't hide the blush on her cheeks. "Ah, sure. Can I have the steak, please?"

Max stared at the way Josie bit her lip, disinterested in the woman next to him.

Just Josie.

His focus on her.

His time for her.

Him at her beck and call.

"And how would you like your steak?"

Josie's lips pursed. "Medium rare but more well done, if you know what I mean."

The waitress laughed. "I understand. And you, sir?"

Max didn't have to look at the menu to know what to order. He had been to Pa La Blue plenty of times and knew which dishes were best. But unlike all the other times he had dined at the restaurant, this wasn't for work purposes.

He'd pay for his and Josie's dinner.

This was for him and them.

Not for his father to pick up his tab.

Max realised just how special Josie was to him.

She was his.

Free of anyone else.

She had never had any romantic feelings for any of his friends.

Never kissed them.

Touched them.

Made love to them.

Josephine Faulkner was his clean slate.

She was the better thing in his life.

The only better thing in his life.

The only love he wanted that made him feel free and honest.

And that knowledge caused his heart to swell in his chest.

"Max?" Josie said, her voice sweet and full of concern.

He blinked at her. "Yeah?"

"You blanked out."

"I did?"

She nodded. "You did. The waitress wants to know what you'd like to eat."

Max craned his neck and smiled apologetically at the waitress for wasting her time. He was sure she had other people to wait on, not just them. "The steak, too, please. Medium rare."

The waitress nodded. "Any other drinks?"

"The water's fine for now," Max answered. "Josie?"

She smiled. "I'm good with water, too. Thank you."

"You're welcome. I'll be back with your steaks," the young waitress said as she picked up their menus and left their table.

"Are you okay?" Josie asked, getting his attention.

He gazed over at her then reached out and clutched her fingers, brushing his thumb over her knuckles. "More than okay."

"What did you mean when you said that you were scared but for other reasons?"

His lips had made a fine line before he answered. "When I was doing my law degree, I already had a placement lined up with my father's law firm. I didn't have an interview. My father

179

told me that a Sheridan couldn't work at another firm. I was scared because I wanted to work at another firm and prove I was as good as my father was. I had to explain that to lawyers who would interview me, and they all said the same thing, that I was what they needed. I walked out of every interview I had actually believing I could work for another firm. But no one called me back. I had to do a year of placement, and I had no other choice than Gordon Sheridan Lawyers."

"You put yourself out there, so you should be proud of yourself," she encouraged.

"I also had to prove myself to all the lawyers at the firm. That I didn't become a lawyer because it was the family business. I wanted to help people. I ended up helping terrible companies. But in the past nine or ten months, it's been about helping good and honest people."

"That's great, Max."

His chest filled with warmth knowing and seeing how proud she was of him in her blue eyes. He wanted that. To see it every day.

"So what kind of advice do you need?"

"The how-to-get-an-interview advice. I have recommendations from a few of my tutors. I kind of lied and told them I had interviews, but I think I'm late in the applying game," she admitted with a layer of shame in her voice. "I just kept putting it off, and I keep hearing everyone securing their placements. I think the top four firms have their graduate positions already filled."

She's afraid to really ask for my help.

"Josephine, I can help you get an interview. Tell me your dream firm and I can call a few of my connections —"

"No, Max. I have to do this on my own. I mean, I appreciate that you'd go above and beyond, but I just need tips on how to approach firms and what to say."

"I can get you a placement," he assured.

"I know, and I appreciate that. I do. Just tell me the things I should avoid saying, and we'll work from there." Then she pulled her hand away and gave him the most hesitant smile he had ever seen.

Max pulled his hand back to rest on the table next to his plate. He realised what he had done.

She needed advice.

Not a handout.

He knew he'd have to speak to his father to see if he could find her a placement at Gordon Sheridan or one of his old associates' firms.

Tomorrow, Max would get her numbers and names so she could set up the interviews herself.

"You shouldn't have paid, Max," Josie said, her big blue eyes staring up at him with that mild hint of annoyance mixed with her appreciation.

He set his hand on the small of her back and led her away from the register. "It wasn't a work dinner, Josephine. I wasn't letting my father pay for me to take you to a dinner you deserved to have."

Just short of the exit, Josie stepped away from his touch and then spun around. "It was *my* rain check dinner. *I* should have paid."

"Then where was your credit card when we made it to the register?" he teased.

"You practically pushed me out of the way, and I had to save Stella's chocolate cake, or I'd be kicked out of the apartment tonight," she explained.

Max chuckled as he walked past her and opened the door. "We can argue in the car if you want."

She turned to face him, but the grin on her face only had him shaking his head at her. "I'm never going to let this go, Max," she declared.

"I hope you don't."

"You're real funny," she muttered as she made small steps until she reached him. Then she turned, and their bodies now blocked the entryway for anyone entering the restaurant. Josie set her free palm on his chest, and Max inhaled sharply.

Did she feel his wild heartbeats against her hand?

Did she notice how he held his breath the moment she touched him?

Did she know he was beginning to love her?

"Promise me something."

Max nodded, afraid of sounding breathless.

Josie licked her lips and took a deep breath. "Promise me you'll let me pay for the next rain check dinner we have. And because I know what you're thinking, I really mean I'll pay for it and not my father. This may have started because of him not showing up, but everything else about us, he or anyone else can't touch."

Speechless.

She made him choke on his words.

A loud, aggressive clearing of the throat had Josie quickly pulling her hand away. "If you two are done with your sweet PDA, we'd like to have dinner."

"Max?" that familiar throaty voice said.

No.

No.

No!

Not now.

Not when Josie just put herself out there.

He turned his head to find Sarah standing next to him with another man by her side. She looked horrified. Maybe even heartbroken. And for the very first time, he honestly didn't care.

He was clean of her.

Then he glanced back at Josie to see her wide eyes.

Because of you.

I'm clean of her because of you.

"Max, who is this?" Sarah asked, but he couldn't take his eyes off Josie.

He waited for her reaction.

To see if she put it together that this was Sarah Collins.

Josie turned slightly, and her eyes found his. She knew. It was so clear in her eyes. So was her sadness. Not for her. No, she appeared sad for him. Then her lips tugged into a small smile, and she walked around Sarah and her latest whatever he was. Max followed Josie out but was forced to stop when a hand wrapped around his wrist.

"*Max!*" Sarah desperately pleaded.

He watched Josie halt, pause for a moment, and then spin around. He silently pleaded with her to understand him. To not

182

judge him right now.

Clenching his eyes shut, he took a deep breath, ready for a confrontation he hadn't been prepared for. When he opened his eyes, Josie gave him a small nod, and he knew they would be okay. That one nod was his reassurance that nothing—not even Sarah—could get between them.

Max pulled his hand free from Sarah's hold and then spun around.

The hurt in her blue eyes no longer affected him. Her blues still held that vindictive gleam because she still wanted to blame everyone else but herself. She hadn't changed at all. It wasn't enough anymore. She wasn't enough anymore.

He knew better.

He knew there was better with Josie.

"Sarah," he acknowledged.

She shook her head in disbelief at him. "What are you doing?"

"Leaving."

"No. What are you doing with a different woman?"

"That's none of your business."

"It is!"

The man next to her let out a growl and hissed, "I'll meet you inside." Then he left Sarah alone with Max.

"What are you doing having dinner with another woman?" she seethed. Her cheeks turned red as her nostrils flared.

"Josephine," Max said. "Her name is Josephine."

"I don't care if—"

"But I do," he interrupted her rant and stepped forward. "I care, Sarah. Her name is Josephine. And it is none of your business who I spend my time with. We're done. We've been done for a long time."

The horror reached her eyes. "No," she whispered. "No!"

Sarah knew.

She knew he was no longer in love with her.

"Not with her. Please, Max, not with her," she begged.

"Her name is Josephine," he reminded. "And I care about her more than I could ever care about you. I don't miss you, Sarah. When I'm with her, I still miss her."

"Does she know what kind of person you really are?" She was trying to discredit him. But she couldn't.

"Josephine does. She knows who you are, what you were, and what we did. Goodbye, Sarah," he farewelled and then spun around to see the bewilderment on Josie's face.

Then that bewilderment softened into understanding, and for a second, he swore he saw adoration in her eyes.

"Ready to go?" he asked.

Instead of saying yes, she said, "I'm incredibly proud of you."

And that there ...

Was the moment he fell in love with Josephine Faulkner.

He no longer liked her honestly.

No, he *loved* her honestly.

Josie

"And I care about her more than I could ever care about you ..."

He cares about me.

"I don't miss you, Sarah."

He doesn't miss her.

"When I'm with her, I still miss her."

He misses me when we're apart and when we're together.

Josie peeked over to find Max staring at her as they walked down the hall to her apartment. The car ride was quiet. She had no idea what more to say than that she was incredibly proud of him for standing up against the woman who had caused him so much pain in his life. The same woman who was beautiful with her long black hair and icy blue eyes. But no matter how stunning she was, Josie knew and saw the bitter woman Max had once loved.

Josie tore her eyes from Max and concentrated on her fast approaching apartment door. Max confessing that he cared about her more than Sarah really added to Josie's confusion.

He had said he missed seeing her.

Missed her when they were apart.

They had admitted they liked each other.

But it all just felt so undefined between them.

It was supposed to be simple with him.

He was her friend and tutor.

184

They shared mutual friends.

But she knew she connected with Max in ways she could never connect with Stevie or Ally.

She had never connected with any man the way she had with Max.

No man made her heart almost weep and beat out of control.

No man understood her and her relationship with her father.

No man looked at her the way Max did.

Am I falling in love with him?

"I'm sorry about Sarah," Max said once they reached her door.

Josie's grasp on the plastic container tightened. He had nothing to be sorry about. Sarah had hijacked their night and let confessions spill out of him. It made her really question her personal feelings for him.

Am I falling in love with Max?

She spun around to see the concern on his face. He'd put so much effort into tonight. He had even worn a black tie with his grey dress shirt. She lifted her eyes to meet his light browns, and she realised they were almost a honey colour. They had a gleam of different emotions to them that she couldn't decipher, but she wanted to. She wanted to look into his eyes and take away every regret he had.

She wanted to wake up to them.

She wanted to look into them when she told him she loved him.

I love him.

The thought had her flinching.

I.

The air was forced out of her.

Love.

The realisation caused her heart to throb.

Him.

It was the only way to explain how she felt. How much her heart yearned for him. How much she missed him. How much the thought of him caused her head to spin. She loved him enough to stand there and watch him confront someone he had loved. Her love was patience. Her love for him made her a more hopeful person.

I.

Love.

Him.

It was true.

So true.

But right now, she couldn't act on her love. Max cared for her. He even missed her. Friends could care and miss each other.

Friends couldn't love each other.

"I'm so sorry about her," he said with so much sorrow in his voice that it pained her.

She felt it.

Her confession on the tip of her tongue.

Stella was right.

She was self-destructive.

She ruined her own happiness.

Because what she wanted to do was tell him and plead for him to love her.

Josie felt her eyes sting as she forced herself to hold back the foolish tears that were forming. She took a deep breath and begged her heart to hold in those three words.

For just a little bit longer.

Not now.

And the anxious set of beats in her chest was all she needed to know that she had to hold it together. To keep it in. To address what was actually said and not what she felt.

"Don't be sorry."

He shook his head. "I am. We were having a good night ..."

"She didn't spoil it."

"She didn't?"

It was Josie's turn to shake her head. "No."

Max sighed in relief, and it caused her to let out a small laugh.

"I'm glad she didn't," he admitted.

Now.

Tell him now.

Josie swallowed hard.

It wasn't time.

She knew it.

Her brain knew it, but her damn foolish heart was intoxicated by the way his eyes softened as he gazed down at her.

"Max," she breathed.

He closed the small distance between them, and her chest heaved at the proximity. Her line of sight fell to his lips and then back to his eyes.

"Yes, Josephine." He sounded as breathless as she felt.

"Do you really care about me?"

His slow smile caused her heart to skip a beat.

"Isn't it already obvious that I do?"

"More than her?"

He nodded. "More than anyone."

Her throat tightened as her breathing became almost impossible. "And you miss me?"

"Even when I'm with you," he confirmed.

Her right hand reached up and wrapped around the back of his neck. "I like you, Max," she confessed; this time, it was a decoy admission of her love. "And I desperately want you to like me the way you miss me when I'm with you."

His hand settled on her hip. "I already like you more than that," he enlightened.

That was it.

The break.

The line had been obliterated.

Confession and feelings were free from their chains.

It was all she needed as she pulled his lips to hers and kissed him.

They didn't move.

Not for a second as they allowed their mouths this connection.

Then he really kissed her.

Lips fluttered over hers perfectly as her hand moved to cup the back of his head.

Heat.

So much heat between them.

He kissed her so passionately that she became delirious.

The moment his tongue traced her bottom lip, she moaned, and he backed her into her apartment door. The sudden impact of her back hitting the door was all he needed to flick the switch, and their kiss went from passionate to desperate.

His tongue passed her lips and found hers.

Strokes were made.

A dance of their own continued.

Then Max's hand left her hip, and his arm snaked around her back and held her to him.

She kissed him back, hoping he didn't taste her love for him on her lips.

"Jesus, Josie, knock like a proper per—" she had heard before the door opened, and she fell slightly into her apartment. Their kiss ended immediately, and Max held her against his body, ensuring they didn't topple over.

Josie clenched her eyes closed. Embarrassed to face her best friend and to see Max's reaction.

"Oh, I see ..." Stella trailed off, the smile evident in her flirty voice. "Carry on," she urged as Max shifted them and the door shut loudly behind them.

There was silence as Josie slowly opened her eyes to find Max's soft gaze on her. His cheeks were red, and he was panting.

Then Josie heard Stella say, "West, you owe me twenty dollars! It happened. Yeah, right outside our apartment. I knew it! I can't believe they waited *this* long."

Josie was mildly annoyed her best friend had made a bet on her friendship with Max. She would have to discover exactly what kind of bet Josie had lost.

Right now, though, the way Max was looking at her with a million questions in his brown eyes had her focusing. To her relief, she saw no regret on his face. Instead, he seemed as if he were in awe like their kiss moved him.

She hoped it had.

Longed for it.

But his silence began to chip away her confidence, and she dropped her hand from its grasp of the back of his head. Then the arm around her fell away from her and space was created. Though it was only marginal, it felt as if oceans separated them.

Max pressed his lips together and made a nod.

She had no idea what that nod meant.

But she watched him turn and make his way towards the elevator.

Every single step wounded her.

Every single step took her breath away and replaced it with thick smoke in her lungs. Watching him walk away was a pain she couldn't comprehend. She hated it. She wanted him to take back the kiss and all his words so she wouldn't have to feel it.

She had discovered marvellous bliss with him, and she hated it.

Hated what it felt like.

What it did to her.

Josie clutched the plastic container tightly, hoping she could redirect her pain. Instead, it made it worse. And she was never one to let herself be hurt by any other man than her father.

She wasn't about to let Maxwell Sheridan disappoint her.

He was allowed to be confused.

Hell, she was that and more.

But he wasn't allowed to be disappointed.

"Max!" she called out, turning her head to the right to find him halfway to the elevator.

He said nothing.

He gave her silence.

"Is that it?" she asked in a small voice.

"No. It can't be," he answered. Then he spun around and faced her, shaking his head. "Not with you."

And before Josie could even register what he meant, he stormed towards her, cupped her face, and gently pushed her against her apartment door.

"Max," she breathed.

He tilted his head to the right and sealed their lips together, kissing her even deeper than before.

His name on her lips was the last word between them before they kissed.

It was perfect.

The way he held her face gently in his hands.

The way his lips touched hers.

The way he couldn't stop kissing her.

He was perfect.

And even if he never loved her, she appreciated knowing just how incredible it was having him kiss her.

"Josephine," he breathed against her mouth and pressed his body against hers, trapping her against the door.

The way her name escaped him was beautiful.

A symphony couldn't do it justice.

He made her world feel like a song.

A beautiful melody.

He was *La Vie En Rose* before her.

A life of pink.

A life of beauty.

A life of wonder.

A life of her love for him.

He graced her in ways no one had before.

A knock was made against the door. "Josie ..."

Max broke their kiss; his heavy breathing only made her want him to continue. She wanted more. She wanted to kiss him and have him believe her love was better than anything anyone else could give him.

He pressed his forehead to hers and gently used his thumb to swipe her bottom lip. Then his thumb rested on the corner of her mouth, and he pulled back to look at her.

Their kiss exposed the brittleness of their friendship.

They had found *more.*

"Can you and Max bring it inside?" Stella asked. "You have a perfectly good bed in your room. Also, can I have my cake?"

He let out a low laugh.

"Answer her," Max urged.

Josie nodded and then swallowed hard. "Just a second."

"Okay." Stella sighed as her footsteps retreated further into the apartment.

Her heartbeat counted the silence between them.

Beat.

Beat.

Beat, beat, beat.

Beat.

Beat.

Beat, beat.

"Josephine ..." His thumb now traced the line of her bottom lip. "I like you too much to let this just be it for us."

Oh, poor foolish heart.

You had no chance with Maxwell Sheridan at all.

"I like you, too, Max," she said with a smile on her lips.

"Then we're on the same page?"

"What does your page say?"

He laughed and pressed his lips against hers in a chaste kiss. It was all her heart needed to affirm that Max was its weakness and strength.

When he pulled away, he answered, "Mine says I want to be with you and that I can't spend another fifteen days without seeing that smile on your face in person. Or to hear your laugh or to kiss the purest lips I've ever had the pleasure of ever knowing."

She inhaled sharply.

Stunned at how a kiss could end up with heartfelt confessions and truths.

"I like you, Josephine Faulkner, and I want to walk away right now so I can let you think of all the positives and negatives of there being more with us. I truly hope you see that this between us could be so right," he said and then pulled away.

Just when she thought he'd leave, his hands settled on the side of her head, and he pulled her forehead to his lips and pressed a soft kiss to her skin, just like he had when she was sick over two weeks ago.

Her heart wanted him completely.

Wanted those three words out of her so he could hear them.

Josie peeked up at him through her lashes.

"You're right for me in ways I can't even comprehend. I hope I'm right for you the way I strongly believe you're right for me." Max took a step back. "That case I've been working on goes to court on Monday. I'll be helping my dad prepare for it all weekend. I hope that's enough time."

She bit her lip and nodded, not trusting the words.

Max, with all his courage and strong posture, couldn't hide the fear that consumed his eyes.

Josie had the words to rid him of it.

But for selfish reasons, and to protect her own heart, she kept them and watched him walk away. When Max entered the elevator and spun around, he waved goodbye, and the elevator doors ensured that her love stayed a secret.

Just for now.

Ally: Hey, Josie! Rob and I are having an engagement

party in like a month. I have an invite for you. I
know you've cut back on some shifts, so can I drop
by soon to give it to you?

Josie stared at the message her boss and friend, Ally Moors,
had sent. For over two weeks, she hadn't been able to properly
hang out with her and Stevie. She felt guilty, but with Josie and
Stevie at university and Ally running one business and learning
another, their schedules never seemed to align.

Josie: I'm so glad you and Rob are finally having an
engagement party. I have a shift tomorrow. Stop by
before I close?

Ally: I know, right? My father has really added
pressure for us to set things right. Eloping really
hurt his feelings, but it was the best decision for us.
I will definitely see you tomorrow!

"Oh, is that Max messaging you?" Stella teased from across
where Josie sat.
"Who is Max?" her mother asked.
Josie shot Stella an "I'm going to kill you!" glare as she set
her phone on the table. "No one, Mamma."
Stella let out an unbelievable laugh. "*No one?* Em, your
daughter, yes, Josie, got kissed by a very attractive man the
other night."
Her mother almost jumped out of her hospital bed and
winced from her fast movements. "What?"
"Stella," Josie scolded.
"You have a man in your life?" her mother inquired.
Josie sighed and slumped in the chair she sat on. "I don't
have a man in my life."
Stella settled her hand on Emily's shoulder. "In the world of
Gilmore, he's a Luke."
Her mother's eyes glazed over. "You found *love?*"
"Mamma," Josie said, hoping the stern tone she used
downplayed the subject of love.
Yes, she was in love with Max.
But she had no idea what to do or how to be in love with

him.

He gave her time to think, and his lack of communication proved he was sticking to his word. After he had kissed her and told her how right she was for him, Josie entered her apartment to find Stella waiting desperately for more information. Josie had said nothing as she handed her roommate the cake and walked into her bedroom. That night she had laid in bed and pressed her fingertips to her mouth, remembering the feel of his lips on hers and the way his kiss changed the rhythm of her heart's beats.

Her heart used to sing his name.

Now her heart pleaded for his name to leave her lips and sear the surface of her heart.

"Are we forgetting that even though we love Luke for Lorelai, he wasn't right for her for a little while?" Josie reminded.

Stella groaned. "That's because the writers wanted to delay the inevitable. I know we never got to see it, but Luke was right for Lorelai. Just like Max is right for you."

"I didn't say he wasn't."

"You didn't say he was at all," Stella countered.

"I want to meet him," her mother announced.

Josie leapt out of the chair. "*What?*"

"Stella, what does Max do for a living?" her mother asked, completely ignoring Josie as she shook her head.

Her traitorous best friend grinned. "He's a *lawyer*."

Her mother's mouth dropped. "A lawyer?"

"Yep! And get this, a complete gentleman. Nothing like the previous callers Josie had at her disposal." Stella stuck her tongue out at Josie. "And he's a great guy. You'll love him, Em."

"I will?"

Stella nodded. "You will. Especially when he all but declared his love for your daughter after he kissed her like he would lose her."

Her mother reached out and took hold of Josie's hand. "Is that true, Josephine?"

Her shoulders fell. "He just said he thought I was right for him."

"I'd like to meet the man who makes my daughter's eyes hold that loving gleam," her mother urged.

Josie sighed. Whatever her mother wanted, she'd give her.

The only problem was that she hadn't told Max that her mother was battling cancer. Besides Stella and West, no one knew. And she wanted to keep it that way.

"He doesn't know, Mamma."

"I'll be out of hospital soon. You don't have to tell him. We can meet for lunch," her mother said with a lot of hope and determination in her voice.

"All right," Josie said, giving in to her mother. She knew that a goal of meeting Max would push her mother to fight harder against her cancer. It was a good thing. A blessing nonetheless. "I'll ask him."

"After you tell him you love him," Stella added.

Josie glanced over at her eyebrow-raising best friend. "*Love* him, Stella?"

"You can deny it all you like, Josie. He's right for you. And you have to tell him. Not to put him out of his misery, but to let you feel what it's really like to have someone think of you as their world. Someone to honestly and truly look at you as if you're the only star worth staring at," her best friend said.

"That's very poetic of you, Stella."

Her best friend shrugged. "I got it off a cereal box."

"Really?"

Her best friend and mother laughed.

"Nah. It's how I feel about West, so … don't make fun of it."

Josie smiled. "I won't."

It had been almost three days since Max kissed her and left her to think about her feelings, the kiss, and what it would do to their friendship.

Friendship.

That was what was at stake. A beautiful friendship she was terrified to be without. With Max, she could be herself. With Max, she felt comfortable and free. He understood her in ways no one else could. If their feelings were only temporary, it would destroy her.

Her love was so sure.

194

But she had no idea how sure he was of her.

Being right for someone didn't mean love.

Being right for someone didn't mean a future.

Her being right for him could be a fleeting affair.

The risk seemed to outweigh the gain.

But that was just it.

The gain was Max.

And realising it could be his heart she got the chance to love, she would obliterate any risks and doubt.

Risk everything for him.

Risk her entire heart for him.

Josie glanced down at the mixing bowl to see the chunks of banana she had just added to the mixture. This one batch would decide. It sounded childish, but she needed to decide. Max had given her tomorrow. She wasn't sure when, but she knew he would expect an answer.

The continuation of their friendship or the exploration of something new.

Something more.

Max wanted more.

With her.

To be with her.

He missed her.

Cared for her.

Liked her, even.

Josie used the wooden spoon to move around some of the banana pieces as she closed her eyes and replayed the way he had kissed her.

Touched her.

Whispered her name.

The way he took away her heart's ability to want anyone else.

He had put himself out there to women who had abused and neglected his affections. But this time, he had chosen Josie.

Opening her eyes, she smiled at the almost ready batch of cupcakes. The thought of him caused her chest to feel lighter. The thought of him caused her stomach to fill with butterflies. The thought of them caused a pang of rightness to erupt in her chest and spread blissful warmth throughout her.

As she reached for the walnuts, she realised that a choice

was on the brink of being made.

"Maybe it's time someone risked everything for him," she said to herself as she tipped the small glass bowl of walnuts and watched them fall into the batter.

But the risk for love worked both ways.

She needed to know he would risk everything for her, too.

Josie knew that was a while away from knowing, but she knew what her feelings were, and they were strong. Mixing the nuts into the cupcake mixture, she told herself to let herself experience this.

She had shut herself off for so long that she was struggling to allow herself to trust that Max wouldn't disappoint her. But he wasn't her father. In fact, Max was the only man who had ever gone out of his way for her.

Nobody claimed her in a kiss as he did.

Nobody touched her with such devotion and gentleness.

Nobody looked at her with that soft gaze like him.

Nobody but Max.

And nobody made her love with a sense of fear and freedom like he did.

And that had Josie setting the spoon down to rest on the inside of the mixing bowl. She reached over and picked up one of her bakery business cards she had brought into the kitchen with her.

Though the cupcakes hadn't made it into the trays, she knew her answer.

She'd just have to wait until tomorrow.

Chapter ELEVEN

Max

Normally, Max would relax on Sunday nights. Either settled on his couch watching whatever Sunday night flick was on or reading whatever book he had picked up from the top 100 picks from the Dymocks bookstore close to his office. There wasn't a real system to what he read. Every year, he had the store employee save him a copy of the list, and he'd pick randomly which book to read. His target was to read at least one book a month. But this year, he had only read four. The books he had chosen were good, but they didn't challenge or provoke him the way he wished. Max knew that next year he'd forgo the top list and try to read every book nominated for the Man Booker Prize Award instead.

But this particular Sunday was different.

He hadn't worked on a Sunday night since his first year of placement at his father's firm. Even then, it wasn't hard, pressurising work. Max's father's case would go to court tomorrow morning, and Max was working through the night to make sure the prosecution couldn't object to their key argument. That the defendant's wife was not dead but in hiding after falsifying her death and framing her husband. Max was sure that the contract imbedded in the countless emails was the key evidence the defence needed to ensure their client was found not guilty. His father had even hired a leading expert in code as their key witness.

Max's job was to make sure none of the evidence was circumstantial and could be dismissed by the judge. Max never intended on doing that task, considering he never wanted anything to do with criminal cases. But his father needed his help, and Max had recently learnt to appreciate the man he was. Gordon Sheridan was the best lawyer in the state for a reason. Though he could scare any veteran in the business, he worked hard to get the right outcome.

And for the very first time, Gordon had come to Max for help.

Max couldn't let him down.

A ping from his MacBook had him glancing up from the printed emails he had in his hands. Max noticed the red balloon on his mail app and twisted in his seat to reach for his laptop to bring it closer. He wasn't expecting any emails at this time of the night.

"Except ..." he said as his heart filled with joy.

Josephine.

She was the only person who would email him on a Sunday night. He knew she had her contracts tutorials and lectures on Monday, and he presumed she needed his help with this week's current readings. He didn't mind that he hadn't heard from her since their kiss outside her apartment.

The very kiss that changed everything.

His heart.

His wants and needs.

His idea of a future.

They all included Josephine Faulkner.

He had wanted it even before she had pulled his lips to hers and coerced every fibre in him to only ever want her.

Max had walked away that night to give them both time to think. And as the hours turned into days, it only had him desperately longing for her in ways he hadn't before.

No woman made him feel this way.

No woman made him miss her smile the way Josie did.

No woman made him miss her heart.

No woman made him love the way Josie could.

No one but Josie.

Excitement bled through him as he pressed on his emails and opened them, ready to answer every question she sent his way.

But the moment he saw the unread email, his heart stopped.

The euphoria of his new love for Josie came to a halt as he saw Andrea's email waiting for him.

Max's breathing heaved as he noticed it was an email from her personal account and not her work address.

A cold sweat blanketed him as he hovered the cursor over her name.

His head told him to delete it.

To forget her completely.

But a small piece of his heart wanted closure.

Max wasn't sure if he should trust that small piece; the piece he hadn't let Josephine touch for fear she'd make it hers.

Swallowing the large lump in his throat, he decided that in order to be fair and love Josephine honestly as he declared, he had to let Andrea go. He had to have closure. Those remaining feelings would have to dissipate into the void of all the other disappointments he had faced in his life.

So he clicked on the email and read the first words she had sent to him in months.

To: MaxwellSheridan@GordonSheridan.com.au
From: AndyWallace@gmail.com
Subject: All the things I should have said.

Max,

I'm sorry this email took a long time to get to you. I'll be the first to admit I handled everything completely wrong. I let my pride overshadow my feelings for you.

I couldn't get myself to reply. I'm so sorry, Max. I read your emails, and they hurt me. You poured your heart out to me, and I exited your emails and disregarded your feelings.

My boss told me that you'd be working in the law department in Boston and I'll be one of your supervisors when I return from Florida.

You're probably wondering why I moved to Florida. Well, I just couldn't see him happy. I had hoped that when Noel went after her, she married her fiancé.

I hoped that when he returned from Hong Kong for the expansion that he'd realize he really did love me more than he loved her.

But I didn't think he could break my heart more than when I found out he married her. I wanted to be happy for them. I really did, Max.

I loved Noel.

I thought he was it.

I thought I would marry him.

New York changed everything.

I kissed you.

I cheated on him even when I didn't have his whole heart.

I felt sick after it happened because I felt more with you than I did with him.

Because I knew that kiss was true, and the kisses and touches he gave me were desperate attempts to forget her.

I was so angry with you for making me feel that.

I was so angry with Noel for loving another woman while he was with me.

I hated Clara for marrying the man I loved.

And I hated myself for not having the courage to face you the most.

I shouldn't have made you go all those months without hearing from me. I just needed to start new. Without knowing

that my boyfriend married another only
months after I broke up with him. I
needed to be away from him and people
who knew what happened. I needed to be
away so I could hate without hurting
his marriage.
I needed to be away from you the most,
Max.
I needed time to think of what one kiss
meant.
One kiss.
That was it.
It was just one kiss.
And you and I both knew it wasn't enough.
But I was Noel's.
He might not have been mine, but I was
his.
And for a brief minute under that tree,
I was yours.
Completely yours.
And now, I have to face the fact that
I have to work in the same building as
the man who fell out of love with me.
A married man.
I still want him.
I still love him.
I still desire to have him leave her
for me.
To return to me.
But I only have these feelings because
of my pride.
I was made a fool.
And what was worse was that I blamed
you.
You, Max.
Innocent, sweet, loving you.
You did nothing but care for me.
And I'm so sorry I wasted that.
So here I am, writing you this confusing
email because hearing that I might

```
see you again made me feel all those
emotions I felt under that tree.
I want to see you.
I want the chance to have everything
you offered me.
I'm so sorry, Max.
Please forgive me for being so selfish.
I let my pride cost me you.
Give me a chance to redeem myself.
```
Yours,
Andrea.

That was it.

All the words he had ever wanted to hear from her.

And that small piece of him that still cared for her burst within him and took his heart with its explosion.

The pain and misery opened his wounds.

The same wounds Josie had soothed and healed.

Andrea helped destroy him.

Josie healed him and made him her equal.

There was a difference between the two.

Andrea might claim a piece of him.

But Josie owned not only his heart but also his mind.

She gave him a brighter outlook on life where he was deserving.

Where he could be her hero and not the villain.

Being Josie's hero meant finding a way to forget Andrea Wallace.

And Max knew to forget her was never to reply to her.

After all, ignorance is bliss.

At nine a.m., Max was sitting in the first row behind his father and his client in the Supreme court. In Gordon Sheridan's opening statement, he had labelled Andrew Walsh a loving husband who loved his wife more than money or possession. He went on to tell the jury that Andrew was a man who dedicated his life to his wife's happiness and couldn't be held responsible for his wife's death. Gordon went on to say that Andrew missed his wife and buried an empty coffin and couldn't be tried for murder if one didn't even occur. At the end of his opening statement, Max's father stated that the truth would be revealed in court. That Andrew Walsh had been framed, and his wife was still alive.

After eleven a.m., a short recess was called after the prosecution had finished questioning the medical examiner. The ME who testified stated the amount of blood found on the kitchen floor was sufficient blood loss to be considered a homicide, and that nothing in the blood tested proved that any tampering had occurred.

"It's not looking good, Gordon," Andrew stated, fear and anxiety written on his face as he and Gordon turned to face Max.

Max got up from the row and nodded at his father. "You did well," Max said.

"He did?" Andrew asked, sceptical.

"Mr Walsh, I can assure you that you have the best defence lawyer in the country. My father knows exactly what to do when he cross examines the ME. It's only the first day of your trial."

Andrew nodded, but the concern in his eyes hadn't faded. "Will you still be here after the recess? Could really use a friend, Max."

"I just have to step out to make a phone call." Max had nodded at them both before he made his way down the aisle and then towards the court doors.

He needed fresh air. How his father was able to sit in a courtroom with stale air was beyond him. Max was glad he hadn't followed in his father's footsteps and pursued a career in criminal law.

Once Max had made it through the arched doors and exited the Supreme courthouse, he went down the short steps until he stepped onto the footpath of William Street. He took a deep breath. The fresh air worked wonders for his lungs and his mild headache.

Reaching into the pocket of his suit jacket, he pulled out his phone to find several missed calls and text messages. He unlocked it to find a few from a number he didn't recognise, some from Julian, one from Noel, and even a text message from Alex.

But no call or text message from Josie.

It was Monday.

He had hoped that three days would be long enough for her to think about them being together.

What if giving her space was all the time she needed to realise we shouldn't be together?

That they should just be friends.

Friends.

The one word he hated when it came to Josephine Faulkner.

They might have started out as friends, but he wanted more.

Desperately wanted more.

The small recess would end soon, and Max would have to go through security once more before returning to the courtroom. So he would have to reply to his best friends once his day in court had ended. Being supportive of his father had cost him an entire day's worth of his own work, but the opening day was the most important day of the trial.

Max opened the mail app on his phone and swiped his thumb down to refresh it. Several new emails appeared, and he was shocked to find another message from Andrea.

Curious, he opened it, choosing to read hers rather than the others sent to him since he entered the courtroom.

```
To: MaxwellSheridan@GordonSheridan.com.au
From: AndyWallace@gmail.com
Subject: The apology that is almost a year
too late.

Max,
    I deserve no reply from you.
    Last night, I reread your emails.
    I read your pain, and I am so sorry I
    hurt you.
    You chose me.
    And it took me a long time to realise
    just how special that declaration was.
    You chose me.
```

He chose her.
I chose you too late and went to Orlando
instead of telling you that.
I was scared another man would hurt me.
You made a lot of promises.
I believed them.
But I also believed Noel when he said
he loved me.
I now know that I made the mistake of
comparing you to him.
Because I get why he fell in love with
Clara.
I get why he made her his wife.
She understands him.
I saw the wedding pictures, and seeing
them as bride and groom was all I needed
to see.
I'm choosing you, Max.
It's been over a year since you last
kissed me.
It's been over a year since I last saw
you.
Please come to Boston.
Please let me explain myself in person.
I treated you wrong when all you did
was try to treat me right.
I'm sorry, Max.
Yours,
Andrea.

Just as he exited her message, he received another. And to
his disappointment, it was from Andrea and not Josie.

To: MaxwellSheridan@GordonSheridan.com.au
From: AndyWallace@gmail.com
Subject: I made such a terrible mistake.

I did.
And I have so much regret.
Please write me back.

```
Yours,
Andrea.
```

Regret was such a powerful word.

And Andrea was a powerful woman.

He had been attracted to her strength and ambitions. He had been attracted to her need to prove herself. They shared many traits.

Regret being one of them.

And right now, as he stood outside the Supreme Court of Victoria, he had one.

He regretted the fact he was tempted to reply and tell her all the lies that had been truths many months ago.

That he still wanted her.

"Don't you think drinks are a bit pre-emptive?" Max asked with a hint of humour in his tone.

His father chuckled. "It was a good day in court."

Max nodded. For him, it would be his last until the final day of court. His father had a whole team who would be there for support if he needed it. Max had made sure his findings were all catalogued and in order for his father. The emails were already submitted into evidence and were available for the prosecution. But so far, they hadn't put it together that the contract for hire was carefully imbedded in the wife's emails. Unfortunately for his father, the cyber experts hadn't been able to locate exactly where the receiver of those emails was. The IP addresses bounced through several different countries, and it was taking some time to pinpoint the exact location. Whoever the wife had hired was a professional.

"There are many days in court left," Max tried to reason.

"So you won't be joining us? The others are already on their way there."

Max shook his head. "I have a lot of work to catch up on. A few redrafts I need to look at."

"Don't stay too late, all right?" It surprised Max that his

father seemed to care about how long he spent at the office. It used to be that Max never spent enough time, but now it seemed the opposite.

"I won't," he promised.

His father set his hand on Max's shoulder and then squeezed it. "The past few weeks, I've never been more proud to call you my son. You've really come into your own."

And before Max could even respond to his father's rare compliment, his father spun around and made his way towards the waiting black BMW. One of the perks of being the state's most sought-after lawyer was being able to afford a car service. However, Max enjoyed driving his Porsche. It was one of the only luxuries he had ever indulged in.

His father was proud of him.

Proud of the lawyer he was.

For the first time, Max felt as if he were worthy of being proud of.

His life had changed since he sat across from Josephine Faulkner that night her father had stood her up for dinner. It was at the same restaurant Max had taken her to on Thursday night. The same restaurant where his ex-whatever-she-was begged him not to love Josie. And the same restaurant they had left and ended up sharing their first kiss and confessions.

He had hoped Monday was enough time for her to decide.

But as Max pulled his phone out from his jacket pocket with one hand and tightened his grip on his briefcase handle with the other, he realised that it wasn't enough time.

It was already after four p.m.

Monday was almost finished.

Her time to think would rollover to Tuesday, and Max was terrified that it would continue for days to come. If not weeks. And that frightened him. He hadn't seen her for fifteen days before their rain check dinner, and he was already missing her. Any more days and he'd do something drastic.

Like demand an answer.

Max walked into Gordon Sheridan Lawyers to find Ruby, the receptionist, behind the desk with a smile on her face.

"Good afternoon, Mr Sheridan," she greeted as he walked past her and headed towards the elevators.

"Afternoon, Ruby," he had said before he stopped in front of the elevator. Max reached forward and pressed the up button.

When the elevator opened, he stepped inside and pressed his floor's button. Once the doors closed, he unlocked his phone and brought up Josie's contact. His thumb hovered over the call icon as the steel box ascended. He wanted to talk to her.

He wanted feelings shared and expressed.

He wanted mutual love with her.

She might only like him, but he hoped someday that like turned into so much more than just love.

The ding of the elevator reaching his floor had him glancing up from his phone. He stepped off the elevator and headed towards his office. On his way, he walked past several of the junior lawyers and interns. They had all addressed him as Mr Sheridan, and he nodded and said hello. Max would have to ask HR for their files to find out their names and their background. He would make an effort to get to know them and give them the chance at forming a work connection. So that if they ever needed help, they could approach him without any fear of repercussion.

When Max reached his office, he pulled his set of keys out of his pocket and unlocked the door. He pushed the glass door open and stepped inside his office. Max approached his desk and noticed a pink box on it. He stepped around the desk, set his briefcase on the floor, and slipped his phone into his dress pants pocket.

The pink box had a white ribbon wrapped around it with a bow on top. Curious, he pulled his office chair out and then lowered himself down to sit on it. Max squinted at the box as he set his hands on it and pulled it closer. Taking in the box, he saw no indicator of who it could be from. Max was used to gifts from his clients. Some he would send back because they were too grand, and others he had donated. But he had no idea which of his clients would send him a pink box.

Max reached up and grasped one of the ribbon ends. He pulled on it until the bow untied and Max could pull the white ribbon away from the box. Then he grasped the lid and lifted it up.

He let out a light laugh at the sight of four cupcakes.

Max knew these rare cupcakes.

They were his favourite from the Little Bakery on Little

Collins Street.

His heart clenched at the sight of them. Only one person knew his favourite cupcake.

Josephine.

She had a box of banana and Walnut Whip cupcakes delivered to him. As he lifted the lid a little higher, he noticed something stuck on the inside of the lid.

It was an envelope.

Max pulled it off and let the lid rest against his desk. Then he picked up the box and set it away from him. He took in the small, rectangular white envelope to find his name beautifully written across it. He flipped it over, ripped the envelope open, and pulled out its contents.

His brows furrowed the moment he saw that it was Josie's business cards.

Why would she send me her business cards?

He stared at the stack of cards.

Then it hit him.

She had written on the back of her card and had left it with the receptionist downstairs when he was out of his office, and she had come to visit him.

Max separated the cards and flipped over the first card to see that she had left him a message. It read:

I'm right for you, Max.

Then he flipped over another.

And you're right for me.

He set the two cards down on his desk and flipped over the last card.

I'm waiting for you to make this right between us.
I'm ready when you are.
I like you, Max, the way I know you like me back.
Josie.

His love and her words hit him straight in his chest. It was a collision like no other. This was what he had always wanted. Someone to care for him. Like him and miss him.

Someone who understood him personally and professionally, and everything between.

Someone right from him.

Someone like Josephine Faulkner.

And her three business cards were the encouragement he needed to swipe the cards off his desk and leap out of his chair.

Because he knew without hesitation or doubt.

I'm ready.

Josie

"*No*," Josie breathed as she stared at the name of the sender of the email that had just landed in her inbox.

Johanna.

She was stunned.

She was the last person Josie had ever expected to get in touch with her. She owed Johanna nothing and had never heard from her. But after fourteen years of silence, Josie was curious to see what her father's wife had to say.

```
To: Josie.Faulkner@hotmail.com
From: Johanna.K.Faulkner@hotmail.de
Subject: Hello, Josie.

Dear Josie,
    I hope this email gets to your correct
email address. I asked your father's
assistant for a means to contact
you. I thought a phone call might be
uncomfortable for you.
    I know I'm the last person you want
emailing you, but I thought it was
time. Your father made it clear that
our meeting was out of the question. He
informed me that you would never come
```

to Germany—which is understandable.
Your home is in Australia.
I wish I had written to you years ago.
I feel like I let time slip and let
your father control every source of
communication.
All I ask, Josie, is that you read this
email.
That's all.
As you already know, your father and I
have two daughters.
Your sisters.
Their names are Heidi and Angelika.
Heidi is the eldest, and she's thirteen.
Angelika is eleven.
They would like to know you.
Your father talks about you to them all
the time. He talked about when you used
to dance and shows them both pictures
of you. They ask all the time when they
can meet you, but I never gave them an
answer. When they were little, it was
easier to feed them the excuse that you
were busy. But now that they're older,
they would like to meet their sister
from Australia.
Their sister who is about to become a
lawyer.
I know I'm asking a lot.
Your father doesn't know I'm reaching
out to you.
I've always wanted you to be a part of
our family, Josie.
I realised too late that we never
formally invited you and opened our
arms out to you.
You have your own life, and I understand
that.
You're an adult and have experienced

many things we haven't.

We don't have to be in yours, but we'd very much love you to be a part of ours—even if it is only through emails. I have attached pictures of Heidi and Angelika in this email. They're learning ballet because they saw a picture of you in your tutu when you were young in Jeff's office.

You inspired them, Josie.

They're sweet girls.

I haven't told them that I am writing to you in fear of getting their hopes up.

I don't want to disappoint them if you don't respond.

Not in the way your father and I have disappointed you through the years.

I look forward to hopefully hearing from you soon.

Johanna.

They want to meet me.

Josie reread the message once again.

It was right before her. The email she had wanted when she was nine. The words she had hoped for when she was a child. To know the sisters she never got the chance to meet.

Heidi and Angelika.

For years, Josie knew of them but refused to let him speak their names. Every time her father would begin to discuss them, she'd cut him off. It wasn't until she was thirteen that she agreed to see him for a few weeks each year. She was an adult now. Her mother believed she was old enough to make her own decisions. And Josie only agreed to please her mother and no one else.

Josie could simply ignore Johanna's email and hope they left her alone. But Heidi and Angelika would only be getting older. Soon, they would be able to go online and find Josie on social media. It would only take one name search, and they'd find everything. Her Facebook, Twitter, Instagram, and even her Snapchat. Only her Twitter and Instagram were available for public viewing, but they'd see her life. A part of her told her to ignore the email. It had already been years, and her German sisters could continue their lives without her. But a bigger part of her felt guilty.

Her bitterness with her father affected Heidi and Angelika. They had questions and were curious about her. Josie didn't want them growing up and resenting her for being selfish. When she was younger, all she wanted to do was get to know them and be a big sister. Her mother was right; she had to know them. They shared the same blood. They might never be real sisters who told each other secrets, but they could be friends.

Josie let out a sigh as she clicked on the picture attachments her father's wife had sent her. When it loaded, she saw two blonde girls in their leotards with smiles on their faces. Unlike Josie, Heidi and Angelika had brown eyes, and she presumed that they must have gotten them from their mother. They were cute, and Josie took in their smiles. They were so young and innocent.

She was torn between giving them a chance at a relationship and giving her father what he wanted. But she had no idea how her mother would really take the possibility of Josie connecting with her father's young German daughters. Josie didn't want her mother to think she was betraying her … or worse.

Abandoning her.

Josie closed the image and returned to her inbox.

The thought of her mother ever thinking Josie could abandon her caused a pang of guilt to explode in her chest. Josie was used to abandonment and disappointment. She wouldn't allow her mother to feel the terrible way it ate at your heart and played with your mind.

She'd spare her mother of that one thing.

But she couldn't expose Heidi and Angelika to it either.

It was a mess.

And she knew the only person who could help her was the man she was waiting for.

Max.

He would give her helpful advice. But she hadn't heard from him, and she presumed his day at court had dragged. The court case his father was on was already all over the news. The media had called it the trial of the decade. Josie had brought the cupcakes to his office early in the morning on her way to university, but he had already left for court. She wasn't sure if she should leave them, but it was Monday. And she had promised a decision.

That he was right for her, and she was right for him.

She just had to hope that Ruby, the receptionist at the front desk of Gordon Sheridan Lawyers, did as she promised and left the box of Max's favourite cupcakes on his desk for him to find. The suspense of not hearing back from him yet was driving her mad. All she wanted to do was message him. But he was in court, and she had been in class all day.

"Here you are, Josie," her contracts tutor, Oswald, said as he stood in front of her table.

She glanced up from her laptop screen to see him holding a stack of papers out to her. Josie reached out and grasped the papers to discover it was her assignment she had handed in two weeks ago. The same assignment she had worked hard on with Max.

"Congratulations, Josie. You surprised me. I'm glad you finally understood the content. You should be proud of that mark," Oswald said as he began to distribute the rest of the papers to the class.

Josie set her assignment on her keyboard and smiled the moment she saw the high distinction grade on the top right corner of the coversheet of her assignment. Then under it, she saw 96% written in red pen. Oswald was one of only a few tutors who liked using the percentage grade along with the standard marking key. He wanted students to understand exactly where they were, and Deakin's standard markings were too vague for him.

The smile on her face stretched as she realised her overall average for her bachelor would remain in the high distinctions, eighty percent and above, if she aced her contracts exam. That goal of graduating with honours could still be realised, and she had Max to thank for that. She quickly dug her phone out of her cardigan pocket and paused the moment she set her thumb on the screen to unlock it.

Max was probably still in court.

He still didn't know her answer.

That she wanted to be with him.

"So has he gotten in touch with you yet?" Stella asked eagerly as Josie held her phone between her shoulder and ear.

She sighed. "No, he hasn't. He might not have even gone to his office after court. He could have gone straight home, which means he won't see the box until tomorrow … and even that's a big *if* he goes to his office before court."

"Argh!" her best friend groaned. "Why can't you go to his apartment then?"

"Because I don't know where he lives."

"How?"

Josie locked her Mini Countryman and hoisted her satchel onto her shoulder. "I've never been to his apartment."

"This is so frustrating. You tell him you want to be with him in the most adorable, sentimental way, and it's just sitting there on his desk, waiting for him to read it. Like come on!"

She laughed as she made her way towards her building's security gate. Josie should be parking in the apartment garage, but the street parking was more convenient for her early morning commute when she drove to campus. Sure, there was a chance her car could be stolen, but her father had paid for it, and she had insurance. It wouldn't be a loss she'd miss greatly because public transport wasn't so bad. When Josie reached the security keypad, she entered the passcode and heard it buzz, announcing it had accepted it. Two steps to the right were made and then she pushed the door.

"Are you still there?"

Josie reached up and grasped her phone in her hand and relieved her shoulder from the cramped position it was in. "I'm still here. I'm just getting home. What do you want for dinner?"

"I'm gonna stay at West's tonight. The school I was at today is probably Satan's devil factory. Every class I taught was horrible. And well …"

She rolled her eyes as she entered the building complex and pushed the gate closed behind her. "You need West to relieve the stress?"

"Exactly. So I'll see you tomorrow once I finish work?"

"Yeah, I'm closing at the bakery. So stop by if you want to."

"If I want to? Oh, I definitely want to," Stella promised.

"All right. I'll see you then."

Josie concentrated on her footsteps as she listened to her best friend say, "When Max gets back to you, call me straight away, okay?"

She lifted her eyes off the concrete and found the man in question sitting on the steps that led into her building. Josie's footsteps halted when she noticed he was staring at the business cards she had left with the cupcakes.

"Stella …"

"No, seriously, I need to know. I've been going insane all weekend!"

"Stella, I'm gonna have to call you back," she said just as Max took his focus off the business cards and directed those light brown eyes to her.

"Is he …?"

Josie couldn't read the expression on Max's face. She couldn't tell if he was here to say 'yes, let's be together' or 'I had time to think it over, and we let ourselves get carried away.'

God, don't let it be the second one.

She removed the phone from her ear and hung up on Stella without a goodbye. Just the sight of him had her heart soaring and aching. It suddenly weighed heavily from the nerves that ravished it.

As she slipped her phone into the pocket of her oversized cardigan, a wave of nausea rolled through her as his silence struck her and only sickened her more.

Max slowly got up from the steps.

Inhale.

Exhale.

God, breathe, Josie.

He closed the distance between them, and she watched him take a deep breath. Then his palms cupped her cheeks; her business cards were soft and cool against her skin.

And before she could say the first words since their kiss outside her apartment door, Max whispered, "I'm ready."

But then he did something she hadn't expected.

He kissed his statement into a promise as his lips found hers.

Chapter
TWELVE

Max

I'm ready.

Two whispered words before Max couldn't take it anymore and had to kiss her.

And what a kiss it was.

Her soft, sweet lips on his.

She kissed him gently as if she were telling him that she was ready, too. Max had dropped a hand from her face and reached the strap of her bag. He pulled it away from her, and her bag fell to the concrete path. It was the only thing in the way of him wrapping his arms around her and pulling her body to his.

The impact of their bodies touching elicited a soft moan from her.

It was music to his ears.

Caused the dizziness in his head.

Josie's hands settled on the nape of his neck, caressing his skin with her precious touch.

The way she kissed.

The way she tasted.

The way everything about her was so different and new to

him was beautiful.

She was beautiful.

"Max," she breathed against his mouth and then pulled away.

When he opened his eyes, her lips were red from their kiss and a stunning shade of pink tinted her cheeks.

But her eyes.

God, her eyes were magnificent.

They were that soft shade of blue.

Full of hope and adoration.

She gazed up at him as if she saw a better man.

The man he was because of her.

"Josephine," he said in a low voice.

He said it with all his love for her. Whether she heard it or not, he knew it was there.

He was in love with this woman.

"I have to tell you something," she announced.

Max stilled and instantly thought the worst. Nothing good had ever followed those words. He knew those six words always ended with something horrible and heartbreaking for him.

Not with Josephine.

Don't let her break my heart.

His jaw clenched, knowing he had given her the power to break him just like all the women before her. But he knew she wouldn't. She hadn't done a single thing wrong since he had met her. The way she was looking at him with that contented expression on her face was the reassurance he needed.

Josie's hands left his neck, and Max took a small step back to give her space. He watched as she bent her knees and opened her bag. Then she took out a piece of paper and stood straight, holding the paper out to him. Max slipped the three business cards he would treasure for his entire life into his pocket and took the paper from her.

"What is this?"

"Just flip it over," she encouraged.

And he did.

His heart had sped up its beats as he took in her name and the assignment title. Then he saw the mark on her assignment, and he glanced up to see the smile on her face. He couldn't take

219

it anymore; he wrapped his arms around her, proud of her for getting the mark she had.

Her arms looped around his neck, and she whispered, "Thank you."

He lifted her, and a giggle escaped her.

"Thank you, thank you, thank you," she breathed.

And his heart broke.

Completely broke for her.

Not in the way he had expected.

But his heart had given up on trying to keep that small spot reserved for another. Josie broke his heart and mended it for it to only beat her name.

He adored her.

So much that he had fallen in love with her.

Max inhaled deeply, content this was what he wanted.

This woman in his arms, he wanted and needed.

Once he had set her on her feet, he kissed her cheek and smiled down at her. "I'm so proud of you."

Her hand moved from his neck to settle on his cheek. "I couldn't have done it without you."

Shaking his head, his palms found her hips. "It was all you, Josie. I didn't write that assignment. You did."

Her thumb brushed along his cheek. "Trust me, Max, I couldn't have done it without you. This whole semester, I wouldn't have survived without you."

She wouldn't have survived without me.

He loved hearing she needed him.

And he loved seeing her appreciation in her blue eyes more.

Max squeezed her hips. "You know I'm always here for you, right?"

She bit down on her lip and nodded. "I know."

"I never want to disappoint you, Josie."

"And you haven't," she assured.

"I never will," he promised as he bent down and kissed her forehead.

"Do you want to come inside?"

Max pulled his lips from her skin and nodded.

They had a lot to discuss.

They needed to get their pages aligned so they could be together.

His hands left the sides of her body, and he bent down to pick up her bag. Then he turned and reached out to grab her hand. She let him. Their hands had touched many times before, but he had never held her hand as intimately as right now. Max's thumb stroked hers as he led her up the steps and into the apartment building.

He smiled, knowing that *this* was right.

Their kiss.

Their connection.

The way their hands fit perfectly together.

She was right for him.

And he was right for her.

To: MaxwellSheridan@GordonSheridan.com.au
From: AndreaWallace@GandMC.com
Subject: G&MC's offer.

Dear Mr. Sheridan,

I understand you are a busy man and work for one of the best law firms in Australia and might not have come across the previous email I sent a few weeks ago. Mr. Gregson would like to speak to you about working for G&MC accounting firm for a short contract. We already have the paperwork done for your visa that will permit you to work. We have also outlined the terms and payment package you will receive (please see attached document) if you do agree to assist us. The recent change in the law department has seen a few lawyers either moved or promoted. Andrea Wallace is one of those lawyers who was recently promoted to become the senior lawyer at our Boston office.

And at the request of Mr. Gregson, we are seeking a skilled and experienced corporate lawyer to oversee and help Ms. Wallace transition into her role as the new senior supervising lawyer. You come highly recommended, and Mr. Gregson is happy to open negotiations to have you and your talents at our firm. I can assure you money is not a problem, so please let us know what your terms are, and I will redirect them to Mr. Gregson.
I do look forward to hearing from you soon.
Again, if you wish to reach out to me personally, please email me at XenaDavenport@GandMC.com with any of your concerns or questions.
Kind regards,
Xena Davenport
Executive assistant to *Andrea Wallace*.
Senior supervisor.
Legal Department.
G&MC accounting firm.

"Can I ask you something?" Josie asked as she walked across the lounge room and sat on the couch next to Max. While she was putting her bag in her room, he had waited on her couch for her and went through his emails.

Max locked his phone and hid the email from Josie. The email meant nothing. He wasn't even going to consider taking the job opportunity in the US. He was where he was meant to be. And though he had good intentions, Max still felt as if he were deceiving Josie. But that was his past.

Andrea was his past.

And he wouldn't reply to any of her emails.

In fact, he wouldn't read any more if she decided to send any his way.

"You can ask me anything," he said as he slipped his phone into his pocket.

Josie handed him the laptop she had brought from her bedroom and took the sticky notes and marker off the keyboard. Max set the laptop on his thighs to see that she had an email opened on the screen.

"What is this?" He glanced over to see her remove the Sharpie lid.

"It's from my father's wife." Then she sighed and set the tip of the marker on the sticky note. "This is the first time she's ever reached out to me."

"And you're surprised?"

Josie's eyes fell to the square note as she began to write something down. "Yeah. I was in class today when I got it. Can you read it and tell me what you think?"

The hopes of talking about them would be put on hold.

He had to take care of her needs, and she needed his advice.

Max nodded then began to read Josie's stepmother's email. In it, Johanna Faulkner wrote of how her daughters wanted to meet Josie. She even wrote of how Josie's father spoke about her and how her sisters had followed in Josie's footsteps by doing ballet. Johanna sounded sweet, apologetic, and genuine in her email to Josie, and Max knew that this email confused her.

He craned his neck to find her staring at him as that unsureness swept the features of her face, her lips even pursing.

"I'm torn," she admitted. "I want to know them. Heidi and Angelika, I mean. But I feel like if I do, I might be betraying my mum or something."

"It's okay to feel that way. It's been just you and your mum for a long time. You love her and don't want to hurt her."

Josie's eyes glazed over. "But I don't want Heidi and Angelika to someday message me about how much they hate me for abandoning them, too."

Tears now rolled down her cheeks, and Max instantly set the laptop next to him and shuffled closer to Josie. He wrapped his arms around her, and she settled her ear to his chest.

"Hey," he said as he rubbed her back.

"I just … What if I did agree to meet them, and then they pull a stunt like my father always does and don't show up? What if my mother feels betrayed? What if this is just a stupid trick to get me to talk to my dad? I … I don't know what to do, Max."

"It's okay," he whispered.

Josie sniffled and moved in his arms. Her chin rested on his chest as she gazed up at him. "Do you think it would be extremely selfish of me not to email her back?"

He shook his head. "I don't think so. It's your choice, Josie. No one is forcing you to get to know them. And I know you want my advice, so I'm going to tell you that you need some time to think it over. I know you don't want those girls to feel the disappointment you've felt, but they live in Germany, and you live here in Australia. It would be hard. But one email saying hello isn't going to make your mother think you're choosing them over her. I know you'll do what's right for you."

Her bottom lip trembled as she blinked her tears to fall. "I knew you'd say the right thing." She splayed her hands on his chest and pushed him to sit herself up. "Can you pass me my laptop?"

Max reached up and brushed the moisture off her cheeks. When the tears were gone, he reached over to pick up her laptop and handed it to her. The sticky note pad in her lap caught his attention, and he picked it up and laughed.

"'*Fräulein emailed me!*'?"

Josie grinned. "It's for Stella for when she comes home tomorrow. We don't like saying her name in this apartment, so Stella just calls her '*Fräulein.*'"

Max set the pad and pen on the coffee table as Josie placed the laptop in her lap. "And are you going to reply to her?"

"Umm … yeah. I think I will. My mum said I needed a lot more love in my life than just hers. That I *deserve* more love. So maybe Heidi and Angelika could love me like a proper sister. None of this was their fault. And if I turn out nothing like my father said I was, then I know I tried. If I write a reply, can you read it before I send it?"

He leant over and kissed her temple. "You write that email, and I'll stick that note on Stella's bedroom door for you." He got off the couch and picked up the sticky note pad and pen. "I'll be back in a minute."

Josie nodded and took a deep breath as she set her fingertips to the letters of the keyboard.

He was incredibly proud of her.

Max knew it wasn't easy for her to be so open to the chance

of being burned by those in Germany. He knew she didn't count them as family, but he heard the tiredness in her voice. She wanted a resolution to her problematic family life. And Max would be by her side, offering his support. Upon reaching Stella's bedroom door, Max peeled the note off the pad and stuck it on her bedroom door with a smile. He tapped the Sharpie on the pad as he spun around and made his way back into the lounge room. When he was behind the couch, he noticed Josie still typing away. She had paused for a moment, groaned, and then he heard her press a button several times. He presumed it was the delete button from the way she attacked it.

Glancing down at the yellow Post-it pad, he smiled, knowing just what he had to do. Max rounded the couch and sat back down. Then he used his free hand and took the laptop from her, setting it on the coffee table before he faced her.

Josie raised her brow, and he saw the humour reach her eyes.

"We've gotta discuss something."

She turned her body to his and crossed her legs. "Okay."

Max took in the curiosity in her eyes. She surprised him. He had no idea he needed someone like her until she left him wanting more. She understood him within seconds of talking to him. She gave him a chance. She opened her heart to him.

She was everything and more.

She was the woman he was sure he could love forever.

Josephine Faulkner was the woman he wanted to love forever.

"I like you, Josephine," he breathed as he removed the cap from the marker.

The smile on her face softened, and she was even more beautiful than before. "I like you, Max."

"And I'm right for you?"

"You're right for me," she confirmed. Then she got on her knees and set her fingertips on his jaw. "You're so right for me, Maxwell."

Maxwell.

No one had ever called him Maxwell except for his parents.

"You're so unbelievably right for me," he stated, and then she pressed a light kiss on his lips.

It was the lightest of kisses, yet he still wanted more with her.

He could never get enough of her.

Josie brushed her thumb along his bottom lip and whispered, "But?"

"You think there's a but?"

She shrugged. "I don't want there to be."

"There's not," he said.

Suddenly, his heart clenched in a pain he had never known. He had lied to her.

It was the first.

There was a but.

And her name …

Andrea Wallace.

"Then what do you have planned for that Sharpie?" she asked, pulling him away from the heat in his chest.

The tenderness in her eyes was breathtaking. He would be worthy of this woman. He promised himself that he would.

He would tell her about Andrea's emails.

But it wasn't the right time.

"I want us to never forget how right this is between us," he said. "I want us to write our initials on our own sticky notes so that no matter where we are, we know we are right for each other."

"Max," she breathed as her hands fell from his face.

He smiled as he brought the sticky note to the tip of the pen. "We'll do it like in *Gilmore Girls.* We'll write our initials in reverse like Lorelai wanted to do on Rory's graduation day."

"Okay, but you write mine, and I'll write yours," she said.

Max nodded and then got to work and wrote:

$$S M \& F J$$

He peeled off the sticky note and handed it to her. Josie held it between her thumbs and index fingers and stared at it. She peeked up at him through her lashes and smiled. Then she got off the couch and stuck the note on her laptop. When she returned, she took the pad and pen from him.

"You can't change yours, okay?" she instructed.

Then she wrote on her note, peeled it off, and handed it to him.

Max looked down at the square piece of paper, and his heart throbbed at what she had written.

You're my La Vie En Rose.

Although she might not realise this meant everything to him, he knew this was her way of telling him that she could love him.

That her heart, soul, and love would be his.

Max glanced up from the note, and he saw the truth in her eyes.

He reached over and set his palm on the back of her neck. Pulling her lips to his, he stifled her small gasp with his kiss.

Because he might be her *La Vie En Rose.*

But she was the love of his life.

Josie

"And you didn't have sex with him?" Stella asked in disbelief.

Josie set her legal practice and ethics textbook down and noticed that her best friend was no longer sitting at the dining table. Instead, she was standing, staring at Josie as if she had said no to a small pox vaccination.

"I did not have sex with Max last night," she confirmed.

Though it did cross her mind how much she wanted to be with him. Feel things no man had ever given her. The way he kissed her made her breathless, so she could only imagine what it would feel like to be intimate with Max. When he had her lying on the couch with his body covering hers, she thought maybe they'd go further than just the touch of their lips against each other. But his ringing phone had him cursing against her mouth. He had apologised as he got off her and answered it.

It had been his father.

Max needed to head back to the office because the police had made an arrest in connection with the Walsh case his father had been representing in court. Max apologised and said he had to go. Josie didn't mind. There was no way she'd let Max stay with him when he was assisting on the trial of the decade. This morning, it was all over the news. However, the media wasn't allowed to say who exactly was arrested in relation to the case. Max had wished her a good day this morning by text. Josie had wished him an exciting day and had desperately wanted to trade shoes so she could sit in that courtroom.

"But you told him you loved him, right?" Stella asked.

Josie pressed her lips together and shook her head. "I didn't. I mean, not really."

Stella set her hands on her hips. "What does 'not really' even mean?"

"It means …" She trailed off as she played the memory back in her head. That awe-like expression that consumed his face when he had read the sticky note she had written to him.

"Don't leave me hanging like that! What did you say?" Stella sounded desperate, and that had Josie laughing at her.

"It means I told him that he's my *La Vie En Rose*."

Stella's eyes widened. "Holy shit," she breathed.

"Yeah."

Her best friend appeared bewildered as she blinked rapidly at her. "Josie, that's *more* than just love to you."

Stella didn't have to tell her twice.

She knew what it meant the moment she wrote '*La Vie En Rose*' on that sticky note and gave it to Max. She gave him her love and her whole heart.

It was 'I love you' and more.

It was 'my life is yours to love with all your beautiful might.'

"Josie, you're in love with Maxwell Sheridan." Stella sat back down on her seat. "He's your *La Vie En Rose*."

"But—"

"But?"

Josie nervously chewed her bottom lip. "We haven't really spoken about what our feelings meant for well … *us*."

Stella's mouth dropped. "You didn't discuss *actually* being in a relationship?" Her best friend sounded horrified.

"No. He had to go before we could actually put a label on it."

"Do me a favour?"

"And what's that?"

Stella set her hand on Josie's arm. "Define it. For God's sake, define it. Make Max yours already, Josie." Then her best friend got up from the chair and made her way out of the dining room and into the kitchen. "So what do you want for dinner?"

Josie brought her laptop closer to her and lifted the screen. She smiled at the sticky note stuck next to the trackpad of her MacBook.

Her fingers traced their initials he had written.

$$S M \& F J$$

"Just like in *Gilmore Girls*," she whispered.

> **Max:** Did you get your legal practice and ethics assignment in?

It was Wednesday, almost two days since she and Max had expressed their feelings. And in those two days, they had only exchanged text messages between clients and her classes. Josie actually wanted to discuss where their relationship was heading, but she felt it was a conversation to have in person rather than through texts.

Josie grabbed the water bottle from the man behind the counter and smiled. She thanked him and made her way to a free table in the food court of her university's student centre. She had just finished her evidence seminar and was happy to get out of there and relax before her next tutorial. Josie sat on the chair, set her phone on the table, twisted the cap off the bottle, and swallowed several mouthfuls of water. Then she put the cap back on and set the bottle on the table. Picking up her phone, she smiled at the text message Max had sent her.

> **Josie:** Handed it in this morning. How's work going?

> **Max:** I'm back at the office for a few hours to meet a client before I go back to the Supreme court. How are classes?

Josie: How's the case going? Evidence seminar was … well … *eye roll*

Max: Josie, I'm not going to tell you about who was arrested. You know I can't. Can I see you tonight?

Josie: I have a study group for evidence tonight. Tomorrow?

Max: Court all day and then a dinner with the clients I'm representing in an arbitration case.

Josie: Ugh. Friday?

Max: Court all day. Firm dinner that night.

Josie: This. Officially. Sucks. I thought you were done in court with this case?

Max: Yeah, I thought so, too. But my dad wants me there. This weekend?

Josie: Too full-on. I have work, seeing Mum, and assignments. Plus, I have exams coming up, so I've gotta work on prepping for them. Next week?

Max: I have court all next week, too.

Josie: It seems as if we might surpass fifteen days without seeing each other.

Max: Don't say that. I'll move things around so I can see you.

Her chest tightened at his determination. He wanted to see her as desperately as she wanted to see him.

But if he were to cancel on clients and dinners for her, she'd feel horrible for getting in the way of his life. In the way of his career. And Josie would not let that happen.

Josie: Don't move things around for me. You have work, and I have uni. The moment you're free, let me know. I've gotta get to my next class. Have a good rest of your day.

Max: Josephine, you're much more important to me than some pointless, redundant dinners. I'll make time for you. I'll let you know when I can get out of this court case and see you. Just so we're clear, and no misunderstandings occur, I miss you. I miss that smile of yours. I miss the way your lips taste when they're on mine. And I miss the way you breathlessly say my name. I miss the way your body felt on mine. I miss all of you.

Oh.
If Josie was unsure of Max's feelings towards her, she wasn't anymore.
She felt her heart warm at his message.
It was intimate.
And sweet.
She could almost hear him whisper it to her.
Josie shoved her bottle in her bag as she got up, ready to head over to her next tutorial.

Josie: I miss everything about you, too, Maxwell.

Chapter
THIRTEEN

Max

Max: It's been an entire week since I last saw you. This is torture. I'm sitting here in my office waiting for my father before we go to court. How does this week look?

Josie: CRAP! Crap, crap, crap!!! I'm running late for my lecture. I slept in. I spent all night reading cases for contracts. I have another memo of advice due this week. What about you? Court all week?

*M*ax sighed.
Seven days of not seeing her frustrated him more. Add that to the amount of pressure he felt with his father's case and his own clients, and Max was losing it. All he wanted to do was see Josie even if it was just for a minute. Her messages weren't enough. But Max wasn't going to pull her away from her assignments just to feel her lips on his once more.

He couldn't be selfish.

Not when Josie's degree was at stake.

Max knew how tough law school was, and he didn't want to add any more strain on her.

Max: Clients this week. A lot of contracts I have to read and go through.

Josie: So maybe next week?

Max: That means three weeks. No, that can't happen. I need to see you. Even if it's for a minute.

Josie: Just for a minute?

Max: Yes.

The moment he had pressed send, his glass door opened and in stepped Josie, cheeks bright red and breathing heavily. Max dropped his phone on his desk as he got out of his chair.

"What are you—?"

She held the box he hadn't noticed higher. "Cupcakes ..." she said between her panting. "Made ... last ... night ..."

Max went around his desk and approached her. He shook his head unbelievably as he cupped her cheeks.

"I only have a minute." She took a deep breath. "Have only a minute. Super late."

I love you.

It was on the tip of his tongue as he watched her struggle to inhale more breaths.

"Did you run to my office?" he asked, finding it comical that she had.

Josie nodded. "Asked Ruby. I really have to go."

"Okay," he said, and then he kissed her. Deeply and passionately. He controlled this kiss. He dominated her under the coercion of his lips, telling her he missed her in such an intimate way than just with words.

Each flutter of his lips only had him wanting more.

More kisses.

More minutes.

More days in the week with her.

"Max," she breathed as she kissed him.

His tongue traced the seam of her lips, and she gave him access to slip inside and find her tongue. The moment they touched, he groaned as their kissing became frantic.

"Late," she muttered. "I'm so late."

He chuckled as he began to slow the exploration of her mouth until he finished with chaste kisses to her lips.

He pulled back and pressed his thumb to her bottom lip. Then he moved it back and forth. "Go," he urged.

The way her eyelids hooded only made him want her to stay longer. He could see it in her lust-filled eyes that she wanted to stay. So to convince her to leave, he dropped his hands from her face and grasped the box of cupcakes. "Go, Josephine."

She nodded, got on her toes, and pressed a sweet, lingering kiss to his mouth. "That was worth being late to my lecture for."

He chuckled as he watched her spin around and race out of his office and then out of sight. Smiling, he walked back to his desk and set the box down. Max lifted the lid to find his favourite cupcakes inside. Then he noticed the envelope stuck on the inside of the box. Max pulled it off and removed the business card that was inside.

His chest tightened when he saw that it was her business card. He turned it over and read what she wrote.

All this time away from you has only made me miss you more.
Josie

Max said goodbye to his latest clients, an elderly couple who were selling their prime city property to developers, on Thursday afternoon. It had now been ten days since that free minute with Josephine. And seventeen days since he really got to spend time with her.

It was torture being away from her, but timing got the best of them.

Max's new client had made an appointment with him to go

over the contract the developers had given them. Max needed to know what they wanted out of the deal to sell their old house and land. It was one of the rare properties in Melbourne, and they received an offer of thirteen million dollars for it. The couple wanted to make sure they wouldn't be taken advantage of, and Max had agreed to look over the contract. He promised to redraft it if he thought his clients were being screwed over. The first thing he would have to do was contact a property surveyor and a real estate agent. He needed to know what their house and land were worth in the current market.

Max picked up his phone and unlocked it to find Josie's unread message waiting for him. He pressed his thumb to the screen and opened it.

Josie: Sorry, I was in a lecture. Can't do tonight. Will be working on my assignment. Tutor gave us until Monday after he noticed just how much he wanted from us. Thank God for small mercies, huh? I want this done so I can enjoy Rob and Ally's engagement party this weekend. I completely forgot about it. How's the trial going?

Max: Email me if you need any help on your memo or if you want me to read it. You've got this, Josie. Their engagement party is Saturday night. You've got plenty of time. Don't stress yourself out. At least I can finally spend time with you. I've been bloody counting the days until I can.

Josie: So I'm guessing you've missed me just a little bit?

Max: You have no fucking idea. Terribly. I've been missing you terribly.

Josie: I'm tempted to bail on my tutorial right now to see you.

Max: Stay put! What's two more days?

Josie: Nineteen days since we last spent time together.

Max: Nineteen days too long.

His laptop made a pinging sound, and he glanced up to see a new email in his inbox. He set his phone down the moment he saw Andrea's name. It had been some time since her last email. It was nothing new. She was apologetic. She wanted him to email her back. He shouldn't have opened it, but he couldn't help it. He wanted to read her suffering. It was only fair after she kept him in the dark for almost a year.

Max glanced back at his phone to see the ellipses on his screen indicating that Josie was replying to him. Taking a deep breath, he pulled his laptop closer to him and clicked on Andrea's email.

```
To: MaxwellSheridan@GordonSheridan.com.au
From: AndyWallace@gmail.com
Subject: I'm willing to fight for you.

Max,
    I leave for Boston soon. I spoke to Noel
    briefly about you temporarily working
    for G&MC. I could really use you there.
    Please consider taking the job, Max.
    He still doesn't know about what
    happened between us—at least, I don't
    think he does.
    I have to admit I'm a little scared
    to return to Massachusetts to see him
    and Clara together. I used to be so
    angry that they got married. But then
    I realised Clara was the better woman.
    She got what she wanted. She waited and
    worked for it. I ran away from who I
    really wanted.
    I never gave us a chance, Max.
    I want you to give me the chance to
    prove to you that I can be the woman
```

236

```
you've always wanted.
All those messages we shared before he
married her meant everything.
You understood me.
You understood my career the way Noel
couldn't.
Please, Max.
I made the mistake of letting you go.
I know that.
Yours,
Andrea.
```

I made the mistake of letting you go.

He was tempted.

For a single moment, he fell back into his old ways and was tempted.

But Max moved the cursor away from the reply button and reached over and pulled his top drawer open. Max reached inside and pulled out his wallet. He took a deep breath, flipped the wallet open, and removed the piece of paper from inside. Max unfolded it and held it between his thumb and index finger, reading the words that reminded him that someone quite possibly loved him more and had always put him first.

You're my La Vie En Rose.

Josie.

His *La Vie En Rose.*

The love of his life.

So Max did right by her and set the sticky note down and deleted Andrea's email.

Josie

Mamma: Good afternoon, Josephine. Will you be visiting me this weekend? I thought we could have lunch on Sunday. I'd like to talk to you about some stuff.

*J*osie saved her assignment and grasped her phone with both hands, reading her mother's message once more. Over a week and a half ago, her mother was finally fit enough to be released from the hospital. The doctor had given her mother orders to rest and not return to work. That was the only day when work and uni didn't consume Josie's life. It was also the only day Max was free to spend their afternoon together, but she had told him she couldn't see him. Josie wanted to be with him, but no matter how much she wanted to or loved Max, her mother came first.

She felt horrible for lying to him.

She felt even worse knowing he was willing to reschedule a client dinner for her.

When Josie drove her mother home, Stella and West were there and had decorated her mother's living room with balloons and a sign. They had even brought a 'Welcome Home, Em!' cake and flowers. Her mother had cried, and Josie had tears in her eyes. Josie had no idea what she would do without Stella and West in her life. They had no idea how much she appreciated it. The moment her mother asked about Max, Josie felt that sick knot tighten in her stomach. She would tell Max the truth about her mother's health and apologise for keeping it from him for so long.

Now that her mother was feeling much better, Josie felt the strain loosen a fraction. There was still a long way to go, but she was confident that with enough rest, her mother could focus on chemotherapy and fighting cancer.

Josie: Hey, Mamma. Yeah, Sunday works for me. I'm almost finished with this assignment. But are you sure you're feeling well enough to have lunch?

Mamma: I'm feeling great, Josephine. Honest. I'll let you get back to your assignment. I love you.

Josie: I love you, too. I'll call you later.

A knock on her front door had her setting her phone down. Josie got out of her chair and sighed. She didn't have time for visitors. She needed to finish her assignment if she wanted to have a guilt-free weekend—especially since she'd see Max at Ally and Rob's engagement party.

Tomorrow night, she'd tell him the truth about her mother, her feelings, and her want to be something more than just friends who missed each other.

She wanted to define them.

For her heart to know that his called hers home.

Sweeping her brunette hair behind her ear, she made her way down the hall and to the front door. She wasn't expecting visitors, and Stella hadn't said she was expecting any either. Upon reaching the door, she set her hand on the handle, twisted it, and then pulled the door open.

"Max," she breathed in surprise.

That smile of his was flawless and one she missed seeing. "I promise this won't take up too much of your assignment time," he announced.

"What?"

Max pushed past her and entered her apartment. Josie closed the door and spun around, noticing that he was staring at his phone and seemed apprehensive.

"Is everything okay?"

He slipped his phone into his pants pocket and nodded. The nervousness in his eyes gave her no confidence whatsoever.

"Every minute counts." Then he stepped closer to her, leant down, and kissed her cheek. "God, it's so good to see you, Josephine."

The truth replaced the nervousness in his eyes, and she smiled.

"What are you doing here? I thought I would see you tomorrow?"

Max's hands settled on her shoulders for a brief second then slid down her arms, and he grasped her left hand. "I'm still seeing you tomorrow, but I needed to see you tonight. Josephine, can I please have two hours of your night tonight?"

She grinned. "Two hours?"

"That means you'll have enough time to finish your assignment, and I won't feel guilty," he explained.

He had her interested. "Okay. You have me for two hours."

"We're going to have to multitask," he said as he held her hand and led her down the hall and to her bedroom.

"Multitask?"

"Yeah." Max opened her door and pulled her inside. Then he let go of her hand, gently pushed her to the door, and cupped the nape of her neck. His lips found hers, and he stole the breath from her lungs with a simple touch. Just as she was about to part her lips, Max pulled away and shook his head. "Sorry, I only pencilled in like ten seconds of kissing. You have to change."

"What?" She was half-surprised and half-humoured by him.

Max stepped back and walked to her walk-in closet. "Trust me, I love seeing you in jeans and a T-shirt, but where we're going, you're gonna want to wear something a little more formal."

Her eyes scanned his body, and she noticed he was wearing a nice, tight white dress shirt that had buttons with anchors on them and black dress pants. His hair was combed perfectly, and she noticed his leather shoes were polished. He was dressed the part, and she wasn't.

Not wanting to disappoint him and the two hours he had planned for them, Josie walked into her closet and took in her clothes.

"So how was your day?" Max asked as he joined her inside the closet.

Josie let out a light laugh as she began to search for something formal to wear. "Is this us multitasking?"

"Yep," Max said as he pointed at the white dress she had pulled aside to look at. "That's the dress."

"Really?" she asked as she took in the chiffon dress. It was an impulse buy. She had been shopping with Stella when her best friend had begged her to buy the long A-line dress with a sweetheart neckline. The bodice had a corset style design to it and chiffon sleeves that fell off the shoulders. Josie never had an occasion to wear such a beautiful dress.

Not until today it seemed.

"Really. It's actually perfect," Max said as he pulled it from her closet. "So how was your day?"

"It was okay. Short lecture today since it's so close to exams. My lecturer wanted us to focus on our assignments and exam prep. How about you?"

Max walked out of her closet and set the dress on her bed.

Then he turned and faced her. "Stressful. Turns out this couple I'm representing was about to get screwed over by developers who wanted to buy their land for an apartment complex. It means negotiations and more contract redrafts. All right, I'm gonna let you change, and I'll be on the other side of the door to continue this conversation."

Josie walked out of her closet and watched as Max left her room and closed the door behind him.

"So yeah, my day's been stressful. But I was happy to see you," Max continued from the other side of the door.

She shook her head as she felt her cheeks warm at his admission. Josie glanced at the white dress and then reached for the hem of her shirt. She lifted it over her head and let it fall to her bed. Then she unsnapped her jeans and shimmied them down her legs until she could step out of them. She frowned when she realised that she was wearing a black bra and underwear set. It would show under the white dress.

Sighing, she returned to her closet and went to her drawers. She pulled the top one open and searched until she found her strapless white lace bra and matching panties. After staring at the two pieces of lingerie, she felt her heart rapidly beat in her chest. She didn't want to presume Max would ever see them, but there was hope. That, and she couldn't wear black underneath white chiffon. Deciding to act before she changed her mind, Josie removed her black bra and panties and changed into the lacy white set. Then she collected her black undergarments and returned to her bed.

She picked up her jeans and shirt and walked to her en suite bathroom. She disposed of the dirty clothes into the hamper and glanced at her reflection. She was glad her brunette waves appeared tame and didn't go frizzy. And she was glad that she had put on some makeup this morning, but it was too simple. Josie pulled the first bathroom drawer open and retrieved her makeup bag.

She didn't have a lot of time, so she had to retouch her makeup quickly. She applied powder where she could, added some blush, and applied a small amount of dark blue eyeliner. Then she curled her eyelashes, coated them with mascara, and reached for her pink glossy lipstick. With the white dress, she decided to keep the colours as gentle as possible. She spread the pink lipstick on her lips and was happy to see that in her rush, her makeup appeared decent. It wasn't the best job she had ever done, considering she was quite good at it after watching hours and hours of YouTube tutorials. Finally, Josie dug her fingers into her brunette locks and shook them back and forth to tease her hair.

She quickly returned to the foot of her bed, leant down, and removed the dress from the hanger. She pulled the back zip down and stepped into the dress. She threaded her arms through the off-the-shoulder straps and reached around to pull the zip up. Her arms started to ache once she struggled to zip the dress higher than halfway.

Josie gave up, rested her palms on her breasts, and held her dress in place as she yelled out, "Max, I need you in here!"

He was in her room within seconds.

"Wow," he breathed when she glanced over her shoulder and saw him with his mouth gaped. His awe-like expression was one she'd never forget.

"Zipper's stuck," she said.

Max swallowed hard and then nodded. "Right," he said and walked towards her.

When he was behind her, her chest heaved as she felt his finger trace a line down her back. It was so intimate. One simple touch and she was dizzy. She felt the zip tug twice until it zipped all the way. Then his hands held her hips, and he whispered, "Change of plans for the next few seconds. Going to sacrifice a few things so I can do this …"

His lips pressed against her left shoulder.

They softly trailed up and settled on the curve of her neck for a few seconds. When he pulled away, his breath graced her skin as if he were tattooing the feel of his lips to her skin.

Then in a soft voice, he said, "You're so beautiful, Josephine."

Her eyelids hooded as she fell in love with the way his voice became hoarse as he complimented her.

It was so hard to hold back her love.

But she had to.

For the remainder of the two hours they had, she had to stick to his plan.

She was sure he hadn't pencilled in 'Josie telling me she loves me' in his two-hour plan. So she took a step away from his touch and then spun around.

"I have to grab a few things and put on my shoes. Meet me in the lounge in a few?"

He nodded. "Sure thing."

Josie grasped the bottom of her dress and lifted it off the ground. Then she made her way back to her closet.

"Josephine," he called out.

She glanced over at her door to find Max standing by it. "Yeah?"

"I just wanted to say that I ..." He closed his mouth and inhaled deeply. "I think you're the most beautiful, genuine woman I have ever met in my life." And then he was out of her room seconds later, leaving her with her need to say, "I love you," on her lips.

Soon, she promised her impatient heart.

She'd tell him everything soon.

Chapter
FOURTEEN

Max

G *oddamn.*

Josephine Faulkner made him so needy and reckless.

He had almost confessed he loved her in her bedroom. It was definitely not the ideal location to tell her.

No one should ever hear an, "I love you," while they were in the closet.

And now, he was confined in his car with her. Her perfume seemed to linger in the air and strengthen the moment he breathed in. Every part of him ached to touch her. To have those big blue eyes look up at him as he whispered how much he adored her.

It had been eighteen days.

Eighteen.

Eighteen days since they were last together in her apartment.

Eighteen days since he had really kissed her.

Max turned off the engine and pulled the key out. He had parked outside a supermarket on the way to her surprise.

"Max?" Josie said.

He glanced over to see her staring at the shop. "We have to

pick up some food."

Then she faced him and asked, "Where are we going?"

Max reached over and tucked her hair behind her ear. "Didn't schedule enough time to tell you. Come on. We've got like an hour and a half left before we have to get you back home to finish your assignment."

"Fine." She sighed and pulled back. Josie pulled on the car door handle and got out.

Max took a deep breath in hopes his erratic heart would calm, but it was to no avail. It only drove that organ in his chest to beat faster. Max got out of his Porsche and walked around it until he stood next to Josie who waited by the passenger side. Countless pairs of eyes were on them, and he heard someone whisper, "Are they famous?" He grasped Josie's hand and led her inside the store.

"What kind of food do we have to get?" she asked as he led her farther into the store to the aisle he was looking for.

"The only kind we can bring with us."

When they had reached the confectionary aisle, she laughed as they walked down it.

"So lollies and chocolates?"

"Yep," he said as he dropped her hand and pointed at the shelves of junk food. "You can only bring your favourite confectionary with us."

"That's easy!" she announced and then pointed to his right. "That pink bag over there."

Max reached up and removed the bag from the hook. Then he took in the picture of the cartoon man with the moustache. "These marshmallows are you favourite?"

She took the bag from him and nodded. "They're filled with this strawberry jelly. They're amazing."

Her eyes twinkled, and he loved the sight of her excitement.

"All right, I believe you. Come on. Checkouts are this way." Max took the bag of marshmallows from her and made his way to the registers, Josie following.

He reached the self-serve machine and scanned Josie's marshmallows through. He placed the bag on the scale and pressed on the screen to pay.

"Oh, hang on, I've got it," she said as she opened her black clutch.

Max ignored her and pulled his wallet from his pocket. He flipped it open, pulled out his card, and tapped it across the eftpos machine.

"Wait, no—"

Max returned his card to its slot and his wallet to his pocket. Then he grabbed the receipt and picked up the marshmallows. He handed them to Josie with a smile. "I sacrificed fighting with you about paying for your favourite lollies so that I can tell you how beautiful you are. We don't have time, Josephine."

The annoyance faded from her face. "Fine."

Max cupped the nape of her neck and brought her lips to his in a chaste kiss as he gazed down at her. "You're so beautiful, Josephine."

I love you, he thought.

But he wouldn't say I love you in a supermarket.

Not when she had given him much sweeter declarations.

Josephine Faulkner deserved the best out of life, and Max was working his way towards giving her everything.

"Thank you," Max said, handing his keys to the man who had held the sign with his last name on it. Even he had to admit that Dominic Gomez had outdone himself. All Max had done was call in a favour from his client, but he was impressed.

"You're welcome, Mr Sheridan," the Arts Centre employee said, eyes gleaming with joy knowing that he would soon be driving and parking a Porsche.

"The Arts Centre Melbourne?" Josie questioned as she tilted her head back and took in the spire inspired by the Eiffel Tower and a ballerina's tutu.

He was a little disappointed that they weren't here later at night when the building was lit up and a stunning sight. But unfortunately, this was the only time he could get his favour done.

"Yep."

Max held the marshmallows by his right side and took her hand with his left. She glanced down at their hands and smiled.

When her eyes lifted to meet his, that smile of hers deepened.

What he had said in the supermarket was true.

She was beautiful.

"And what are we doing here at the Arts Centre?"

"The Australian Ballet," he announced as he led her towards the front entry.

Josie hurried her footsteps to meet his. "We're seeing the ballet?"

"We're seeing their dress rehearsal for a new show," he clarified.

When they were at the front doors, Max saw his client waiting for them with a bouquet of red roses in his hands. Max led Josie to him, and Dominic Gomez smiled. He was one of the world's most talented male dancers. And at twenty-eight, Dominic had danced for the world's greatest ballet companies.

"Ah, you must be Miss Faulkner," Dominic said. Max saw the desire fill his green eyes. He appreciated what he saw, and Josie in that goddamn white dress of hers was a beautiful goddess.

"Oh, my God," she breathed next to him. She pulled her hand away from his, and he turned to see her hands covered her mouth. Her blue eyes were wide in shock and disbelief. "You're ... you're ..."

Dominic smiled and glanced over at Max. "I think she knows who I am."

Josie removed her hands from her mouth and said, "Of course, I know who you are. I saw your performance with the Paris Opera Ballet on TV last year. I read an article online that you had left the company."

"Wow," Dominic said, sounding surprised. "I had no idea Mr Sheridan knew a beautiful woman so interested in ballet."

She blushed. "I'm sure that's not true."

"Don't be so modest. You're beautiful, Miss Faulkner. I've been Mr Sheridan's client for a few years now, and he has never once asked me for a favour. I've offered to give him tickets to my shows numerous times, but he's always declined. So his call was definitely a surprise."

"Dominic, I told you; it's Max."

"And I told you it was a sign of my respect for you, Mr Sheridan." Dominic stepped forward and handed Josie the bouquet of roses. "These are for you, Miss Faulkner."

"For me?"

He nodded. "Of course. Mr Sheridan insisted that I be the one to give you his flowers."

Josie gazed down at the roses and then turned to face him. The tenderness in her eyes was a sight of their own. So beautiful and bright. "These are from you?"

Max beamed at her. "That okay?"

"Incredibly okay."

He hated that he didn't pencil in enough time to really kiss her.

Then the doors opening and a woman stepping out caught his and Josie's attention, breaking the connection their eyes made. "Dominic, they're ready," she announced.

"Ah, yes. Thank you, Susanne. You both ready to go inside?"

Josie nodded enthusiastically.

Max grinned, knowing she was about to experience something unique and tailored just for her. She followed Dominic inside, and Max quickened his pace to walk next to her.

"Wow," Josie breathed as they made it down the hall. She had stopped for a second to take in the pictures on the walls.

"Have you ever been here before?" Max asked.

She shook her head as they continued to follow Dominic. "No. I've always wanted to, but I couldn't. I don't know. It sounds stupid, but I couldn't get myself to commit to seeing a show here."

"Have you ever seen the ballet performed live?"

They walked downstairs, and he noticed Josie bite her lip. Finally, when they reached the bottom level, she said, "I went to the Royal Palace Theatre with my father when I was eight and saw a performance. It was beautiful. It was one of the last things we did together before he left us and went to Germany."

"Oh, I'm sorry."

Josie shook her head with a smile. "Don't be, Max."

"Just in through here," Dominic said. He held the door open, and Josie stepped away from him to enter the theatre with Max right behind her.

When they stepped inside, he heard Josie's sharp inhale.

"Welcome to the State Theatre," Dominic said. "Follow me

to your seats."

And they did.

They went down the stairs until they were close to the stage. They reached the fifth row when Dominic stepped aside and pointed at the row.

"Your seats are reserved."

Max glanced over at the row to find two reserved signs on the seats in the middle.

Josie slid into the row first, and Max stood there a moment to face Dominic.

"Thanks for this, Dominic." Max held out his hand, and the ballet dancer grasped it and shook it firmly.

"You got me out of my contract with the Paris Opera Ballet so I could come home early when my father was sick. I'm the one who's thankful, Mr Sheridan. Because of you, he was able to see me dance before he passed away." Dominic smiled and then ended their handshake. "She's beautiful, Mr Sheridan. I hope you both enjoy the performance."

"And ...?"

"It's all ready to go," Dominic assured with a grin. "We tweaked and used an old routine to make it work."

Max sighed in relief. "I appreciate it."

"I can see that. Go sit with her. It'll start in a few minutes."

Max nodded, turned, and made his way down the row to find Josie already sitting in her seat, staring up at the high ceilings.

"This is so incredible. There are like five levels!"

The wonder in her eyes and the amazement in her voice had him sitting down in his seat and setting the bag of marshmallows next to him. Then he reached out and grasped her hand and squeezed.

"It's about to start."

Josie lowered her chin, and that tenderness in her eyes from before didn't disappear. It had stayed and magnified as her blue eyes shimmered before him. "Max."

"Yeah?"

"This is the most incredible, thoughtful thing anyone has ever done for me."

He shifted in his seat, and with his free hand, he cupped the side of her face with his palm. "The show hasn't even started."

249

"I know. But even if this was it. Just us sitting in the theatre where so many of the world's best ballet companies have performed would have been more than enough."

Max leant in close and whispered, "That wouldn't have been enough. Even after we watch this show, it's not enough."

Her free hand wrapped around his wrist and in a low voice, she said, "You're absolutely more than enough for me."

A pang of guilt erupted in him.

He wasn't.

Not just yet.

But he would be.

Josie

I wish I was more than enough for you.

It had almost slipped from her lips.

Her insecurity over her worthiness of Maxwell Sheridan made an appearance. He had gone to so much effort to plan a two-hour activity together. And it was beautiful and thoughtful and everything that made her love him more.

Suddenly, she felt her clutch vibrate in her lap. Josie pulled away from Max's touch, picked up her clutch, and opened it. She took out her phone to see a new message from Stella.

> **Stella:** Why aren't you home? Have you been abducted? I see no ransom on my door. I thought we were going to have ice cream sandwiches for dinner after you finished your assignment. *plotting your demise*

Josie laughed and showed Max the screen.

He read the message and chuckled. "You should reply to her before the show starts, or she might think you really did get abducted."

She giggled. "You're right."

> **Josie:** Max took me to a dress rehearsal for the Australian Ballet.

Stella: THE. Australian. Ballet?

Josie: Yes.

Stella: Do you realise who Max is?

Josie: Huh?

Stella: In the world of Gilmore, he's a ...

Josie: This is NOT the time!

Stella: LUKE.

Stella: He IS Luke.

Josie: Shhh! I'll see you at home.

Stella: Nah. I've already walked out of the apartment. I've just packed my things, and I'm gonna spend the weekend with West. Which means you get some peace to finish that assignment. Also, pics that you're with Max or it didn't happen.

Groaning, she glanced over to see Max staring out at the stage.
"Max ..."
He craned his neck and smiled at her. "Everything okay?"
"Stella wants a proof picture."
"Really?"
"Yep," she said with a laugh.
But it wasn't just for Stella. Josie wanted one for them. They didn't have any pictures together, and she wanted to remember this moment. She wanted proof of the most wonderful thing anyone had ever done for her.
"All right," Max said as he shifted closer to her.
Josie opened her camera and held it in front of them. They smiled, and she pressed the button to capture the image. Then she craned her neck slightly and looked at him. The soft smile on her lips mirrored his as his eyes found hers. Then she heard

the sound of her camera's shutter, realising Max had reached out and pressed the button on her screen.

"Don't send this one to her," he whispered as he kissed her.

The sounds of her phone's camera taking their photo echoed in the empty theatre. Josie pulled the phone away from him and concentrated on the feel of his lips. Her phone ended up on her lap as she cupped his face and deepened the kiss. He made her so needy and desperate.

He made her want to tell him she loved him without fear of consequences.

Maxwell Sheridan made her defenceless when it came to him.

He dragged his lips over hers slowly until their kiss ended with the soft flutter of his lips to hers.

She smiled against his mouth when he asked, "How did I ever live without you?"

Josie pulled back and wiped his bottom lip with the pad of her thumb. "I believe you managed to suffice."

"Barely," he said between his heavy breaths. Then he rested his forehead on hers.

The loud sounds of a drum roll filled the theatre, and Josie broke away from him to watch the curtains part. Mystified at the black stage in front of her, Josie sat in her chair and held her breath, waiting to see just what happened. She had heard the new Australian Ballet performance was an original production and not the classics that would be performed on opening night at the Arts Centre next week.

That drum roll she heard faded into the strum of a guitar.

It was soft.

And suddenly, the darkness slowly faded into light, and in the middle of the stage was a ballerina in a white and silver romantic tutu. Her arms wrapped around her as the guitar played the soft song. The ballerina turned her head, and Josie followed to see Dominic Gomez on stage. He was to the right of the stage with his back to her. Then Dominic made a soft, perfect turn, and he found the ballerina. His palm settled on his chest as he gazed at her.

His face softened, and his arms reached out to her.

The ballerina untangled her arms and curtsied in a low bend. She was poised and graceful. It was beautiful to see her body move. Then she extended her foot behind her as if to tell Dominic it was time.

Their love could begin.

The violins began, and Dominic and the ballerina moved in sync. Their positioning was phenomenal as they transitioned to each move so fluidly that it was breathless.

And when they met it was magical.

Dominic set his hand on her hip and held her close to his body as if it weren't close enough.

His other hand settled on her hip, and then he lifted her so flawlessly that Josie gasped in awe.

The violins continued to play as they danced before her.

"What is that song?" she wondered out loud.

Max grasped her left hand and whispered, "A violin version of Elvis Presley's 'Can't Help Falling in Love.'"

"Really?" Josie couldn't take her eyes off the dancers as they leapt together in a series of perfect jetés.

"The show is called *A Testament to Love*. It's all about love songs and the power they have."

It was love song after love song.

It transitioned from Dominic and his female love interest to several dancers coming on stage trying to tear them apart until finally, at the final song, they found each other in the middle of the stage and his arms wrapped around her. It was beautiful. The lights dimmed, and Josie jumped out of her seat and applauded, not caring that her phone fell out of her lap and onto the floor. Her vision blurred as she noticed she had begun to cry. She reached up and quickly wiped the tears away before they could fall down her cheeks.

She had been incredibly moved by the show.

It was so beautiful and perfect.

The beauty and freedom.

The connection and grace.

The turns and artistry.

It was everything she remembered about ballet.

For years, she had resented the art.

But right now, she respected it.

Then something appeared on stage. It was a hologram of a scripture on the stage wall. Josie glanced up to see that it was projected from above.

She watched the curves disappear, and then suddenly they spelt out.

For Josephine.

She gasped at the sight and just as she was about to turn and throw her arms around him, the message disappeared, and the dancers returned to the stage. They stood in front of her and Max and held their arms out to them. Then the strumming of a guitar returned, and they began to dance freely and beautifully to the music that played.

And she recognised that tune.

She recognised each chord and each unsung lyric.

"*La Vie En Rose*," she breathed as tears consumed her eyes.

Her eyes fell closed as she listened to the way her heart beat to the gentle music. She swayed as she took in her mother's favourite song. Slowly, she opened her eyes to see Dominic gently caress the ballerina's cheek as the song came to a slow end. And when it did, he hugged her tightly.

The two dancers parted and turned to face Josie and Max. They curtsied and bowed then walked off the stage, leaving them alone in the empty theatre.

Her heart pounded in her chest. It was anxious. It demanded the freedom the dancers had on the stage.

Josie slowly turned and faced Max. He was so beautiful. No Dominic Gomez with his dancer's body and talent could ever reach the beauty of Maxwell Sheridan.

And the way Max looked at her as if he truly did see her as remarkably beautiful had her breathing out, "I love you."

His eyes widened, and lips parted slightly.

Suddenly, she couldn't breathe.

His silence made it hard for her heart to make another beat.

Her eyes stung as tears threatened. Josie had exposed herself to heartbreak. To another one of life's rejections. But it was the truth. She was so in love with Max. And maybe she had crossed a line, but she couldn't hold it in anymore.

To her relief, Max's lips slowly spread into a smile as he uttered, "I love you, too, Josephine."

He loved her.

Max loved her.

He bent his knees and wrapped his arms around her back, and she looped her arms around his neck, and he lifted her.

"I love you, I love you, I love you," she whispered in his ear.

"I love you, Josephine," he said the moment he set her down, and his palms cupped the nape of her neck.

And she believed him.

His thumb pressed against her jaw as he said in a soft voice, "I love you. I love you. I love you, Josephine Faulkner."

And his lips found hers and continued to whisper his love between small moments of their passionate kiss.

On the drive back to her apartment, Max kept his fingers entwined with hers. She would sneak peeks to find the contented smile on his face and would breathe out a sigh of relief that her love wasn't unrequited.

He loved her.

She loved him.

And after that earth-shattering kiss, he held her tightly and said he had to get her home so she could finish her assignment. He also made promises about taking her to the ballet on opening night to see the full show. Max had told her that the *La Vie En Rose* dance was just for her and wouldn't be featured in the actual performance. That Dominic and the other dancers had made small tweaks from a previous routine to fit *La Vie En Rose* specially for Josie. For a second, she was sad she wouldn't see it again, but she knew it was a performance made just for her.

Josie unlocked her apartment door and pushed it open. Then she spun around and faced Max who was holding her bouquet of red roses and the marshmallows he'd bought her but hadn't had the chance to eat. The ballet performance they had watched was so intoxicating she couldn't take her eyes off it. The way the two danced and symbolised each love song was spectacular.

"Do you want to come inside?" she asked, hoping he'd say yes.

Max's eyes shimmered as a small smile tugged at his lips.

"Sure. I'll stay for a bit, and then I'll go."

She nodded as she spun around and made her way farther into her apartment. Max stepped inside, closed the door behind her, and followed her down the hall and into the kitchen. Josie watched as he set her roses and marshmallows down with a smile. He was so careful not to bend or destroy the bouquet. As she took him in, she couldn't help how moved his "I love you" was. She replayed it over and over again in her head.

Josie set her clutch down next to her flowers and set her hand on his arm.

"*Josephine* ..."

She shook her head.

His love made her want more.

His love made her heart desperately plead for more.

His love made her want him in every possible way.

Pulling him away from the counter, she set her hands on his strong arms and looked into his eyes. The love was there. Bright and breathtaking. The gleam was one she'd never forget.

"I love you, Max," she whispered as she walked them back and in the direction of her bedroom.

His eyelids hooded. "Your assignment ...?"

She shook her head. "Almost done. And right now, it is the last thing I want to do."

Max's large hands found her hips. "And what's more important than your law degree?"

"*You*," she breathed. "You're more important."

"God, I love you," he uttered as he pulled her body to his.

Josie gasped at the contact, and he quickly pressed his lips to hers, taking her by surprise. She smiled against his mouth as he dug his fingers into her hips.

He kissed her with sheer abandonment as if this was the last time he'd ever kiss her.

Each flutter of his lips made her heart ache and soar.

And when she playfully bit his bottom lip, he groaned and broke their contact.

"Are you sure?" he asked, panting.

She nodded, and her hands left his jaw, and she reached out and held his hand. Taking a deep breath, she decided that tonight she would give herself to him. All the parts. The raw. The needy. The selfish. And most importantly, the entirety of her heart. She was Max's, and she intended to be his in every intimate way. Josie led him to her bedroom and opened the door. She stepped inside and let go of Max's hand. The moment he closed the door, she spun around to find his fingers against the sticky note she had stuck on her door.

The same sticky note he had written for her.

S M & F ⌣

Max turned and faced her. "Why is it on the back of your door?"

Heat consumed her cheeks as she dropped her eyes to her hands, afraid to tell him the truth. Afraid that he'd think it was childish and stupid.

Max set his index finger under her chin and lifted her eyes to find his. "Why is my sticky note on the back of your door?"

He made her so breathless under his curious gaze. Josie licked her lips, took a deep breath, and answered, "So that when I start my day, I always know we're right for each other. I walk out of my room knowing that you're right for me and I'm right for you. And I return knowing just the same."

"That's beautiful," he said in a hoarse voice, and his lips found hers again.

This kiss was so different from all the others.

It was soft.

It was ruthless.

It tasted like love as her heart clenched at the feel of his hands tugging at her dress zipper. Max's tongue swept across her lip, and she moaned his name and allowed his tongue to find hers.

His tongue slid perfectly against hers.

Over and over.

Josie felt hot all over as she grasped his shirt and brought him even closer to her. The air between them was thick and heavy with lust and need and want.

"Max," she begged, and her fingers found the button of his shirt, urging him.

Max pulled the zipper of her dress down, and it loosened around her. He took a step back, and her hands fell to her sides. He seemed conflicted and amazed.

Feeling brave, Josie freed her arms from the straps and shimmied out of the dress, standing before him in her white strapless bra, underwear, and her heels. Max balled his fists as he swallowed hard.

Josie reached around her and found her bra clasp when Max stepped forward and shook his head. "Turn around, Josephine."

And she did.

She glanced over her shoulder to see him step towards her, and his finger traced a horizontal line above her clasp. She heard him murmur, "Beautiful," as he unclasped her strapless bra and it landed on the floor. Josie stepped out of her heels and missed the height it gave her. She turned around and tilted her head back to look into Max's eyes. His irises had darkened when he took in her naked breasts, and she noticed the flash in his brown eyes when she pressed her thumbs into the elastic band of her lace underwear.

Josie heard a small inhale as she bent her knees, pulling the lingerie down her legs and to her ankles. When she stood straight, she stepped out of them and tucked her hair behind her ear.

Before she was even able to say a word, Max's hot lips were on hers, and he walked her back, kissing her relentlessly until the back of her legs hit the edge of her bed. She let out a gasp, and Max gently pushed her down on the bed, his hard body pressed against her. Josie widened her legs and his erection pressed against her, causing her to moan. The urgency in them built as they continued to kiss and her hands skimmed the sides of his body. Max's palms cupped her breasts, and his thumb circled her nipple. Josie was losing it. Normally, she controlled the pleasure, but with Max, she fought for it.

He took the power from her and tortured her with calculated moves. Max's lips left hers as he pressed open-mouthed kisses on her chin.

To her neck.

Lower.

A kiss pressed against her collarbone.

Even lower.

Until his breath caressed the swell of her breasts.

Her hands left his hips and cupped his head as Max dragged his tongue across her left nipple, causing her fingers to grasp his hair as he licked, nipped, sucked, and kissed each breast.

"Max," she begged.

His hips bucked, and his hardness pressed against her core.

She let out a moan of frustration when he pulled away.

She needed so much more.

She needed him inside her.

Max got off the bed, kicked off his shoes, peeled off his socks, and his hands found his belt buckle.

Josie had sat herself up and licked her lips before she asked, "Do you have a condom?"

He nodded and reached into his pocket and pulled out his wallet. Josie reached out and took it from him. Max began to undress as she opened his wallet to find a yellow sticky note stuck in front of the card slots.

Her heart came to a roaring stop as she took in the note she wrote him.

You're my La Vie En Rose.

And how true it was.

Her love for him written down long before she expressed the words for him to hear. She blinked away the tears that made an appearance, completely touched that he kept it with him.

"I take you with me," he said, getting her attention. Josie looked up to see him pull his shirt over his head. "You go where I go, Josephine."

God, she loved him.

The truth in his eyes had her heart throbbing in her chest.

She needed him.

Desperately.

Nothing she could say could truly express what his words meant to her. Josie watched as he unfastened his belt, unsnapped his black dress pants, and pulled them and his underwear down. He stood gloriously naked before her.

Her eyes fell to his length to find him hard and impressively long and thick.

She pulled out the condom from the notes slot and let his wallet fall to the floor. Then she handed him the protection and shuffled back to the middle of the bed.

Max tore the condom packet with his teeth and pulled

out the rubber. He had wrapped his fist around himself and pumped twice before he expertly and flawlessly rolled the latex down his hard length until it was properly on. Then Max climbed onto the bed and covered her body with his.

Josie reached up and wrapped her fingers around his arms as he kissed her. The moment he slid his erection against her core, she gasped, and his tongue thrust into her mouth, mirroring the movements of his hips.

"Max," she pleaded.

Thrust.

Slide.

Her fingers dug into his skin as she bucked her hips.

Wanting.

Needing more friction between them.

"Oh, God … Josephine …"

"Please," she whispered against his mouth, and she opened her eyes to see him pull back and nod.

Her hand had fallen away from his right arm before he shoved a hand between them and fisted himself. Then she felt him nudge at her entrance, and her chest heaved in anticipation.

His eyes met hers. "Are you sure?"

She smiled. If she wasn't so desperate to have him inside her, she'd laugh. Instead, she nodded and breathed, "Yes."

Max slowly pushed inside her, and Josie gasped.

It had been so long.

So long since she'd felt the touch of another.

But never had she felt the touch of a man who loved her.

She had never been *this* intimate.

This slow.

This loving.

She had never had this connection before.

The sweet burn from him stretching her had her clutching his hips, urging him for more. Max took the hint, and with a hard thrust, he completely filled her to the hilt.

She was full.

So incredibly full.

Max's body fell on hers, and she felt his heart beat against hers as his lips found her neck. He stayed still, allowing her the time to adjust to his size.

Josie needed him to move.

She needed to feel more.

She grasped the side of his head and pulled his lips from her neck to return to hers. She kissed him with urgency.

With crazy desperation.

It was as if Max had snapped. He pulled out of her and slammed into her, causing her to gasp so loudly.

Then he inched out and entered her slowly.

Hard.

Slow.

In.

And out.

Again.

And again.

He discovered his rhythm, finding that sweet spot as he slid inside and out of her.

Her hips met each thrust as she moaned into his mouth.

He gave her pleasure.

He tortured her when he slowed his pace and then sped up.

"God, Max!" she cried as his hips flexed, and she felt him throb inside her.

"You, Josie," he groaned and pulled back to look at her. "I love you." Then he shoved a hand between them and rubbed circles above where they joined. She clenched around him and began to writhe.

He entered her and whispered, "I love you."

He pulled out of her and groaned, "You …"

She exploded to a thousand songs playing in her head when he had breathed, "Are my *La Vie En Rose*."

And Max finally came with the words, "Are the love of my life," leaving his lips and pressing against hers.

Chapter
FIFTEEN

Max

"*Max!*" Josie moaned as his fingers dug into her hips and moved her up and down his hard length. "Oh, God ... right ... there ..."

Last night, after their first time together, he had reached for his wallet and noticed that he had run out of condoms. Josie had told him that she had an unopened box in her drawer. After checking the expiry date and seeing they were still good to use, he had made love to her twice more before she led them to the shower and he brought her to orgasm with his tongue. When she had come down from her high, they took turns slowly washing each other until the water had turned cold and the steam had dissipated. It was crazy just how insatiable they were.

They couldn't get enough.

Max couldn't get enough.

"Christ, *fuck!*" he cursed as she rode him harder. Max wrapped an arm around her and sat up. Josie's hands found his jaw as she rode him, eyes never leaving his.

God, she was beautiful.

Sweat glistened her breasts.

Her blue eyes had that love to them.

And her cheeks flushed.

This was the second time this morning that they were making loving.

He had woken her up with the kisses he peppered on her lips, cheek, jaw, neck, and chest.

"Max, I'm … close … oh, God. Oh, God!"

His hips snapped up, taking over and thrusting into her again and again until he felt her tighten around him, and she came, moaning his name.

He flipped them over so she was on her back, satisfied with that slack smile on her face. Max grasped her waist and flexed his hips, pumping into her until he felt the familiar tingling at the bottom of his spine.

Josie grasped the back of his neck, whispered, "Come for me, Max," and bucked her hips to meet his thrusts.

It had taken two lazy thrusts before he came, shooting his release into the condom. Max collapsed on top of her, squashing his chest against her breasts. He was short of breath and needed a minute. Josie reached up and stroked the back of his head.

"What time is it?" she asked in a soft voice.

Max pressed his hands into the mattress and lifted himself off her, realising he was probably too heavy for her.

"I'm not sure." He reached out and picked up his phone from her bedside table. He pressed the home button to see he had missed calls from Rob and Noel. He ignored them and took in the time. "It's just after six."

She sighed and pulled her hand away from the back of his head. "I have to go open the store. Nadia already prepped all the batter for this morning."

"So we can't stay in bed?"

"I really wish we could," she said, and Max rolled off her. "Do you want to shower first?"

"You don't mind?"

Josie reached out and brought the blanket up to cover her naked body. "I'm sure. While you're in there, I'll grab you a towel."

Max leant over and kissed her on the lips. Then he got out of bed and made his way into her en suite bathroom, closing

263

the door behind him. Max went to the toilet, pulled off the condom, and threw it into the bowl. He had ripped off some toilet paper, cleaned himself up, and dropped it in the toilet before he flushed it and made his way to Josie's shower.

Josie handed him his belt as he dropped the towel she had given him onto her bed. He grasped it in his hand and ducked down and kissed her full on the mouth.

She whimpered the moment he pulled away.

"You sore?"

She opened her eyes and bit back a grin. "A little."

Max reached out and grasped the sash of her silk dressing gown she'd put on while he was in the shower. "Really hate that you have to go to work."

"Me, too. But I can't call in sick. I don't want to stress Ally out just so I can spend today in bed with you. It's her engagement party tonight," she reminded.

"Her *make-up* engagement party to please her father," he corrected. "Trust me, Rob and Ally don't want any of this."

Josie gripped his wrist and pulled it away from her dressing gown sash. "Can you do me a favour?"

"Anything."

"My laptop is in the dining room. My emails should still be up. I have my email to Johanna drafted. My password is EdithPiaf. It's one word. Do you mind reading it while I shower just to see if I sound reasonable and not a horrible person?"

He kissed her cheek and then nodded. "Yeah, I'll read it now." Then he threaded his belt through the loops of his pants and watched Josie go to her bathroom. When the door closed behind her, Max buckled his belt in place and made his way out of her bedroom. Max combed his damp hair back and walked towards the dining room.

He pulled out the seat and sat down on it. He pressed the space bar, and the laptop came to light. Max typed in Josie's password, EdithPiaf. He knew she was the French singer who first sang *La Vie En Rose*. He had discovered it when he had

asked Dominic Gomez of the Australian Ballet to play it last
night for Josie. Even Max had to admit he was moved by just
how beautiful Dominic and his wife danced together on stage.

When her MacBook accepted the password, her Safari
browser was already on the screen. He noticed all her open tabs.
They were all civil court cases that had to do with contracts. He
was impressed to see some of the names of the cases. She was
going beyond the recommended readings and finding her own
cases for her assignment and references. Max clicked on the tab
for her email and began to read the draft on the screen.

```
To: Johanna.K.Faulkner@hotmail.de
From: Josie.Faulkner@hotmail.com
Re: Hello, Josie.
```

Dear Johanna,
    Thank you so much for reaching out to
    me. I must say I was actually shocked
    to find it was from you. In the fourteen
    years since you met my father, you have
    not once reached out to me. In fact,
    I had to hear about your engagement by
    reading the paper.
    I'm pretty sure the title was: *Australian
    Ambassador to Germany set to marry
    German political leader's daughter.*
    And the first sentence was: *True love
    has hit the diplomatic world with the
    Australian Ambassador set to marry into
    German political royalty—in a move that
    is set to benefit the Australian/German
    relationship.*
    If I sound bitter, I am.
    But I think I'm *allowed* to be bitter
    for a minute.
    Anyways, I'm over it.
    Why?
    Because a very wise man in my life told
    me that I knew what the right thing was
    and that I would do it.

I understand why you haven't told my father of your desire to get in touch with me; I'm not on speaking terms with him. I need some space from him. He's disappointed me for far too long, and I have a lot in my life he will never understand. Just like I won't understand parts of his life.

The truth is he isn't my father anymore. He's Heidi and Angelika's.

They've had thirteen and eleven years with him, respectively.

I had eight.

I'm going to be twenty-three.

He's missed a whole lifetime.

Sometimes people do things out of spite, and that leaves them bitter.

I am that person.

I did things to hurt him. I went out of my way to do those things, and that, therefore, hurt my mother. I dated men he would never approve of. I was scared to date men who treated me well because I was afraid that meant my dad would win. That he would approve and that my rebellion would be over.

But life has a funny way of putting you in your place.

And well, I was already re-evaluating my choices before I connected with this particular man in my life, but he made me be a better person. I never want to disappoint him. So to honour him and do right by him, I am going to do the right thing.

I would like to get to know Heidi and Angelika.

And you, too, Johanna.

I have not been particularly fair to you.

You're my half-sisters' mother.
My stepmother.
When I was younger, I said awful things, but I just wasn't mature enough to understand that you love my father. You wouldn't have spent fourteen years with him if you didn't.
Someday, when I can be guaranteed that my father won't disappoint me, I will consider coming to Germany to meet you, Heidi, and Angelika.
For a long time, I hated that they did ballet when I had to give it up. He saw their recitals, and I had an empty seat stare at me when I was on stage.
I don't think you or him will ever understand that feeling of abandonment. They had a father all their lives.
I had mine abandon me when I was eight.
It was just me and my mother.
All I wanted was to get to know you all when I was a kid, but I never got the chance. You never asked me to be a part of their lives, and that hurt. I know it takes a lot of courage to apologise first, and I do appreciate your email. And I'm sorry I wasn't welcoming of you.
I was just a little girl who got her heart broken by the first man she ever loved over and over again.
My dad was my hero until he became my villain.
Countless moments in my life he never saw.
There will be many more he will never see because I deserve to have a happy life, too. And keeping him away from my life as an adult protects me from getting my hopes up again.

I know all about disappointment,
Johanna.
And I don't want your daughters to ever
experience that because of me. So I
promise you that I want to get to know
them. Give them my email address and
have them send me emails when they're
ready.
Best wishes,
Josie.

"So …?" Josie's voice had him turning in his seat to find her towel drying her long brunette hair. "Does it sound like I really want to get to know my stepmother and half-sisters?"

Max got out of the chair and set his hands on her shoulders. Parts of her damp, white top met his fingers. "You should send it. It's perfect."

She tilted her head at him and smiled. "You think?"

"It is." He slid his hands up her neck and cupped her jaw. Then he held her face steady as he pressed a kiss on her forehead.

"That man in my life …"

He pulled back and gazed down at her. "Yeah?"

He already knew, but he wanted her to confirm it.

Me.

"The one I wrote about …"

"Yes, Josephine."

"That man is *you*," she revealed.

Max smiled. "I already knew."

"Good because I was already in love with you when I wrote that email yesterday. I've been in love with you for some time, Max."

"Far longer than last night at the ballet?"

"Far longer," she confirmed. The towel she held fell to the ground as she wrapped her arms around his waist and held him close.

He let out a small groan. "Really need to get you to work, Josephine. Before you say you love me and I haul that body of yours back to your bedroom."

She giggled and got on her tippy toes. Her lips were almost

touching his when she whispered, "I love you." Then she pressed her lips against his in a chaste kiss. "I love you." And then another kiss. "I love you."

Before he could even kiss her back, she pulled away and picked up the towel off the floor, stating she needed to brush her hair and finish getting ready for work.

She was that kind of love tease.

And he was more than happy to be wrapped up by it.

Max held the box tightly as he made his way through the ballroom doors of the Oslo. It was the newest five-star hotel in Melbourne that had recently opened on the Docklands, and tonight, it would be the venue for Rob and Ally's engagement party. The same engagement party they both didn't want. Max knew this because Rob had messaged him many times to make sure he was coming tonight. He also knew they were only having a party to please Ally's father, David O'Connor.

What most people didn't know was the pair had actually eloped three months ago while in New York. The gift he'd chosen was courtesy of the gift registry on their website. Ally had thought it was unnecessary, but her mother had taken control of the engagement.

When Max glanced at the gift registry, he laughed at the idea of his best friend, the Men's Single Scull World Champion, having a pashmina throw rug. He knew it was Mrs O'Connor who had chosen the registry gifts. So Max played along and actually bought what he thought they might need. Bowls were useful. He especially hoped a two-thousand-dollar crystal bowl would bring them joy throughout their 'engagement.'

"Ah, good evening, sir," a woman dressed in a white top and black pants said as she approached him. "Would you like me to take that off you and set it with all the other gifts?"

Max handed it over, happy to be free of the heavy present. "Thanks," he said as the woman walked away.

He scanned the ballroom to find a band playing and several people already dancing. He couldn't see the couple of the hour.

Pulling out his phone from his pants pocket, he smiled the moment he saw Josie's message on the screen. He unlocked his phone and read it.

> **Josie:** I am so sorry. I know we said we'd meet out the front, but I'm running really late. I'm currently changing at my place. I'll see you soon.

> **Max:** It's okay, Josephine. I just got here. I'll be inside. Definitely missed you. I redrafted the same contract about three times just counting down to see you tonight. Kissing you goodbye outside the bakery was not enough.

> **Josie:** I promise I'm rushing my makeup and quickly putting on my dress just so I can get to you quicker.

> **Max:** Seriously, Josephine. Hurry.

> **Josie:** Go mingle!

> **Max:** Fine. You'd better find me the minute you get here.

> **Josie:** You can bet on it.

> **Josie:** OH!

> **Josie:** To get you through until I see you …

> **Josie:** I love you. I love you. I love you.

> **Max:** Don't even worry about makeup. You're beautiful without it. Just get here because those I love yous are torture to read. Need to hear them.
> **Josie:** Go mingle, Maxwell. I'm doing my hair now. I'll see you soon.

"Max!" He heard someone yell his name out. He glanced up from his screen to see Julian wave his arms for his attention.

"Max! Max, I'm here!"

Knowing he'd probably slow Josie down even more if he texted back, he returned his phone to his pocket and made his way towards one of his best friends. When he had almost reached him, Julian ran up and wrapped his arms around Max, causing him to chuckle.

"Uhh … Hey, Julian."

"Where have you been?" Julian tightened his arms around him. "Max, I've missed you." Then he pulled back, and his light blue eyes scanned his face. "You have no scars or bruises, and you've not gone thin, so you've been taking care of yourself. So where have you been?"

Max glanced over to see Julian's fiancée playfully shake her head at Max. "He's just upset he hasn't seen you at PJ's lately."

"So?" Julian asked, seeking Max's explanation.

"I've just been busy with clients and the court case. It's the final week of court, so my dad's needed me more often," Max explained, leaving out the part where he had been spending any possible free minute with Josie.

Julian nodded and removed his arms from around Max. "Okay. Good. I just thought you found a new best friend."

"I have a few best friends," Max stated.

"One best friend who you've been ignoring for weeks."

Max winced, knowing that voice anywhere. He spun around to find Noel Parker standing before him with a grin on his face. Max hadn't seen him since he left for his honeymoon almost ten months ago. He chuckled and then hugged Noel. Max was glad to see him. There was still a lot Max was sorry for when it came to Noel. Not only had Max made a move on his then-girlfriend, Andrea, but Sarah had been the reason Clara had ended things when he and his wife were first seeing each other. They had kept their love a secret, afraid that Alex, Clara's brother and Noel's best friend, would not approve and tear them apart. But Sarah Collins had fed Clara lies, and then it was over. Clara was about to marry Ally's brother, Liam, until Sarah told Max the truth and he forced her to come clean.

"What are you doing back here?" Max asked when their embrace ended.

"Couldn't make it to Worlds to see Rob compete, so I had to be here for his engagement party."

"Is Clara here?"

He nodded, love for his wife still bright in his green eyes. "She's with Ally and her family catching up. They still love her."

"Liam here, too?"

"Nah. He apparently hasn't been back since he left for Singapore. No one has really heard from him." Noel shrugged. "Clara was nervous to see him, so him not being here means she doesn't have to be careful about flaunting our marriage in his face."

"Julian, come get a drink with me?" he heard Stevie ask behind.

"'Kay," Julian said, and then he stepped next to Max. "We're all catching up the minute I get Cranky Pants a drink."

"Cranky — what?"

"You heard me, Blondie. You're just mad that your mum and I had a great time FaceTiming today," Julian teased. He shot Noel a wink and then spun around and left.

"Julian, we seriously have to discuss you talking to my mother. It's not normal," Stevie yelled as Julian quickened his steps to get away from her.

Noel laughed. "To think, when I last left Melbourne they had no idea what they were. Now they're engaged."

"Yeah," Max agreed.

"Max!" Clara said out of nowhere. He shifted to the right to see Noel's wife with a large smile on her face, those big brown eyes of hers sparkled. She threaded her fingers through her husband's, and Noel kissed her cheek. "I've been looking for you all night."

"I just got here. When did you guys land?"

"A few days ago."

"A few days ago?"

Noel nodded. "Tried calling you but no luck."

"Sorry. Work's been hectic. I haven't been able to see anyone. Have you guys? Did Alex come out with you both?"

Clara shook her head. "My brother doesn't want to leave my nephew's side. He said they'll be here for the wedding. And we've been getting over jet lag, so we're just seeing everyone now."

"You guys staying at your old place?" Max felt his phone

vibrate in his pocket, but he ignored it.

"Yeah. It's nice being back in Clara's old room at Stevie and Julian's. It's more their place than ours," Noel said.

Just as Max was about to ask how it felt being back in town, Rob, Ally, Stevie, and Julian had joined them. For the next ten minutes, they all caught up. It was like old times, but for Max, it was a little different. He didn't feel guilt holding him back from connecting with his friends. Self-pity didn't cripple his ability to join in on the conversation. He finally felt right with them.

When he felt his phone vibrate once again, he pulled it out to see that Josie had messaged him. He noticed Ally staring at him with a small smile on her face.

"Excuse me, I've gotta take this," he announced to his friends.

"Wait, Max. We have to discuss G&MC tonight," Noel said.

Max nodded, knowing it was a conversation he couldn't avoid now that Noel was back in Australia. Max stepped away from the group and opened her messages.

Josie: I'm leaving my place now. See you soon.

Josie: I'm here. Just got to the doors. Where are you?

Max scanned the room, but he couldn't see her with all the people on the dance floor. He pushed past until he made it through the sea of people. Then he noticed her, staring at the phone. He waited a moment and took her in, oblivious to the fact he had found her. She wore a light blue off-the-shoulder dress that hit past her knees. The sleeves connected to the bust to make a crisscross pattern on her dress. Josie's hair was up in a bun with a few strands by her face.

Raising his phone, he snapped a picture of her and sent it to her. Josie's brows furrowed, and then she glanced up.

The slow, radiant smile on her face was absolutely beautiful.

He quickly closed the space between them, and she managed to say his name before his hand gripped her shoulder and he yanked her into his kiss.

Josie giggled against his lips, and her hand settled on his hip as if to stabilise herself. She had kissed him with as much longing as he had before she pulled back. Josie reached up and wiped the lipstick he presumed had spread across his lips from her kiss.

"Don't worry," she assured. "There's none on your lips. Long lasting and kiss proof."

Max wrapped his fingers around her wrist to stop her thumb's soft strokes. "I've missed you."

"You saw me this morning," she reminded.

"I made love to you this morning."

"I was there."

He bent down and pressed his lips against hers in a chaste kiss. "I love you," he whispered. "I love you. I love you. I love you."

"Holy shit!" he heard Julian shriek behind him.

"How the hell did we miss this?" Stevie asked.

Josie bit her lip, and he mentally cursed his best friend. Max straightened his posture and moved his fingers from around her wrist to thread through her fingers, connecting their hands. Max then turned around to see the shocked expressions on Stevie and Julian's faces.

Max squeezed Josie's hand to reassure it was okay that they knew.

"Since when?" Stevie asked, the shock still in her eyes.

"Since you guys were in France, really," Max said as he glanced over to see Josie staring up at him, love still bright in her eyes.

"We need the full story," Stevie added.

"Look," Max breathed as he nodded at Josie, pleading with her to trust him. Then he turned and faced his two friends. "This is new. Although there's been something between Josephine and me for months, it's new."

"How new?" Julian squinted at Josie.

"Since last night," Josie answered. "And can we not make this a big deal? This isn't about us tonight. It's about Rob and Ally."

Stevie and Julian turned to face each other. They both stared at each other as if they were having a silent conversation. Then Stevie faced them first.

"I like this," she declared. "The two of you together. I *really* like this. So we'll keep your relationship on the down-low. Just keep the kissing to a minimum or in the shadows if you don't want people like Clara freaking out—who is here with Noel."

"Just to add, I'm freaking out on the inside," Julian announced. "I thought I was the only love in Max's life—"

"Julian," Stevie hissed. "Don't put the 'L' word on them right now."

"It's okay," Max assured. "She already knows I love her."

"You do?"

Josie nodded. "As of last night, I did."

"How long has this *really* been going on?" she asked, sceptical.

"Since Noel and Clara's wedding," Max stated. "But we lost contact until you all went to France."

Stevie smirked. "Ah, that wedding seems to have brought so many of us together. Well, Julian and I are going to go elsewhere. We'll see you both later."

Then Stevie and Julian giggled like schoolgirls as they headed over to the bar and left Max alone with Josie.

"So my best friend and his fiancée know." Max released Josie's hand and turned to face her.

She smiled. "Is that a bad thing?"

"Definitely not."

"I don't want to tell Clara just yet," she announced. "I'd like to catch up with her before I do."

"All right," he agreed, wanting to kiss her once again. "Do you want to go our separate ways for a little bit and meet up at the bar?"

Josie closed the distance and pressed a kiss to his cheek. "I'll see you at the bar."

Josie

In her search to find Rob and Ally to wish them congratulations, Josie had made several rounds of the ballroom. Each time she passed Max, he'd send her a wink, or he'd reach over and squeeze her hand when no one was looking. All Josie wanted to do was steal him away from whoever he was talking to and leave the party.

Memories of last night and this morning continued to replay in her thoughts throughout the day. She wasn't sure how she was able to get through her shift at the bakery. All she could think about was how Max touched her so intimately. How he drove into her with such need and desire. And how he whispered how much he loved her as he reached his high.

"Josie?" she heard a familiar voice say.

She spun around to see Clara Parker behind her with a wide smile on her face. "Clara!"

They hugged for a long time, Josie hating that she hadn't seen Clara the last time she was in Melbourne.

"How are you?" Josie asked when their embraced ended.

"I'm good. How's uni going?" Clara brushed her brunette curls over to one shoulder. The emerald green halter neck dress she wore fit her perfectly. Josie was still envious of Clara's natural beauty.

"Good. I have exams coming up. How long are you staying in Melbourne for?"

"Not long," she said. "We're here for Rob and Ally's engagement party. Then we're going to catch up with my dad, Noel's family, and then Noel's got some business he has to take care of here."

"Business?"

Clara sighed. "Yeah. Recruitment. Boring stuff."

"And how are you and Noel?"

"Good. Really good. He made this grand gesture of us moving back for me to take some of those offers I had."

"So you guys are moving back?" Josie asked too eagerly.

Clara laughed. "No. It was sweet of him to offer, but there's too much in the States for me to walk away from now. I have my nephew, and I want to be in his life. I love seeing my brother every fortnight. I miss you and all the girls, but I have a pretty great life in Boston. My career in the culinary arts has suffered, but that's my fault. I guess I'm just not meant to be a dessert chef."

Josie's heart broke for her. "So are you working in any restaurants?"

"No," she said in a small voice. "But it's okay. I'll figure it out."

"Why don't you give up the business degree and open your own restaurant or bakery? You're wasting money going to Boston University, Clara. Your tuition fees could pay for rent on a place."

"You sound like my husband," she teased.

"Because your husband is a smart man."

Clara's eyes softened. "Yeah. He is."

"You should go tell him that."

"I will."

Josie noticed Max staring at her behind Clara's shoulder. His lips were pursed, and he raised his phone up as she felt hers vibrate in her clutch. She opened her bag and pulled it out. She glanced down to see he had sent her a text message.

"New guy you're seeing?" Clara asked.

Josie held her phone closer to her and away from Clara's prying eyes. "It's just my roommate," she lied. "I'd better take this."

She could tell Clara didn't believe her. Right now, Clara had other problems to worry about than Josie and Max being together.

"Okay, sure. You'd better reply to your *roommate*."

Her cheeks heated, knowing that Clara didn't believe her. She cleared her throat and asked, "Have you seen Rob and Ally?"

"Ally had to go take her medication, and Rob went up to their room with her. I think they're just tired of this engagement party and wanted some alone time. They'll be back before the end of it to say their last thanks and everything. Noel and I are gonna head out, too."

And as if on cue, Noel was by Clara's side. "Hey, Josie," he said with a smile. "All right, baby. Ready to go? By the time we get back to the apartment, you'll have time to FaceTime with Will."

Clara's eyes flashed with excitement. "Okay, let's go. We'll catch up with you later, Josie?"

She nodded. "Definitely. I'll see you both. Tell Alex and Keira I said hello."

"I will," Clara promised, and then Mr and Mrs Parker turned and headed for the ballroom's exit.

Josie watched them walk out, and she glanced down at her phone to read Max's message.

Max: Come back to me. This is torture.

She laughed at his message.

Josie: Get over here. I'm yours.

Lifting her chin, she raised her brow at him from across the dance floor. Max peeked down at his phone, smirked, and slipped it into his pants pocket. As she watched Max make his way to her, Josie dropped her phone into her clutch and snapped it close the second he stood in front of her.

"So ..." he drawled.

"So," she said as he took her clutch from her.

"I think we should dance."

Josie laughed as he walked over to the table she assumed was his and set her clutch down. When he returned to her, he set his hand on her hip and brought her close to his body. Josie wrapped her arms around his neck and bit back a smile as his other hand settled on her hip.

Then the music from the live band came to a halt, and there were groans and yells from people. But Josie didn't care. She just loved the feel of her arms around Max as he looked into her eyes.

Love was a many wondrous thing.

But love with Max was the most beautiful kind of wonder imaginable.

A strum of guitar echoed in the ballroom, and then suddenly she heard it, her heart clenching at the guitar playing the chorus.

"La Vie En Rose."

It was no longer just her mother's favourite song.

It was *theirs.*

"No," she breathed as she glanced over to see a man in formal attire playing an acoustic guitar.

"Yes," Max said with a grin when she looked back at him. "Asked him if he knew 'La Vie En Rose' and promised him a generous tip if he could perform it when he saw us together."

"You're insane," she whispered as their song played so beautifully.

Max hummed. "Suppose I am. But if insanity gets me that look in your eye, then I'm all for it."

Josie rolled her eyes.

When the guitarist played the last chords, she whispered, "I love you, Maxwell Sheridan." She got on her toes and pressed her lips to his in a sweet kiss. "You're my *La Vie En Rose*."

"And you mine, Josephine." Then he kissed her forehead and let his lips linger on her skin for a long moment.

Her poor heart was so in love with him.

"Want to go?" he asked when he pulled back.

Josie nodded.

"I'll grab your clutch."

She watched as he spun around and made his way to his table. Josie pressed her hands against her warm face and smiled. It was crazy how badly he affected her. But everything he did was so right and beautiful. It'd be more frightening if she didn't fall in love with him. Josie made her way towards him and frowned when a woman she had never seen before stepped in front of him, and Max went rigid in an instant.

"What are you doing here?" he asked.

Josie stopped her steps just close enough to hear him.

"I had to see you," the woman said.

Josie could just see her face. She was beautiful. Dark brown hair, fair skin, and blue eyes. She was the kind of woman she saw in the *Victoria Secret's Fashion Show* each year. She and Stella would watch the models walk down the runway as they ate chicken wings and talked about how great it was to love food.

"You can't be here," he hissed. "How did you know I'd be here?"

"Gregson sent me, and he told me that Noel would be here."

"So you flew from the States to tell me what?"

Josie flinched.

No.

She can't be Andrea.

Can she?

But Josie felt it in every bone in her body. Her heart refused to believe so, but her brain knew.

"To tell you that I choose you, Max. I want to be with you."

Josie's heart dropped to her stomach, and she struggled to inhale air into her lungs.

"This isn't fair, Andrea!"

Andrea.

Josie felt dizzy.

And nauseous.

"I know. But I need you, Max. I need you, and so does Noel. Please."

Max shook his head. "You have to go. Please, Andrea, just leave."

"Please, Max," she begged. "I need to explain. I came all this way. You've ignored all the emails I've sent you for the past month."

Emails.

She sent him emails.

He never told her that Andrea had sent him emails. He had kept that from her.

"I've ignored them for a reason. You can't be here. You can't just show up a year later and expect me to give in to you now."

Andrea inhaled sharply. "I'm staying at the Crown Promenade. I can explain, Max. I want to make this right with you … and Noel. Please just give me a chance." Then she took several steps back, spun around, and made her way out of the ballroom.

Max let out a sigh and turned. His eyes were wide as if he were surprised to see Josie standing there.

She felt raw standing in front of him.

She felt weak that she was envious of the hold Andrea still had over Max.

She felt her tears want to be shed, but she forced them away with a tight smile.

"So that was Andrea?"

Max nodded and took two steps to her. "Yeah."

"She's here in Melbourne," Josie said, stating facts.

"Yeah, she is."

The regret and guilt that swirled in his eyes caused her heart to clench. She knew what she had to do.

She had to give him and her the opportunity of closure so that he could be with Josie without any regrets.

"You should go after her."

"What?" He shook his head.

"Go and get closure, Max. She's emailed you more than once in the past month, and you've kept that from me. Obviously, there are things left unsaid, and you deserve closure. And I don't deserve just parts of your heart when I gave you all mine last night. So go."

"Josephine," he breathed, and she heard the pain and panic in his voice.

She knew how loyal Max was. And she knew how much he wanted forgiveness for the things he had done to his best friends in the past. It would be terrible for her to take away his chance at redemption.

"She said something about Noel. And if it affects Noel, it affects Clara, Max. And she's my friend. If it affects her, it affects me. You need to discover why she was sent to come find you," Josie urged. Then she reached up and cupped his face in the palm of her hands. "You need this, Max. I'll be waiting."

"You promise you'll wait for me?"

Josie smiled then let her lips touch his ever so briefly. "I promise." She dropped her hands and took her clutch from him. "I love you, Maxwell, and this is me putting you first."

Max pulled her in and wrapped his arms tightly around her. "I love you," he whispered. "I love you. I love you. I love you."

Chapter
SIXTEEN

Josie

In the distance, she heard a phone ringing loudly.

Josie groaned and wished the sound away.

To her delight, it stopped.

But then it rang again.

Josie threw her arm in the direction of the sound. When she found what felt like her phone, she grasped it and brought it closer to her. Prying an eyelid open, the high brightness instantly blinded her. She saw a number she didn't recognise on her phone's screen and answered the call.

"Hello," she murmured, irritated that her sleep had been interrupted.

"Miss Faulkner?"

"That's me," she confirmed.

And then Josie heard words and not sentences as her heart ripped apart. Tears dragged down her cheeks as she flung the blanket off her body and said, "I'm on my way," before throwing her phone onto her bed.

Josie raced to her closet, flicked on the light, and pulled open a drawer. She removed the first pair of jeans she found and slipped them on. She now cursed herself for being stupid enough to sleep in just her underwear and a long sleeve shirt. Josie grasped the zipper of her jeans and tried to pull it up.

She had tried twice before her body began to heat in frustration and anger.

"Fuck it!" she cursed as she left her jeans unbuttoned and pulled a coat off a hanger. Then she slipped into a pair of flats, grabbed her phone off the bed, and raced out of her bedroom. On her way out of her apartment, she swiped her keys off the hallway table and raced out, unsure if she locked the door behind her.

How Josie didn't have an accident as she drove with tears in her eyes was beyond her.

She had found parking close by the electronic doors, got out of her car, and shoved her keys into her blue coat pocket.

When she found the desk, she raced towards it, and the nurse gave her a tight smile. She wasn't sure if it was Kristy or Kirsty, but she did know that the double choc fudge cupcakes were her favourites.

"Hello, Josie."

"Someone called," Josie said, getting straight to the point. "They didn't say—"

"I'll page Dr Frederickson now," Kristy/Kirsty said.

Josie pushed off the desk and covered her face with her hands. She took several deep breaths, hoping it would calm her, but it was no use.

She shook in fear.

Her chest pained because it seemed to know the truth.

And her eyes stung from the relentless number of tears that kept being produced and kept falling.

She wasn't sure how long she had been crying when Dr Frederickson pulled her hands away from her face and led her through double doors to a quiet hallway.

The doctor had set his hands on her shoulders and apologised.

Then he spoke words that had her fall to her knees, sobbing.

He broke her heart with a sentence.

He tore out her soul with a statement.

He ruined her with the truth.

Dr Frederickson sent her home.

He gave her papers to read.

He offered her his support and comfort.

And Josie gave him silence.

It was a blur.

She had no idea what time the hospital had called her.

And she had no idea what time it was when she walked through the security gate of her apartment building.

Her heart was no longer in her chest.

It was left crushed in that hallway.

Josie's throat was raw from her cries and shouts.

Her tears came and went.

But the immense pain stayed.

When she glanced up from her feet, she noticed Max sitting on the step.

In light of the circumstances, something in her found hope and warmth at the sight of him.

A faint smile began to cross her lips but was halted immediately when Max lifted his eyes to hers, and she saw the pain in his brown eyes. His eyes glazed over and his bottom lip trembled.

"*Josephine,*" he pleaded as he slowly got to his feet.

Pain struck her.

She knew.

She knew what he would say.

What remained of her heart tumbled from her chest to fall deeper.

And deeper,

and deeper …

Until it no longer beat for her.

Josie covered her face with her palms and sobbed.

Not Max.

This could not be happening to her.

Not after everything.

Arms were around her as she shook.

She wanted to push him away.

She wanted to scream at him that this wasn't fair.

She wanted to tell him what she had just walked out of.

She wanted to yell that a doctor broke her heart and Max killed her off.

"I'm sorry," he whispered.

She didn't believe him.

He was selfish.

So selfish.

He had no idea what sorry was.

"I have to go with her."

He was choosing Andrea.

She hated him.

So much.

With all her charcoaled heart, she hated him.

Josie wanted to push him away, but her knees gave way, and he held her.

"I love you."

You're a liar!

But she remained silent.

"Please believe me. I love you."

He wounded her with more pain.

"You promised you'd wait for me."

But she wouldn't.

She wouldn't wait for a liar.

"You're my *La Vie En Rose*," he promised, and that got a reaction from her.

Josie pushed off his chest and slapped him hard across the face.

He had insulted her.

He had insulted her mother.

But most importantly …

He had insulted her love for him.

He had no idea what being someone's *La Vie En Rose* meant.

She watched his mouth tell her lies.

She saw them, but she didn't hear them.

Then he whispered, "Goodbye, Josephine."

It wasn't the first goodbye she'd heard today, but it was the first she had heard from his lying lips.

And with the first goodbye he had ever given her, she realised her love for Maxwell Sheridan was by far the worst disappointment she had ever experienced.

Then he left her.

Just like her father.

And just like her mother.

Chapter SEVENTEEN

Max

Max had done it.

He disappointed the only person who mattered the most in his life.

Devastated the only woman who had ever loved him the way he wanted.

The way he craved.

And needed.

I should turn back.

I should beg Josephine to take me back.

But Andrea's words wouldn't stop repeating: *Help me fix this.*

I have to do this.

I have to go with her.

Not for him.

And not for her.

For Noel.

To earn his forgiveness.

To be the man Josephine had so much faith in.

Too bad that very man broke her heart and walked away.

All because Max needed redemption.

All because he made the stupid, selfish mistake all those months ago to try to take what was never his.

And in turn, he lost it all.

Max lost the one love he found on his own.

I lost Josephine.

And he could only hope that when he returned, she'd forgive him.

Please, God, let her forgive me.

THE END OF
With the First Goodbye.

Continue the story in the final book of the *Thirty-Eight* series,
With the Last Goodbye.

Read on for an excerpt of Max and Josie's upcoming concluding novel.

With the last
GOODBYE

It's time to say goodbye.

To Max …

And to Josie.

Find out how it all ends in *With the Last Goodbye.*

COMING SOON
JANUARY 24th, 2018

Prologue

Max

The day Maxwell Sheridan broke Josephine Faulkner's heart was a sunny Sunday morning.

It was early.

Skies as blue as her eyes.

The wind was cool and refreshing.

But as Max sat outside on her apartment building's step, the beautiful day was a façade to what he knew was impending.

He felt the pain of his decision weigh heavily on him.

It made it hard for him to breathe.

His heart begged him for a change.

It pleaded with him that redemption wasn't worth the destruction he'd ensure.

Max had spent all night replaying his verbal promise to Andrea Wallace.

He was going to Boston, Massachusetts.

Not for her.

Not for her love or affections.

He was going to put away the demons.

His demons.

Put them finally to rest.

Seek redemption and forgiveness for the things he had done in the past.

Reveal the truth to his two best friends and hope to God they would someday forgive him for the awful things he had done to them.

Although he wasn't going to claim Andrea's love, he was going to seek her forgiveness, too.

He had pursued her when her heart wasn't his to chase.

To want.

To desire.

To believe he could have.

Andrea Wallace was never meant to be his.

It had taken over a year to understand it.

Because her name wasn't the name his heart whispered to have.

To want forever.

Max stared at his hands as he waited.

He felt the end creep toward him.

He knew it was close.

The wait broke his heart even more.

He wished she was home.

He had knocked on her apartment door and waited. When he got no answer, he returned downstairs and sat on the step, waiting for her.

Then he heard it.

Faint, slow footsteps that eventually came to a stop.

Max lifted his chin to find her standing before him.

Her eyes had glazed over with tears.

She knew.

She knew what he had decided.

She had put him first, and Max had deemed her last.

His lip trembled at the wounded expression on her face.

It was horrible to see the one person he loved the most look at him with such pain.

He inhaled a sharp breath and whispered, "Josephine," as he slowly got to his feet.

Max watched as she winced.

A painful wince he even felt.

Because he had heard it in his voice.

The pleading for her forgiveness and understanding.
The pleading for her.
Just her.
Josie covered her face with her palms and sobbed.
He felt her slowly fall out of love with him.
Unable to stop himself, he closed the distance and wrapped his arms around her.
She shook.
Her pain he felt and knew.
Her pain was one he had caused.
Because he felt her heartbreak.
He felt her love for him and the devastation.
Because I chose Andrea and not her.
Josephine Faulkner was the name his heart whispered.
She was his solace.
His entire heart and being.
But he gave her up for his morality.

COMING SOON
JANUARY 24th, 2018.

Acknowledgements

Ah, please don't hate me!

I know, I know, A CLIFFHANGER! I'm the worst. I'm so sorry *With the First Goodbye* had to end this way. But don't worry, *With the Last Goodbye* will be out before you know it. When I started writing the *Thirty-Eight* series I had no idea it would turn into a six book series. I thought Noel and Clara would be it. But my readers weren't having it and wanted more. And when it came to Max, I had no idea how his story would pan out. It took a while before I was able to write him a story. That's why it took so long for his book to be published. I wanted Max to find his true love, to have a story worthy of writing and reading.

And his story was complicated.
And it included someone new.
His story was always entwined with Josie's.
Josie is Max's clean slate.
And in *With the Last Goodbye*, you will find out how their story ends.

I promise it'll be a story worth waiting for.

Right.
Now to the acknowledgements.

Thank you so much to my parents for being so supportive. Can I just say, my mother is a champion! Thank you, Mum. Your support is an absolute gift.

Thank you to Dennis, Leslie, and Emily. You three. Thank you for the laughs and for keeping me grounded and helping me sort out this book so it makes sense. I couldn't ask for better siblings.

As always, Jaycee Ford. I couldn't do this all without you, Jaycee. Thank you for not only being my author friend, but for being my best friend. And thank you for walking me down the streets of New Orleans when I had too much of a good time. I blame the Hurricanes. I miss you!

To Veronica Larsen. We clicked so quick and instantly and reached best friend status within a blink of an eye. Thank you so much for not only being my friend, but for being such a great supporter and always being there for me. Veronica, I think you are an amazing woman and talented author. You are going places, and I am so happy and honoured to be part of that journey. Stay amazing!

Thank you to Danielle Woodside for beta reading ALL OF MY BOOKS. My life is better with you in it. And thank you so much to Tarsh Smerdon for also beta reading Max's book and helping me out with the ballet aspects of this book.

My editor, Jenny Sims, THANK YOU! Thank you for always putting all your hard work and time into my books. They are always better after they've been in your hands.

Thank you to Najla Qamber for *With the First Goodbye's* cover. The last minute change you did with a snap of your fingers and it is so perfect. Thank you for everything, Naj.

A massive thank you to my publicist, Veronica Adams. Seriously, Veronica, thank you for all your hard work and getting Max and Josie's book out there. Ever since we partnered up my life has been better. I owe you so much and I don't think a simple thank you would ever be enough. But just know I appreciate you and everything you do so much. I won't ever stop saying thank you.

My formatters at *E.M. Tippetts Book Designs*. Emily, you and your team are amazing. Thank you for always making the interior of my books so amazing and beautiful.

Thank you so much to all the bloggers who shared all the teasers, excerpts, cover reveal, and the release of *With the First Goodbye*, THANK YOU SO MUCH! You are all amazing.

To my readers. God, where would I be without you all. Thank you all so much for your support, your time, and your love. I am so blessed to have you all. I get teary thinking of all of you. So thank you so much for being by my side. I love you all so much.

My *Lenatics*, you are my family. Thank you for reading my random posts and all your love and support. You are all very special individuals who I love wholeheartedly.

And to you. Yes, you! Thank you for buying and reading *With the First Goodbye*. I hope you enjoyed and loved Max and Josie's story. Don't worry, you'll see them both in *With the Last Goodbye* in January!

This isn't a goodbye from me, but a see you until the next book!

Love,
Len
xo

About the Author

Len Webster is a romance-loving Melburnian with dreams of finding her version of 'The One.' But until that moment happens, she writes. Having just graduated with her BBusCom from Monash University, Len is now busy writing her next romance about how a boy met a girl, and how they fell completely and hopelessly in love.

She is also not a certified explorer, but she's working on it.

Connect with Len
Website: www.lenwebster.com
Facebook: www.facebook.com/lennwebster
Twitter: twitter.com/lennwebster
Instagram: www.instagram.com/lennwebster
Goodreads: www.goodreads.com/author/show/7502135.
Len_Webster

Want exclusive teasers, giveaways, excerpts, and news?
Join Len's private reader group and be part of the family!
Len Webster's Lenatics

Or you can join Len's newsletter for all the need to know!
There's giveaways and all the news you might have missed.
Subscribe to Len's newsletter

Printed in Great Britain
by Amazon